# The Money Tree

## *Vault of Verdancy*

*By*

*RANDEEP PAHWA*

**Disclaimer**

This book is a work of fiction. All views, opinions, and interpretations expressed are those of the author and do not necessarily reflect the opinions or beliefs of any individual, organization, or entity.

Any resemblance to actual events, places, or persons, living or dead, is purely coincidental. The content is intended for informational/entertainment purposes only and should not be considered professional advice.

The author and publisher disclaim any liability for errors, omissions, or any outcomes resulting from the use of this material. Readers are encouraged to exercise their discretion and consult relevant professionals when necessary.

## Prologue

The world remembers gold as wealth, but Marcus Chen had always suspected it was something else entirely.

Buried in forgotten texts and whispered across fractured civilizations were fragments of a single story, of a tree whose roots ran deeper than history itself. Not a myth, not a metaphor, but a design: etched into stone, carved across cultures that had never met yet somehow shared the same secret.

In the sterile hush of the British Museum, the air hummed with static, faint and metallic, like the breath of something old. Beneath glass and catalog tags, gold glimmered in patterns that seemed to pulse when no one looked directly at them. The hum made his skin prickle, alive, electric, wrong.

He'd chased that pulse for years. Tonight, he and his team would try to seize it. They'd planned everything: one artifact, one night, one clean escape.

But some treasures aren't stolen. They awaken.

And when they do, the world holds its breath.

Tonight, the roots of the Money Tree would wake.

# Preface

In an era where technology and ancient mysteries collide, "The Money Tree" takes readers on an extraordinary journey that begins with a daring museum heist and evolves into a multidimensional adventure. Through the eyes of archaeologist Marcus Chen and his elite team of specialists, we explore the consequences of awakening forces that have lain dormant for millennia.

What starts as a simple theft transforms into a desperate race against time as the team discovers that some artifacts hold powers beyond human comprehension.

As they navigate parallel worlds and confront moral dilemmas, they discover that the true price of power is often one's own humanity.

This tale delves deep into the complexities of human nature, examining how greed, loyalty, and sacrifice intertwine in the face of extraordinary circumstances. The Money Tree redefines our notions of wealth, power, and responsibility, posing urgent questions about the true cost of progress and the lasting impact of our choices.

In a world where the boundaries between ancient wisdom and modern ambition blur, this story reminds us that every discovery, no matter how magnificent, carries with it the potential for both salvation and destruction.

# Table of Contents

## Chapter 1: The Failed Heist

Suspended from the ceiling of the British Museum's restricted section, Marcus Chen fought to keep his breathing steady as a bead of sweat threatened to fall from his brow. The last thing he needed was a telltale droplet alerting the guards below to his presence.

"Security rotation in forty seconds," Sofia's voice came through his earpiece, crackling slightly. Her fingers flew across multiple keyboards in their van parked three blocks away. The soft glow of her monitors reflected off her face as she tracked every camera feed, every electronic lock, and every security guard's position in real time.

"Copy that," Marcus whispered, his muscles straining against the harness that kept him hovering fifteen feet above the marble floor. From his vantage point, he could see the artifact case housing their target: an ancient golden tablet, its surface etched with markings unlike any recorded in known civilizations.

"Ghost, status?" Marcus exhaled softly into his comms.

"Perimeter secure," came the clipped response from James "Ghost" Thompson. The ex military man stood in the shadows of a doorway across the street, his trained eyes continuously scanning for unexpected visitors. "Two police cars on routine patrol passed five minutes ago. Next round is due in twelve minutes."

Footfalls echoed through the marble halls, growing louder. Marcus held his breath, perfectly still in his black tactical gear.

"Incoming guard," Sofia warned. "Leo, you're on."

"Already on it, darling," Leo's smooth voice purred through the comms. The former magician turned con artist appeared at the far end of the hall in a pristine security uniform, walking with the confident stride of someone who belonged there.

"Evening, mate," Leo called to the guard approaching him, in the most polished British accent he could muster. "Rough night, eh?"

From above, Marcus watched, fascinated, as Leo deftly struck up a conversation with the guard. With practiced ease, Leo deflected suspicion, spinning a perfectly crafted story about a security breach in the Egyptian Wing.

"Marcus, you've got three minutes while Leo keeps him busy," Maya's voice came through, precise and focused. The anthropologist monitored the situation from her post in the research library one floor below. "Remember, the surface of the tablet is extremely delicate. According to the museum's documentation, it's made of an unknown alloy that"

"Maya," Sofia cut in sharply. "Lecture later. Heist now."

A slight smile touched Marcus's lips as he began his slow, silent descent toward the display case. The team dynamic hadn't changed much Maya still let her academia spill into the job.

"Thirty seconds until the next camera sweep," Sofia warned. "Ghost, any movement on your end?"

"Negative. Street's clear."

Marcus reached the case just in time, his gloved hands steady as he retrieved a small device from his belt one Sofia had built specifically for this job: a frequency emitter designed to disable the case's pressure sensors, at least long enough for him to act.

A soft click signaled the lock's release.

Marcus's heart pounded as he hovered above the case, the weight of the moment pressing down on him as heavily as the harness. The stakes had never felt higher. Failure here meant not just the loss of an artifact, but the potential collapse of everything he had fought for the respect of his peers, the thrill of discovery, the bond he shared with his team.

What if he was caught? The thought twisted his stomach. He could already envision the headlines: *Archaeologist Turned Criminal* splashed across every newspaper. This wasn't mere theft it was a desperate gamble, a high stakes risk where their very lives hung in the balance. Each minute hovering there, heart racing, reminded him that one slip one wrong move and it could all come crashing down.

He scanned the room, every flicker of movement amplified in his mind. The guards were trained. The cameras were relentless. The sensors were tuned to detect the faintest disturbance. Adrenaline coursed through him, making him acutely aware of the sweat pooling at the small of his back. If he failed to retrieve the tablet, they wouldn't just lose their chance they might alert forces far more dangerous than museum security.

"Think, Marcus," he whispered, forcing down the rising panic. "Focus." He knew the risks, knew the consequences. And yet the thrill of the heist pulled at him like a siren's call. He couldn't hesitate. He had to trust his instincts, trust his team and above all, trust himself.

"I'm in," Marcus whispered, reaching for the tablet.

"Be careful with the lower right corner," Maya cautioned, her voice tight with concern. "There's evidence of micro fissures in the metal that"

"Movement!" Ghost's sharp warning cut her off. "Two unmarked vehicles just turned onto the street. Black SUVs. Government plates."

"That's not scheduled." Sofia's voice held an edge of concern as her fingers flew across her keyboard. "These aren't regular security. Marcus, abort"

"Almost there." Marcus had already seized the tablet from its resting place. The metal felt curiously warm against his gloves. For a moment, he could have sworn a faint glow pulsed along the strange symbols.

"Leo, get out now," Sofia ordered. "They're breaching the east entrance."

"Bit busy here, love," Leo replied, his accent thick as he worked to distract the guard.

Marcus slipped the tablet into his specialized pack and started to climb. The warmth of the artifact seemed to grow, bleeding through the fabric into his back.

"Multiple heat signatures entering the building," Ghost reported. "Professional formation. These aren't museum security they're tactical."

"Marcus, you've got forty seconds to clear the room," Sofia said tightly. "I'm triggering the smoke screens on your mark."

The tablet's warmth was undeniable now its heat pulsed even through the thick padding of his pack. This wasn't normal. This wasn't

In an instant, a flash burst from Marcus's pack, rivers of golden light spilling out and bathing the room in miniature sun brilliance.

"What the hell was that?" Ghost demanded.

"Marcus, they saw that!" Sofia warned, just as cries of alarm rang through the museum halls.

"Abort, abort!" Maya's voice was urgent. "Marcus, the tablets never displayed any photometric properties in previous studies. This is unprecedented"

"Save the research for later," Marcus grunted, already swinging toward his exit point as the thunder of boots filled the corridors below. "Sofia, we need that smoke now!"

"Triggering in three, two"

Smoke billowed through the corridors, alarms blaring as chaos erupted. Marcus Chen understood instantly the heist was spiraling far beyond anyone's expectations. The tablet pressed against his back, pulsing like a second heartbeat, and deep down he knew they had uncovered something far greater than a simple museum theft.

The real question was: would they live long enough to find out what it was?

With Leo keeping the guard occupied at a safe distance, Marcus dropped the final few feet to the display case. The golden tablet gleamed within, its etched surface catching the faint light piercing the smoke. Up close, the markings were even more extraordinary unlike any ancient script he had ever studied.

"Maya, are you seeing this?" he whispered, adjusting the micro camera on his shoulder.

"Fascinating," Maya breathed. "Those symbols they're not consistent with any known ancient writing system. The upper quadrant almost resembles early Sumerian, but the lower patterns… they're completely unique."

"Less analysis, more extraction," Sofia cut in. "You've got two minutes before the next guard rotation."

Marcus drew Sofia's custom bypass device from his belt and attached it to the security panel. The screen flickered with shifting numbers as it worked to crack the code.

"Thirty seconds," Sofia updated.

The bypass emitted a soft beep, and the locks clicked quietly as they disengaged. With practiced precision, Marcus lifted the glass housing, careful not to leave a mark.

It all went wrong the moment his fingers touched the tablet.

A piercing whine filled the air as hidden security measures activated. Red warning lights flared across the restricted section, and a heavy metal gate began to descend at the entrance.

"Multiple alarms tripping!" Sofia's voice tightened. "These weren't in any of the schematics!"

"Must be a separate system," Ghost snapped. "Marcus, incoming. Multiple guards converging on your position."

Marcus's fingers brushed the tablet's unexpectedly warm surface. "Leo?"

"On it," Leo replied smoothly. Even through the comms they heard the rustle of his tools. "Ladies and gentlemen, it's showtime."

Small explosions and thick smoke erupted in the next hall as Leo unleashed his magician's arsenal. Confused shouts echoed as security scrambled between the alarms and Leo's distractions.

"East exit's still clear," Ghost reported. "But police responders are three blocks out."

Marcus sprinted toward their planned escape route, the tablet secured in his pack. The gate was halfway down he'd have to slide under it.

"Wait!" Maya's voice cut through. "The tablet's showing strange readings some kind of energy"

Her warning ended as Marcus's pack suddenly grew hot. Golden light bled through the fabric, casting flickering shadows on the walls.

"What the hell?" he muttered, diving into a roll beneath the gate just as it slammed shut behind him.

"Multiple teams converging," Sofia called, fingers flying across keyboards. "Taking control of ventilation smoke in three, two"

Smoke poured from the vents, thick and choking, cloaking Marcus as he darted through the corridors. Behind him, chaos swelled Leo's diversions weaving into the rising shouts of security, a symphony of disorder chasing at his heels.

"Ghost, status on that exit?" Marcus called as he rounded a corner.

"Compromised," Ghost replied. "Tactical teams laying a perimeter. You'll need the secondary route."

"The maintenance tunnel," Sofia said quickly. "Cameras disabled. Go now."

Marcus veered off, the tablet burning hotter with every step. The golden glow had grown intense, piercing through the smoke.

"Marcus, right turn ahead," Maya guided. "Tunnel entrance is behind the Roman exhibition."

He nearly collided with two guards before Leo appeared beside him, hand flicking in a practiced flourish. A flash of sparks exploded, sending the guards staggering back.

"Everybody, scatter pattern Delta," Sofia ordered. "Rendezvous at Point B in thirty minutes."

Marcus tore through the Roman exhibition, the glow from the tablet illuminating his path and marking him as a target.

"Maya, what the hell is going on with this thing?" he panted.

"The energy readings are off the scale," she replied, her voice tinged with awe despite the crisis. "This is unprecedented. The tablet appears to be reacting to"

"Later!" several voices shouted across the comms.

Marcus reached the maintenance tunnel and yanked the disguised latch Sofia had flagged on the blueprints. The door swung open just as he caught sight of Leo vanishing into another passage, the guards left in confusion.

"Ghost, you clear?" Marcus asked, dropping into the tunnel.

"Already mobile," Ghost answered. "Sofia's packed up. Maya's heading out the library exit."

The tunnel was narrow and dark, but the tablet's glow provided all the light he needed. Marcus ran, heart pounding. Their well planned heist had just become something much bigger something far more dangerous.

The tablet's rhythmic pulse pressed against his back like a heartbeat, and Marcus couldn't shake the unnerving sense that they had just stolen something more profound than they could possibly understand.

The only light in the tunnel came from the tablet. Its glow pulsed brighter and brighter, edging toward brilliance almost painfully so. Fierce heat radiated through the insulated pack, burning Marcus's back as he ran, breath ragged in the stale air.

"Marcus, stop!" Maya's voice cut through his earpiece. "The energy readings are critical. The tablet's molecular structure is destabilizing!"

"What does that mean in non academic terms?" Marcus grunted, skidding to a halt.

"It means drop the damn thing before it melts through your pack," Sofia snapped. "I'm seeing thermal readings that shouldn't even be possible."

Marcus yanked the pack off and lowered it gently to the tunnel floor. The seams glowed white hot as molten light seeped through.

"I should document the symbols," he said, pulling out his specialized camera. "Maya, can you receive the feed?"

"Affirmative," Maya replied. Her voice quickened. "The markings they're changing! The surface patterns are shifting in response to the energy fluctuations."

The camera clicked relentlessly as Marcus captured the transformation. Symbols shimmered and flowed like liquid gold, rearranging themselves into dazzling, alien configurations that strained his eyes.

"Marcus, multiple teams are closing in," Ghost warned. "They're tracking the energy signature. Two minutes, maybe less."

"One more sequence," Marcus muttered, adjusting the settings for the intensifying glow.

"Forget it!" Sofia shouted. "The heat just spiked. That tablet's about to"

A blinding flash filled the tunnel, preceded by a high pitched whine that rattled Marcus's teeth. The tablet hovered inches above the pack, suspended in a column of golden light.

"Marcus, run!" Leo's voice cracked through the comms. "Whatever that is, it's not worth dying for!"

There was no choice. A surge of energy exploded outward, hurling Marcus off his feet. He scrambled upright, abandoning the pack and the hovering artifact as a deep, otherworldly hum reverberated through the tunnel walls.

"Split protocol initiated," Ghost barked. "Everyone to your exits. Standard comms blackout in six hours."

Marcus bolted, racing through the narrow passageways on instinct. The golden glow darted through the tunnels like a living thing, casting restless shadows that seemed to chase him.

"Team check," Sofia ordered. "Sound off before blackout."

"Ghost clear. North route."

"Leo clear. West."

"Maya clear. Southeast."

"Marcus, status," Sofia demanded.

"Still mobile," he panted, veering into a narrower passage. "The tablet it's affecting the tunnel. The walls are… changing."

He wasn't imagining it. The concrete rippled with golden light. Symbols blazed across its surface before dissolving into smoke like wisps.

"Documentation received," Maya said, her voice thick with excitement. "The symbols align with multiple ancient civilizations, but their configuration suggests"

"Maya!" several voices shouted at once.

"Right. Escaping now," she said quickly.

Marcus reached his exit point a maintenance hatch leading to a quiet alley three blocks from the museum. He climbed the ladder, sirens and helicopter rotors thundering above.

"Ten seconds to blackout," Sofia called. "Rendezvous at Safe House Beta in six hours. Sofia clear."

One by one, the comms went silent as each member ditched their device. Marcus emerged into the alley, peeled off his tactical gear, and slipped into the casual clothes he had stashed there.

As he walked away, forcing a casual pace, a final pulse of golden light erupted from the museum. Every streetlight in a three block radius flickered out. For an instant, the sky itself was etched with fiery symbols echoes of those on the tablet. Then the lights blinked back on, and the night was ordinary again.

But Marcus knew nothing about this was ordinary. The impossible energy readings, the shifting symbols this was no artifact. It was something far greater, and far more dangerous.

Blending into the London night, Marcus's thoughts raced. What was the tablet? Why had it awakened? And most importantly what had they just unleashed?

Six hours. That was all the time he had to clear his head before facing the others. Their failed heist had awakened something ancient and powerful, something that could change the course of human history. And Maya, of course, would be obsessed with the symbols.

The rendezvous couldn't come soon enough.

Six hours later, Marcus climbed the creaking stairs of an abandoned Victorian townhouse in South London. The safe house, a dusty three story with boarded windows and *condemned* notices, had been Ghost's idea. No one would suspect a demolition site.

The others were gathered in what had once been a drawing room. Sofia sat cross legged on the floor, surrounded by glowing laptops pulling news feeds and security footage. Ghost stood at the window, pulling a board aside to check the street. Leo paced back and forth, his smooth composure fraying at the edges. Maya, as expected, was immersed in a sea of photographs and texts, her tablet aglow with ancient scripts.

"Well," Leo finally broke the silence, "that was a brilliant failure."

"We got the photographs," Maya countered without looking up. "The historical significance of those symbols alone"

"Historical significance doesn't pay off my gambling debts," Leo snapped. "We had one shot, and we blew it."

"The mission parameters changed," Ghost said calmly. "The tablet's behavior was unpredictable."

"Speaking of which," Sofia interjected, swiveling one laptop toward them. "Every camera in a three block radius went down. The power grid spiked. And get this" She pulled up an infrared satellite image. "The energy signature was visible from space."

Marcus sank into a threadbare armchair, dust puffing around him. "Maya. What have you found?"

Maya finally looked up, her eyes blazing with fervor. "It's extraordinary. The symbols you photographed they're not one language. They're many. I've identified Sumerian, proto Elamite, and what appears to be an entirely unknown script."

"That's interesting," Leo said, dripping with sarcasm, "but it doesn't"

"Let her finish," Marcus cut in, leaning forward.

Maya projected her tablet's display onto the peeling wallpaper, turning the faded surface into a flickering canvas of ancient secrets. "The symbols were moving, changing but not randomly. Look at this sequence." She played a clip from Marcus's camera footage. "They're cycling through different ancient writing systems, but the meaning stays consistent across translations."

"What does it mean?" Ghost asked, finally turning from the window.

"That's the fascinating part." Maya enlarged one image. "This pattern here I've found it in numerous ancient texts, always tied to discussions of dimensional gateways or portals to other worlds."

Sofia snorted. "You're not suggesting"

"I'm not insinuating anything," Maya cut her off. "I'm showing you what the data shows. And that's not all. The tablet's material makeup doesn't match any known metal or alloy. And those energy readings? They defy several laws of physics."

Marcus rose and paced toward the projection. His voice was quieter now. "The heat… it wasn't just heat, was it? When I was holding it, it felt alive."

A heavy silence settled over the room as they all absorbed the weight of that thought.

"Here's what we know," Sofia said at last, pulling multiple windows onto her screens. "We've got photographs of an artifact with impossible writing and impossible energy output. Every major security agency is now interested in what happened at the museum. And we don't have the actual artifact."

"We have something better," Maya countered. "Proof. Everything I've been researching everything I lost my academic standing for it's real. The symbols, the energy readings, they validate my theories about advanced ancient civilizations."

"Theories don't pay bills," Leo muttered, though less firmly this time.

Ghost stepped into the center of the room. "We need to make a decision. Do we walk away or do we pursue this?"

For a long moment, Marcus watched the symbols dance across the wall. The memory of the golden light, the way it had seemed to reach for him, the strange patterns traced across the night sky all of it lingered in his mind.

"Maya," he said slowly, "how long would it take you to translate the symbols?"

"With enough resources? A couple of days, maybe a week." She was already pulling up research databases.

"Sofia, can you keep us off the radar that long?"

Her fingers flew over the keys. "Already have. False trails leading to Spain and Egypt. We've got breathing room."

"Ghost?"

"Safe house is secure. I'll arrange supplies."

The look turned to Leo. He shrugged, throwing up his hands. "Fine. But this had better be worth more than the tablet would've been."

Marcus nodded. The decision was made. "Maya, you have one week. Find out what those symbols mean, and what that tablet really was. Sofia, track similar energy signatures worldwide. Ghost, secure us more safe locations. Leo"

"Yes?"

"We'll need your skills sooner than later. I get the feeling we're not the only ones interested in what we found tonight."

The team dispersed, the failed heist evolving into something far more dangerous and far more intriguing.

Morning light filtered weakly through the boarded windows as Marcus sat in silence, watching Maya work. The glow of her screen lit her eyes, mirroring the cryptic symbols that flickered across its surface.

They had failed to steal an artifact. But perhaps they had discovered something infinitely more valuable a mystery powerful enough to rewrite history.

## **Chapter 2: Ancient Secrets**

Three nights after the failed heist, Maya's ad hoc office in the attic of the safe house had devolved into an academic war zone. Every surface was buried beneath ancient texts and printouts, while sticky notes in every color created a rainbow tapestry across the walls. Holographic projections of the tablet's symbols swirled through the musty air.

It looked like the fever dream of a mad professor, Marcus thought wryly as he climbed the narrow stairs. Not far from the truth.

Maya sat cross legged on the floor, surrounded by open books and her laptop.

As Marcus took in the chaos, he reflected on what had driven each of them here.

Maya's relentless passion for uncovering the past wasn't just about discovery it was about redemption. Years earlier, she had lost her academic standing for daring to challenge conventional narratives. This wasn't just a heist to her. It was her chance to validate her theories and reclaim her place in a world that had cast her aside. Marcus knew that if they succeeded, she would shine but he also sensed how dangerous her desperation could be, for her and for the team.

Then there was Sofia the tech wizard whose calm exterior masked a fierce determination. She could navigate the gray waters of technology and legality with ease, but beneath her confident façade lay a painful scar: her brother had been wrongfully imprisoned after a museum security breach. For her, this was more than code or clever hacks. Every system she cracked was part of her quest for justice.

Ghost, the stoic ex military man, carried the weight of comrades who hadn't made it home. Combat had given way to shadows and subterfuge, but the burden of the past never left him. He wasn't here for money or glory he was here for the team. Protecting them had become his new mission, and failure would mean losing the only family he had left.

And Leo, the charming con artist, had his own demons. A lifetime of deception, of charming his way in but never belonging, had left him searching for something deeper. For him, this was a chance to prove he could be more than just a trickster. The heist, and now whatever lay beyond it, was his shot at belonging to something real.

Together, they weren't just a crew they were fractured souls bound by purpose. And Marcus felt the weight of their broken pieces pressing on him. This path would test not only their skills, but their bonds.

Maya's dark hair was pulled into a messy bun, held by a pencil. She hadn't changed clothes in at least twenty four hours. She barely looked up as Marcus entered, Sofia right behind him with a fresh batch of computational analyses.

"Play it again," Maya said, gesturing toward the projection of the tablet footage. "Stop at marker forty seven."

Sofia slipped into her corner, a command center of computers and glowing monitors, and pulled up the enhanced feed. The hologram displayed the moment the tablet began to glow, symbols flowing across its surface like molten quicksilver.

"There," Maya pointed, tracing a sequence of characters with her finger. "That pattern. Sofia, enhance the contrast."

Sofia's fingers flew across her keyboard, sharpening the image until the symbols gleamed against the tablet's surface.

"Look at this." Maya dragged a worn book from a pile and flipped to a marked page. "These symbols match an ancient

Chinese text describing the *Legend of the Money Tree*. Now, here's where it gets interesting the same pattern appears in Sumerian tales of the *Divine Treasury* and in Egyptian hieroglyphs about the *Vault of Infinite Wealth*."

Marcus leaned closer, studying the comparison. "Different cultures, same story?"

"More than that," Maya said, her eyes burning with excitement. "They're not just similar stories. They're describing the same artifact. The tablet. It's a key."

Sofia turned from her screens. "A key to what?"

"According to these texts," Maya said, shuffling papers, "there's a repository of wealth beyond imagination, created by an advanced ancient civilization. Different cultures reinterpreted it through myth, but the core elements stay the same: a hidden vault, a golden key, and wealth that 'flows like water.'"

"That would explain the tablet's properties," Sofia said, pulling up a fresh analysis. "The energy signature it emitted it created ripples in the quantum field my instruments can't even measure. Here." She projected a graph of oscillating wavelengths.

Maya's head snapped to another book, flipping rapidly before holding it up. Her eyes widened.

"The pattern matches this." She revealed an illustration of concentric circles filled with symbols. "A Babylonian text describing pathways between worlds. They called it *the key that bridges the gap between the mundane and the divine*."

Marcus replayed the footage in his mind the heat, the glow, the uncanny sensation he'd felt while holding the tablet. "It wasn't just energy. It was responding."

"To you," Maya said softly. "The texts mention chosen bearers those who can activate the key. What happened when you touched it was no coincidence."

The attic fell silent. Sofia's computers hummed. From downstairs, faint sounds drifted up Leo practicing his card tricks, his nervous habit.

"There's more," Sofia said, pulling up another screen. "I've been tracing similar energy signatures worldwide. They're faint, nothing like the museum's surge, but they're there. Look."

A holographic map shimmered to life, dotted with pulsing points of light.

Maya sprang to her feet, nearly toppling a stack of books. "The locations… they align with ancient trade routes tied to the Money Tree legends. Routes that supposedly lead to the entrance of the Divine Treasury."

Marcus studied the map, his mind racing. "So the tablet isn't just a key it's a map."

"A map, a key, and maybe a test," Maya said, pulling up more references. "The legends speak of trials tests for any bearer who dares to seek what lies beyond."

The reaction of the tablet might have been only the first step.

Sofia's computer chimed with an alert. "Speaking of steps, we've got movement. Multiple organizations are mobilizing archaeological teams to these locations. Someone else is connecting the dots."

"How long until they figure it out?" Marcus asked.

Her fingers flew over the keyboard. "At current rates three days, maybe four."

Maya glanced at her overflowing research piles, then back at the glowing map. "I need more time. These translations, the correlations there's still so much left to understand."

The symbols drifted lazily in the air as Marcus studied the holographic display, his thoughts circling back to the strange patterns that had burned across the London sky. They had stumbled onto something ancient, something powerful something that had been waiting to be awakened.

As the team debated, tension thickened. Maya's excitement was palpable, but Sofia's brow furrowed. She couldn't shake the feeling that the tablet was changing Marcus in ways none of them could yet define.

"Marcus," she said quietly, unease in her voice, "you need to be careful. This isn't just an artifact it feels alive. The energy readings were off the charts. I can't stop wondering what it's doing to you."

Marcus shrugged, brushing off her concern, but Sofia's eyes lingered. She had seen how the tablet pulsed against his back, how he seemed drawn to it like a moth to flame. The warmth had been intoxicating but was it dangerous? While the others were entranced by the possibilities, Sofia felt an ominous shadow creeping closer, one that could devour them if ignored.

Outside, the shadow already waited.

The Watchers had come.

Figures cloaked in darkness moved silently through the alleys, their forms blending seamlessly with the night. Their eyes glowed faintly, an unearthly light that pierced the gloom like distant stars. They radiated a stillness so absolute it bled dread into the air.

They were the guardians of forgotten knowledge, keepers of secrets buried in time. Their presence was a stark reminder: Marcus was not alone in this quest.

Inside, the air grew heavy. Shadows lengthened along the walls as the team caught fleeting glimpses through cracked windows. A chill crept into the room. Marcus felt the hairs rise at the back of his neck under the Watchers' silent gaze scrutiny that seemed to dissect every choice they made.

"What do they want?" Leo murmured nervously.

"I don't know," Maya whispered. "But they're here for a reason. And it may be tied to the tablet."

Their unseen observers loomed, a silent pressure that made every discovery feel dangerous. The stakes were climbing, and the artifact's grip on Marcus only tightened.

"We don't have time," Marcus said finally, cutting through the tension. "Maya focus on essential translations. Anything that tells us where to go next. Sofia predict the energy signatures. I'll brief Ghost and Leo."

He turned to leave, but Maya's voice stopped him. "Marcus the legends all say the same thing: the bearer of the key must be worthy. Whatever the tablet woke in you it wasn't coincidence. Be careful. Ancient forces don't like to be hurried."

Marcus nodded, his hand brushing his side as if he could still feel the tablet's warmth. Their failed heist had opened a door to something far greater than they imagined. Now they had to decide what waited on the other side before someone else reached it first.

Maya's research web had outgrown the attic, spilling into the safe house's second floor. Digital displays flickered with swirling symbols, while strings and pinned photos stretched across walls, a three dimensional map that looked like the fevered work of a conspiracy theorist.

"Look at this pattern," Maya said, projecting a series of images. "It appears in Sumerian cuneiform from 3000 BCE, then resurfaces on Chinese oracle bones eight hundred years later the same exact sequence."

Marcus watched the flowing projections. The symbols seemed to breathe, alive, shifting with organic rhythm. "Coincidence?"

"Once, maybe. But look." She swiped through more images. "Egyptian hieroglyphs, Indus Valley script, Mayan codices all containing the same symbolic sequence. Civilizations with no contact, yet sharing this knowledge."

From her glowing array of monitors, Sofia spoke without looking up. "The geography is even stranger. I've mapped every find location." She tapped a key, and a world map lit up, smothered with pulsing points of light. "They form a pattern. Like a circuit board etched into the Earth itself."

"Speaking of patterns," Ghost rumbled from the doorway. He stepped in, carrying a thick folder stamped with military classification. "My contacts in geological survey units found this. Electromagnetic disturbances. Specific points around the globe."

He spread half a dozen thermal images across the table swirling vortices of heat and light that defied explanation.

The points matched Sofia's map exactly.

"Those patterns," Maya breathed, reaching for one of her reference books. "They're identical to the designs on the tablet. But these aren't etched into metal these are massive, carved directly into the Earth itself."

Leo appeared, idly fidgeting with a deck of cards. The click and shuffle of them was his nervous tell, though he wore his usual smirk. "My sources in the antiquities black market are already buzzing. Word is spreading fast. Artifacts like our tablet are surfacing all over the world same golden metal, same impossible composition. Every single one is causing bizarre phenomena upon contact. No one can explain it, but they all whisper it's dangerous."

Sofia's bank of computers chimed in a rising sequence as her algorithms finished their runs. Her eyes lit up as she spun one monitor toward the group. "I've cross referenced the electromagnetic disturbances with ancient trade routes and historical line maps. The alignment is precise mathematically precise. There's a geometric logic to the placement. This isn't natural. Whatever it is, it was engineered."

Maya summoned a three dimensional model on her laptop, her voice quickening. "Those symbols we captured from the tablet they're not an alphabet. They're coordinates. Each civilization carved its piece of the map into their culture, disguising it as language or myth. What we thought were stories are fragments of a far larger design."

She cycled through digital scrolls. "The Chinese called it the *Money Tree*. The Sumerians called it the *Divine Treasury*. In Indian texts it was the *Well of Infinite Abundance*. Different names, different myths, but the same underlying description: a vault of endless wealth, safeguarded by powers beyond human comprehension."

Ghost spread more classified photos across the table. "These energy readings see here? They spike every four hundred and fifty eight days, like clockwork. The military has been tracking them for decades. They thought it was natural activity, or foreign weapons tests. But look closely at the wavelength patterns."

Sofia overlaid Ghost's charts with her own data. The graphs locked together seamlessly, wave for wave. "A perfect match," she confirmed. "The tablet's emissions are identical to these global events. It's all connected the symbols, the nodes, the cycles. Somebody, or something, built a worldwide network thousands of years ago, and we've been walking over it blindly ever since."

Leo unfolded a series of black market photographs, laying them carefully in line with Ghost's files. His usual bravado had slipped into something more serious. "Every piece my contacts found shared the same impossible properties: a metal we can't replicate, strange heat signatures, and symbols that… move. But only when no one's watching directly."

"They're all keys," Maya said, eyes blazing with academic fervor. "Each civilization was entrusted with one, a fragment of the puzzle. A key to their own node in the network. But the tablet we found it might be the *master key*, the one that links them all together."

Marcus stared at the flood of data cascading across Sofia's monitors. His mind drifted back to the moment he touched the tablet and felt it respond heat, light, a heartbeat against his hand. "Why now?" he whispered. "Why is all this surfacing in our time?"

Maya pulled up an astronomical chart, stars and arcs glittering in the projection. "Because of the cycle. Every ancient culture recorded it a great cycle when the network would awaken. The spikes Ghost tracked? They're growing more frequent, more intense. Whatever this system is, it's waking up."

"And we're not the only ones noticing it," Sofia added grimly. She flipped through a stream of surveillance footage: satellite captures, intercepted transmissions, grainy photographs of excavation teams. "Multiple organizations are mobilizing their best archaeologists and scientists. They don't yet know what they're chasing, but they're circling the truth."

Ghost studied the world map, his eyes narrowing. "These nodes... they're not random. They form a sequence. Each one has to be activated in a specific order."

"Like a combination lock on a planetary scale," Leo murmured, his deck of cards hanging forgotten in his hand.

Maya nodded, sliding new translations into view. "The texts all warn of it. The order matters. Activate a node incorrectly and the results could be catastrophic disasters of mythic proportion. The ancients left warnings carved into stone, painted onto walls, hidden in chants and hymns."

Sofia's algorithms pulsed out a fresh pattern, the lines on her screen glowing like veins of light. "Based on the frequency of the signatures and their symbolic resonance, I can predict the sequence. The first node is in the Gobi Desert."

Maya's fingers danced across her tablet as she pulled up cultural records. "An ancient crossroads where Chinese, Mongolian, and Central Asian routes converged. The legends say the desert holds the first trial for those who seek the Divine Treasury."

Marcus stood at the center of the room, surrounded by flickering holograms and scattered files. The magnitude of what they were discussing pressed on him like a weight. They had uncovered not just a relic but a hidden infrastructure of civilizations long gone, a lattice of power woven across the Earth. It wasn't merely the discovery of a lifetime. It was something that could rewrite human history and reshape the world's future.

"How long until the next spike?" he asked quietly.

"Three days," Sofia said without hesitation. "When it hits, every major research institute and government on Earth will be able to track these signals. If we're going to act, it has to be before then."

Marcus scanned the faces of his team: Sofia, eyes sharp with both fear and resolve; Maya, glowing with unbridled excitement; Ghost, calm but tense with unspoken duty; Leo, anxious but hiding it beneath his wry charm. They had come together for a heist, but now they were guardians of something far larger.

"Then we have three days," Marcus said, "to reach the Gobi Desert and figure out how to awaken that first node."

The race had begun a desperate contest against time itself.

The safe house attic had been transformed into what the team called their *war room*. Afternoon light seeped weakly through the boarded windows, slicing across the holographic projections floating in the center of the space.

"What we're about to show you," Maya said, sweeping her hand across the display, "turns upside down everything we thought we knew about ancient civilizations."

The hologram shifted, the world map now dotted with dozens of glowing red points. "These," she continued, "are the recorded locations of catastrophic natural disasters."

Sofia picked up seamlessly, her fingers flickering over her controls. "I've cross referenced those disasters with our energy signature map. The overlap is… disturbing."

New layers unfolded across the projection: earthquakes, volcanic eruptions, inexplicable collapses of cities. The patterns interwove with geometric precision, superimposed against historical disaster zones.

Marcus leaned forward, recognition flashing. "Wait I've seen this before." He dug into his satchel, pulling out a worn field journal from his archaeological work in Turkey. He flipped to a page marked with hand sketched diagrams. "Here. Five years ago. We found the same geometric carvings beneath a site thirty meters deep. Local legends called it *The Gate of the Gods*."

"That's not all," Maya said, her voice taut with urgency. She summoned images from multiple excavation archives. "Look every major collapse in human history coincides with these nodes. Mohenjo daro. Göbekli Tepe. The Mayan classical decline. Each event aligns with massive energy spikes at these exact points."

Even Ghost, usually implacable, shifted uncomfortably. "My contacts in military survey divisions recorded identical spikes days before modern disasters as well. Classified, of course. The official line was 'unknown weapon tests.'"

"It's not a weapon," Maya shot back, pulling up her infamous academic paper the one that had ended her career. "It's a network of dimensional doorways. The ancients masked them as sacred sites, but they were gateways, woven into the fabric of their civilizations."

Leo let out a skeptical laugh. "Dimensional doorways. That theory's what got you tossed out of academia, wasn't it?"

Maya's gaze didn't waver. "Yes. Because no one believed it then. But this proves it. They weren't myths. They were building something real something we're only beginning to understand. The Money Tree wasn't just legend. It was the access point to resources from another dimension. A vault, a treasury, a bridge between worlds."

Sofia projected another layer of data, fresh lines of energy overlaying the map like veins of fire. The room glowed with their discovery.

What they were seeing was more than history. It was revelation.

"The energy signatures we're reading share striking similarities with theoretical models of dimensional rifts," Sofia said, her voice steady but low. "The mathematics holds up even if the implications sound impossible."

Marcus opened his worn journal to a page filled with detailed sketches and annotations. His fingers lingered over the symbols he had painstakingly documented years earlier. "These markings I found in Turkey they're not decorative. They're equations. Formulas. Instructions." He looked up, meeting Maya's eyes. "Your paper was right. These aren't religious texts. They're technical manuals."

"Exactly," Maya replied, almost triumphant. She pulled up more comparative images, the glow from her screen reflecting in her eyes. "Every ancient culture encoded the same data in its own way. The *Egyptian Book of the Dead* isn't simply funerary text it's a guidebook for interdimensional passage. Chinese legends of the Money Tree? Not mythology at all, but technical specifications cloaked in folklore. These stories were survival manuals disguised as religion."

Ghost laid out his classified photographs across the console, their margins stamped with thick black military seals. "Look at these readings," he said, tapping a finger against the sharp spikes. "The energy levels aren't stabilizing. They're building. Stronger, faster. It's as if the system is powering up."

"Or waking up," Marcus said quietly, recalling the tablet's unnatural pulse in his hands the way it had seemed to recognize him.

Maya nodded, her tone firm. "That fits. My paper theorized these weren't designed as permanent installations. They were dormant until the right time, waiting for specific triggers. They were meant to awaken only under the proper conditions." She called up astronomical charts, overlaying their lines of data with ancient calendars. "Like now."

New alerts pinged on Sofia's computers. "The tablet we recovered it's not just a key. It's an activation device. The sequences we photographed match startup patterns described in Maya's work. It wasn't just symbolic it was literal."

"But there's a catch," Maya said, her excitement giving way to gravity. "Every civilization that attempted to force these portals open too soon was annihilated. Their collapses weren't random. They were system failsafe mechanisms designed to punish unauthorized access."

Marcus exchanged a weighted look with Ghost. "That explains the military surveillance. They must have detected buildups. They've been circling this for decades without understanding what they're chasing."

"Multiple agencies are already investigating," Sofia confirmed, pulling up surveillance footage blurred images of dig teams, convoys of equipment, satellites sweeping over desert landscapes. "But they're piecing together fragments. They don't have what we do. They don't have the key."

"The tablet reacted to Marcus," Maya said suddenly, her gaze fixed on him. "It recognized you. Just as I theorized. The system selects its own operators when the time is right."

Leo shuffled his cards with twitching fingers, the steady rhythm betraying his nerves. "So, what happens if we activate these portals? Do we get a golden door and walk into infinite money? Happily, ever after?"

"Or," Ghost said flatly, "we trigger one of those failsafe and end up like the civilizations that came before. Ashes."

Maya held up one final image, sketched in her notebook with painstaking care. An intricate design interlocking circles, lattices of lines, and cryptic symbols. "The ancients left detailed instructions. The portals must be activated in sequence. By the right operators. At precise moments in time. Deviate from those instructions"

"And we join the ruins of history," Sofia finished grimly.

Marcus stared at the glowing holographic displays, tracing how every thread connected their past excavations, Maya's exiled research, the shifting tablet in his pack. None of it was coincidence. They had been drawn into a story written thousands of years ago, one now entering its final chapter.

"Your paper," he said slowly, turning back to Maya. "It wasn't just theory, was it? You knew."

She nodded, her voice quiet but unflinching. "I found references across every major civilization. They all pointed to *this* cycle. The system isn't just waking it's fulfilling its original purpose."

"Which is?" Leo asked, his voice little more than a whisper.

"To open a door," Maya said, pulling up the last page of her banned paper. The words shimmered on the projection: *A threshold between the mundane and the divine.* "Not just to wealth, but to knowledge and power beyond imagination. The ancients built this network as a test. If we follow their instructions precisely, we prove ourselves worthy of what lies beyond."

Silence fell heavy across the room. For the first time, the entire team felt it not just the thrill of discovery, not just the danger, but the sheer scale of the choice before them. They weren't chasing treasure anymore. They were players in a millennia old design, participants in a test that could elevate or obliterate humanity.

Marcus glanced down at the tablet photographs, the symbols still shifting as if alive. "Then we'd better make sure we pass."

The weight of history and the burden of the future settled on the team like an iron shroud.

Suddenly Sofia's triumphant shout shattered the pre dawn silence. "I've got something!"

Within minutes, the others crowded around her workstation. Half a dozen monitors pulsed with seismic data, her algorithms painting crossing waves across the globe. Sofia's hands flew over the keyboard as the display came to life.

"Look at this," she said, enlarging the data into a rolling timeline. A time lapse visualization appeared, stretching across five thousand years of history. Pulses of seismic activity swept across the globe not random quakes, but rhythmic, patterned, like the steady thump of a colossal heartbeat.

"That's impossible," Ghost muttered, leaning close. "Earthquakes don't behave like that."

"They do when they're engineered," Sofia countered. She overlaid the pulses with their global map of ancient nodes. The two patterns fused seamlessly. "Every catastrophic seismic event in recorded history follows this sequence. It isn't chaos it's a clock."

Maya grabbed her tablet, cross referencing against her astronomical calculations. Her voice trembled as the pieces locked together. "The Mayan Long Count. The Hindu Yuga cycles. The Egyptian Sothic calendars. They were all referencing the same thing not the end of the world, but the countdown to activation."

Marcus watched the seismic heartbeat ripple across the projection, each wave inching closer to the present day. "How long is the cycle?"

"Five thousand, one hundred twenty five years exactly," Sofia said, pulling up a diagram of overlapping cycles. "The precise length of the Mayan calendar. And we're in its final stage."

Leo, unusually silent, finally spoke. His cards slipped in his hands. "How final are we talking here?"

A countdown clock flared across Sofia's screens. Her voice was tight. "Based on the acceleration of seismic events and intensifying energy signatures, we have twenty eight days. That's when the cycle completes."

"The tablet's reaction makes sense now," Maya said, enlarging her translated sequences. "The symbols weren't random. They were following the activation order. Marcus when you touched it, you triggered the first phase."

Ghost spread more of his classified documents across the table. "Energy spikes are ramping up everywhere. The system is building toward something. It's not stopping."

Sofia pulled up yet another data overlay. "And I've pinpointed the first portal. All the seismic and energy patterns converge here." She tapped the screen, and an image of barren dunes filled the projection: a remote sector of the Gobi Desert. Satellite imaging revealed geometric carvings cut deep into bedrock, half buried under shifting sand.

"*The Gobi Gate*," Maya whispered, clutching an ancient Chinese chronicle. Her fingers trembled as she read the archaic script aloud. "The *Door of Heaven's Treasury*. The first trial the obstacle every seeker of divine knowledge had to face."

The words hung heavy in the room. The first trial awaited, and the clock was already ticking.

Marcus studied the satellite images projected across the table. His eyes narrowed as he traced the etched geometry. "Those patterns… they're the same as what I found in Turkey, but on a massive scale. This isn't just a door. It's the first key in a sequence."

"But here's the problem," Sofia said, overlaying thermal imaging data across the map. Pulsing lines of red and orange spread like veins through the desert. "The energy readings are off the charts. If we misread them, if we make even one mistake in the activation sequence"

"We could cause a catastrophic seismic event," Ghost finished grimly.

Leo flicked his deck of cards restlessly, the rhythmic shuffle sharp in the silence. "Maybe," he said with forced levity, "we should forget all this and find ourselves a nice, simple bank to rob. No earthquakes. No end of the world scenarios."

"We can't," Maya cut in, her voice steady, unwavering. "The cycle is going to complete whether we act or not. If no one initiates the sequence correctly, it will trigger automatically under failsafe protocol."

"Causing what, exactly?" Marcus asked, though his gut already supplied the answer.

Maya brought up a series of historical overlays: floods, crumbled cities, ancient ruins. "Every previous cycle ended the same way. When the portals weren't activated properly, energy built up until it was catastrophically released. Floods.

Earthquakes. Volcanic eruptions. Civilizations wiped away in a single generation."

Sofia's predictive models glowed across half a dozen screens. "Based on current readings, a failsafe event this time wouldn't just devastate one region. It would be global."

The silence that followed was heavy, suffocating. They were no longer chasing treasure. They were racing to stop the clock on an apocalypse.

"We've got competition," Ghost reminded them, his voice cutting through the tension. "Multiple teams are chasing the same energy trails. They'll find the Gobi site soon enough."

"But they don't have this," Marcus said, holding up the tablet photographs. "They don't have Maya's translations. Or Sofia's sequencing algorithms. And they don't have" He stopped.

"You," Maya finished softly. "The tablet chose you, Marcus. That wasn't random. The ancients built in safeguards only selected operators can trigger the portals. And you're one of them."

Leo leaned back against the peeling plaster wall, tossing a card between his fingers. "So our choices are: gamble on waking up an ancient portal system that might kill us all… or sit on our hands and watch the world burn in twenty eight days."

"Twenty seven days, fourteen hours," Sofia corrected without missing a beat, glancing at the relentless countdown running across her screen.

Marcus stood, scanning the faces of his team. They had started as thieves bound by greed and adrenaline. Now, somehow, they had become the world's last hope. "The Gobi site," he asked Sofia, "how long to reach it?"

"Three days, by conventional routes," she replied. "But desert conditions mean we'll need modified vehicles. And specialized equipment for the energy fields."

"My contacts can arrange both," Ghost said, his tone clipped, assured.

"I can track the movements of the other teams," Sofia added. "If they close in, we'll know."

"I can refine the activation sequences," Maya said, holding up her translated texts. "But it has to be exact. One wrong symbol and the failsafe could trigger."

All eyes turned to Leo. He groaned, throwing his cards onto the table. "Fine. I'll bring my… talents. If any of these private security types get in our way, I'll make sure we slip through."

Marcus nodded. His decision was made. "We leave in twelve hours. Sofia, gather every scrap of data on the temple complex. Maya, refine the sequences. Ghost, arrange transport and supplies. Leo"

"Yeah?"

"We'll need you ready to outplay whoever's waiting for us."

As the others dispersed, Marcus returned to the satellite feed, his gaze locked on the carved patterns beneath the Gobi sands. This wasn't just another archaeological site. It was the first key in an ancient system a system that could save or doom humanity. In twenty seven days, they would either succeed or vanish into catastrophe, unsung and unknown.

The countdown ticked on, relentless.

Downstairs, the safe house basement had become a staging ground. Crates of supplies and neat rows of desert gear lined the walls. Weapons, climbing rigs, ration packs every item tagged and ready.

Ghost stood at the center, hunched over a makeshift tactical table. Maps of the Gobi spread before him, marked in thick ink. The team gathered around as he pointed with a calloused finger. "Three insertion points," he said, marking them with red circles. "These areas," he added, circling again in blue, "are patrolled heavily. Chinese military units. My source also confirms at least two private security firms active in the area."

"Four firms now," Sofia corrected, her eyes glued to her laptop. "Satellite sweeps show two more encampments. Someone's throwing a lot of money at this." She froze, a flicker of hesitation crossing her face, then quickly minimized a window on her screen.

Marcus caught the movement but didn't press. He had seen similar flickers of secrecy from others whispered calls, encrypted messages in the dead of night. He wasn't the only one carrying hidden truths.

"Equipment's sorted," Leo said, tossing a thick envelope onto the table. "Favors called in. Desert gear, climbing rigs, comms, and…" He patted a black case with unusual tenderness. "Special items."

Ghost's eyes narrowed slightly, but he said nothing.

Maya laid out her translations, papers rustling under her fingers. One leather bound journal she kept tucked firmly to her side. "The activation sequence has to be performed just before dawn. The desert's blue hour. That's when the energy resonance peaks."

"That's a razor thin window," Ghost said, scanning the coordinates. "And the risk of exposure will be highest then."

"Speaking of exposure," Sofia interjected, spinning her laptop toward them. "I've been intercepting chatter Chinese Antiquities Bureau, private researchers, military traffic. But there's something else." She hesitated before continuing. "I picked up communications I can't crack. They're using quantum encrypted channels."

"Government level?" Ghost asked.

Sofia shook her head. "Higher. This is beyond state tech. Whoever they are… their capabilities don't belong to this Earth."

Marcus studied his team. He saw the tension in their faces, the weight of secrets pressing on each of them Maya's hidden notes, Sofia's private hesitations, Leo's "special items," Ghost's shadowy contacts, his own unspoken discoveries. The tablet's choice hadn't been random. They were all bound to this in ways they didn't yet understand.

"Resources," Marcus said, his voice cutting through the silence. "Ghost, what's our timeline for transport?"

"Military cargo flight departs in eighteen hours. Unofficial, off the record. It'll drop us fifty miles from the site."

He pulled out a satellite phone and stepped away, his voice low, controlled, inaudible.

Leo shuffled his cards with nervous energy, the sound sharp against the silence of the basement. "My contacts gave me some interesting extras," he said finally, eyes flicking toward the black case at his side. "Stuff that could… help with any competition." His voice trailed off, but his gaze lingered on the case with a mixture of pride and unease.

Maya barely glanced up, her pen scratching furiously across the worn pages of her private journal. She angled the pad away from the others, her words for her eyes alone. "The temple complex will have its own defenses," she said. "Ancient, but still active. The texts describe trials tests designed to weed out the unworthy."

"Modern security I can handle," Sofia muttered, still typing furiously at her console. "But these energy readings… they're unlike anything in my databases. Almost as if" She stopped suddenly, her fingers hovering over the keyboard, before she snapped a window shut with deliberate finality.

Uneasy silence followed, thick and suffocating. Only the hum of servers and the rhythmic clack of Sofia's keys filled the basement. Each of them avoided the others' eyes, but furtive glances betrayed the truth: suspicion simmered beneath the surface. A card slipped too carefully into a sleeve, a journal guarded too tightly, a call taken too far out of earshot. They were a team, yes but also a collection of secrets waiting to collide.

Far above the safe house, the silence wasn't theirs alone. A stealth drone floated in the night sky, its quantum sensors sweeping the building with inhuman precision. Every word, every gesture, every flicker of hesitation was captured and beamed across the globe to watchers' unseen. Somewhere in darkened rooms, eyes studied the team with surgical intensity, waiting.

"One more thing," Marcus said at last, breaking the tension. His voice carried the weight of command and unease. "Once we start this sequence, there's no backing out. It has to be completed or the consequences…" He let the unfinished sentence hang, the implication heavy as stone.

"We're all in," Maya said quickly, though her hand pressed protectively over her hidden journal, as if guarding her thoughts from the others.

"Absolutely," Leo added, forcing a smile as he tucked a card not quite casually into his sleeve.

Ghost returned from the far side of the basement, sliding his phone into his pocket. "Transport confirmed," he reported. His face gave nothing away, and no one knew he had made a second call, his voice hushed, his loyalties perhaps not as straightforward as they appeared.

Sofia shut down a row of encrypted feeds, locking them behind invisible firewalls. "Satellite coverage secured. Once we enter the zone, we'll be dark." She didn't mention the hidden protocols she had embedded, safeguards accessible only to her.

Marcus studied each of them, one by one. They were the best at what they did experts, specialists, misfits bound together by fate. But they were also liars, each playing their own game. And at the center of it all, the tablet had chosen him. Why? What had the ancients seen in him, Marcus Chen, to deem him worthy of bearing their key? The question gnawed at him, heavy and relentless.

"Wheels up in seventeen hours," he said finally, his voice cutting through the weight in the air. "Sort your gear. Once we're on site, we move fast."

The team dispersed, scattering to their own corners of the safe house. Marcus watched as they drifted apart noticing the way they avoided eye contact, the way they gave each other space, the care with which they guarded their secrets. They were united, yet distant. Trusting, yet mistrustful.

Miles away, in a surveillance hub bathed in cold fluorescent light, a figure leaned back in her chair, surrounded by a wall of screens. Dozens of feeds showed the team's every move, every word. "They're moving earlier than predicted," she said into a secure line, her voice calm, professional, detached. "Adjust the timeline. Keep distance. They're sharper than expected, and far more cautious."

Back in the basement, Marcus sifted through the tablet photographs once more. The symbols shifted beneath his gaze, as if alive, writhing and reconfiguring when he blinked. The weight of destiny pressed on him the realization that whatever lay ahead, there was no turning back.

In less than twenty four hours, they would step into the desert, toward a temple buried in sand and legend. Toward a trial that could save the world or bring it to ruin.

Above the safe house, the drone drifted silently, one of countless unseen eyes fixed upon them. Across the world, others watched and waited, tracking this unlikely coalition of thieves, scholars, soldiers, and liars each driven by ambition, by desperation, by secrets they dared not share.

The countdown ticked steadily onward, not just toward their departure, but toward revelation. Toward betrayal. Toward survival or annihilation.

**Chapter 3: The Pattern**

The military cargo plane banked sharply over the jagged ridges of the Gobi Altai Mountains, its steel hull groaning against the thin air of high altitude. Through a small oval window, Marcus stared out at the landscape sprawling below a savage tableau of peaks and valleys untouched by civilization. The rising sun bled across the horizon, painting the stone in hues of amber and blood red. Shadows stretched long and sharp, dancing across the terrain as though alive, flickering like sentinels warning of what lay ahead.

Ghost sat in the cockpit beside the pilot, his tactical gear bristling with specialized equipment. His headset crackled softly as he toggled between frequencies, monitoring a chorus of signals. "Three bogies on long range radar," he reported flatly. "Military craft two confirmed Chinese, one civilian tracking us from a distance, holding position."

In the cargo hold, Sofia had transformed one corner into a mobile command center. Six glowing monitors surrounded her, streaming live data: drone feeds, satellite sweeps, magnetometer readings, infrared scans. Her hands blurred across multiple keyboards, orchestrating a symphony of information into something coherent.

"I'm getting anomalous readings," she called out suddenly, frowning at one display. "The magnetic field around the target zone isn't behaving normally." She brought up a 3D model swirling lines of electromagnetic activity spun across the screen like smoke caught in a wind tunnel. "It's almost like it's… breathing."

Maya leaned in, her fingers tracing ancient glyphs across her notes. "The texts mentioned this. They called it *the dragon's breath*. A protective phenomenon designed to disorient navigation and confuse intruders."

Leo, pale from turbulence and gripping his harness as if it were a lifeline, groaned. "Wonderful. Anything else we should know? Fire breathing statues? Angry sand spirits?"

"Multiple cave openings detected," Sofia said, ignoring him. Her drone feeds displayed jagged mouths carved into the mountainside. "But only one matches the geometric ratios from the tablet." She highlighted a formation nestled among outcroppings barely visible, yet precise enough to betray the hand of design. "There. That's our entrance."

Ghost's voice crackled over the intercom, clipped and urgent. "Fifteen minutes to insertion. Beginning descent toward the drop zone."

Marcus studied the footage. At first glance, the cave looked natural, just another shadow in the rock. But the longer he stared, the more its unnatural symmetry revealed itself. The ancient builders had sculpted architecture to mimic geology, weaving artifice into the bones of the earth.

Suddenly Sofia's screens erupted in red. "Spike of energy!" she shouted as alarms shrieked. "Something down there just activated."

The aircraft jolted violently as instruments went haywire. Needles spun. Dials flickered. The pilot cursed in Russian, wrestling with the controls as turbulence slammed them sideways.

"It knows we're here," Maya whispered, clutching her harness. "The system is aware of us."

Ghost switched his visor to thermal. "Heat signatures in the cave network. At first glance, geothermal vents…" He paused, adjusted. "No. Too precise. Too evenly spaced. They're machines mechanisms buried in the rock."

Sofia's drones plunged deeper, their cameras revealing what lay within. Marcus leaned closer as the feed stabilized. The walls of the cavern pulsed with shifting symbols identical to those on the tablet only here, they moved freely, flowing across the stone like molten metal, rearranging themselves in response to the drones' presence.

"Look at this," Sofia whispered, enhancing the footage. The camera pulled back, revealing a chamber vast and echoing, its ceiling vanishing into darkness. At the center rose a structure that defied human logic: a towering pillar of impossible geometry, its surface rippling with light and patterns that seemed alive.

"The First Gate," Maya breathed, awe softening her voice. Her hands shook as she flipped through her notes. "Exactly as described. 'A tower of living stone, awakening to the presence of the worthy.'"

Ghost's voice snapped them back. "We need to move. Those helicopters will have ground teams deployed in less than an hour."

Sofia pointed at her map, multiple points lighting up. "Three possible entrances. All converge on the chamber. But two show signs of recent collapses."

"Deliberate blockages?" Marcus asked.

Maya studied the footage, brow furrowing. "Not deliberate. The system is… reconfiguring itself. It's alive, adapting to us."

The plane began its final approach, descending toward a plateau half a kilometer from the cave mouth. Ghost strode back into the cargo hold, checking rappel lines and weapons. His calm, practiced movements belied the tension in his eyes.

"Temperature's plummeting," he reported. "Storm front inbound from the northwest. Visibility will be near zero."

Sofia's models confirmed it, storm systems spiraling on her screen. "This isn't natural," she murmured. "The system's generating weather cover, manipulating temperature gradients to create the storm itself."

Marcus stared through the window as the clouds churned like a living creature. Lightning flickered unnaturally inside them, illuminating the ridges in quicksilver bursts. The ancient builders hadn't simply raised monuments they had shaped the very earth and sky into weapons.

"Final checks," Ghost ordered. The cargo ramp lowered with a deafening roar, bitter wind slamming into the hold. The air carried the sharp scent of ozone, metallic and alien, prickling Marcus's skin like static.

Sofia recalled her drones, docking them into charging cradles. She slid on her helmet, her voice steady. "Underground mapping is active. Helmet cams are synced. I'll monitor your positions relative to the chamber."

The plane touched down hard, its wheels grinding against rock and snow. The team surged forward, gear strapped tight, eyes on the storm shrouded ridges ahead. Through the curtain of snow and mist, Marcus glimpsed the cave entrance. Strange lights pulsed around it, their rhythm eerily synchronized with the shifting symbols captured on the tablet.

"It's not waiting for us," Marcus thought, his pulse quickening. "It's calling us."

The storm closed around them, camouflage woven from cloud and electricity. High above, Chinese helicopters circled helplessly, their instruments scrambled into blindness.

The First Gate awaited.

The wind screamed through the mountain pass as the team established their base camp. Weather beaten tarps snapped overhead, concealing a nest of high tech equipment hidden in the rocks. Ghost oversaw the perimeter, laying sensor arrays so seamlessly they vanished into the stone.

"Keep everything inside the magnetic dampening field," Sofia instructed, adjusting a device that looked half satellite dish, half Tesla coil. Sparks crackled along its coils. "The interference is growing stronger. We've already lost three compasses."

They had come prepared quantum sensors, ground penetrating radar, even unmarked hardware from Ghost's shadowy sources. Every piece was customized to counteract the waves radiating from the caves. The earth itself seemed alive, whispering in magnetic pulses, daring them to enter.

And in the distance, beyond snow and shadow, the First Gate pulsed like a heartbeat, waiting.

Maya crouched near the cave entrance, her breath clouding in the freezing air as she photographed a series of markings carved into the stone. At first glance they looked like ancient script, but when she shifted her angle, they seemed to move subtle, unnerving. "These aren't just decorative," she said, brushing snow from a line of symbols. She compared them against her notes, her voice quickening. "They're warnings… but they're also measurements."

Marcus knelt beside her, his own instruments buzzing with chaotic readings. "Measurements of what?"

"Time," Maya said, frowning as she traced the grooves with gloved fingers. "But not time as we understand it. This is a record of dimensional intervals markers between worlds."

Leo staggered up the incline, lugging a heavy case of scanning equipment. He set it down and flipped open the lid, but froze when the machines whined like dying animals. The scanner's display flickered violently before dying in a wash of static. "Uh, guys?" His face paled. "That's the fourth unit we've lost." He stepped forward again, only to hear the metallic buckles of his boots vibrating, humming like tuning forks.

From her mobile command center, Sofia watched a wave of interference ripple across her screens. "The magnetic field isn't random anymore. It's forming patterns like it's… trying to communicate." Energy waves bloomed across her display, arranging themselves into fleeting shapes that eerily resembled the tablet's shifting symbols.

The mountain rumbled, a deep growl reverberating through stone. Pebbles skittered down the slope, clattering like bones. Ghost's perimeter sensors flared amber, warning of seismic disturbance.

"Minor quake," Sofia reported. "Magnitude two point three. But…" She stared hard at her readouts. "The wave pattern's unnatural. Too regular."

Maya snapped a series of frantic photographs as the glowing symbols on the cave wall seemed to brighten in rhythm with the tremors. "They're responding," she breathed. "The markings are reacting to vibration. This entire site, it's a tuning fork!"

Leo backed away, his scanning gear already failing. "Everything electronic within five meters is toast. But look at this." He pulled a simple wristwatch from his pocket, its hands spinning backward at a frantic pace.

The ground shuddered harder, knocking snow loose from the ridge. The earth didn't feel random it recoiled, alive, like some vast creature shifting in its sleep.

"Movement in the cave system," Ghost's voice snapped through comms. "Multiple chambers... shifting configuration."

Sofia's ground penetrating radar redrew itself in jagged sweeps, tunnels reconfiguring in real time. "He's right," she said, awe and fear mingling. "The cave network is moving. Reorganizing itself into... something else. A puzzle, solving itself."

Maya's face glowed with excitement. "It's responding to us. The system isn't just active it's testing us."

Marcus stared into the entrance. The shadows inside twisted unnaturally, flickering in defiance of the storm's light. "Sofia, status on those helicopters?"

"The storm's holding them back," she replied, fingers flying across her keyboards. "But they've deployed ground teams on the far ridge. We've got three hours maybe less before they find their way in."

Another quake rattled the ground. This time the tremors pulsed deliberately: three beats, a pause, then two more. The pattern repeated, like the measured thump of a colossal heart.

"The intervals are expanding," Maya said quickly, scanning her notes. "The texts described this. These pulses are part of the awakening sequence. It's beginning."

Leo, keeping well clear of the interference zone, gestured to the markings. "These patterns they're stronger than anything we saw on the tablet. It's almost like the tablet was a key, and this..." he swept a hand toward the cavern mouth..."this is the lock."

Ghost trudged back from his perimeter check, frost collecting on his gear. "We need to move soon. The storm won't cover us forever. These tremors will draw more eyes."

New readings surged across Sofia's monitors. Energy spikes climbed in brutal leaps, approaching levels her instruments weren't built to measure. "It's building toward something," she said. "Exponential increase across every channel."

The symbols on the rock flared brighter, their glow pulsing in rhythm with the quakes. Marcus felt the weight of the moment the sense that this was no ordinary threshold. It was a lure and a trap, an invitation and a warning, all carved by hands long turned to dust.

"Primary setup," Marcus ordered. His voice steadied the chaos. "Sofia, map every centimeter of that entrance. Maya, translate everything, cross check with the tablet. Leo, find a way to shield the essential equipment. Ghost..." another tremor shook the mountain, "secure a fallback route. If this goes wrong, I want us alive."

The mountain trembled again, steady, deliberate. It wasn't seismic it was breathing.

Sofia expanded her holographic display. The tent filled with spectral light, showing the mountain's interior in shifting transparency. The layers of stone twisted in impossible spirals, looping back into themselves like knots. The patterns pulsed, not inert, but animate.

"These structures can't exist," Sofia muttered, pointing to one formation. "The rock isn't folded it's woven. Interlaced like fabric threads."

Marcus studied the 3D projection, his pulse quickening. For a split second, the hologram distorted and the stone itself seemed to move. The formation bent, flexed, as if alive.

"The magnetic fields are forming a lattice," Sofia said, layering fresh data over the image. Blue lines crisscrossed into a shifting grid. "It's a network, but the geometry won't hold still. It changes every few seconds."

"Like it's breathing," Ghost said, his normally impassive voice edged with unease. His own military grade sensors calibrated for hostile environments lit with impossible readings.

Leo, crouched near a jagged outcrop, lost his balance as the rock vibrated beneath his touch. "Whoa did we just *do* that?" He jerked his hand away, shaking out his fingers. "The stone's humming. Vibrating at a pitch sharp enough to rattle my teeth."

Maya hurried over with her instruments, but as soon as she neared the spot, her devices shut down. Dead screens. Batteries drained in seconds. She hissed in frustration. "The energy field's stronger here. And look."

She lifted her notebook. The ink on her sketches of the symbols was moving lines shifting across the page, rewriting themselves into new patterns.

A low hum coiled through the cavern air, too deep to hear clearly, but strong enough to press against bone. Equipment failed in rolling waves: screens flickered, rebooted, died, then flared back to life. Sofia swore under her breath as her main console restarted three times in succession. On the third reboot, lines of code filled the screen programs she had never written. Strings of data scrolled in alien syntax, as though the system itself were responding to something, or someone.

The cave was no longer dormant. It was awake.

"Guys?" Leo's voice cracked with a note of controlled panic. He held up his deck of playing cards, the ones he never went anywhere without. They floated above his palm, spinning slowly, arranging themselves into impossible geometric patterns that mirrored the shifting cave symbols. "Uh, pretty sure they're not supposed to do that."

Ghost stiffened as the tactical gear strapped across his body flickered, powering on and off of its own accord. "Temperature drops every thirty seconds ten degrees, then back to normal." His breath fogged the air in sharp pulses that lingered unnaturally, curling into shapes that hung too long before dissolving.

Marcus staggered slightly, gripping the wall. A pressure had settled inside his skull, as though the mountain itself was pressing words into his mind half whispers he couldn't quite catch, but could almost feel.

The tablet in his pocket grew hot. He pulled it free, and the photographs on the screen weren't static anymore. The symbols shifted, reconfiguring themselves in real time as if alive, as if watching him back.

"The magnetic fields are converging," Sofia called, eyes locked on her glowing displays. "Waves of energy are spiraling inward forming a containment lattice around the entrance."

A deep tremor shook the ground. It wasn't a natural quake; it felt like the mountain resettling, adjusting its weight. Equipment toppled from shelves, but instead of falling cleanly, some objects hung mid air for a heartbeat before clattering down.

"Look," Maya breathed. The shadows around the cave mouth thickened, no longer behaving like absence of light but writhing shapes that bent into ancient glyphs. "The threshold it's activating."

Ghost's motion sensors screamed warnings. "Multiple contacts." He toggled to thermal. His jaw tightened. "Visual feed negative but you need to see this."

On his thermal display, human shaped figures drifted through the camp. Their outlines shimmered in and out, tall and deliberate, moving with eerie precision. They didn't stumble. They didn't hurry. They *watched.*

Maya whispered, almost reverent: "The texts called them Watchers. They appear at the beginning of the final sequence."

Leo's deck scattered from his palm, freezing in the air as if caught in invisible threads. The cards spun into a three dimensional model of the cave system, every tunnel mapped in eerie detail.

Sofia's computers erupted with cascading lines of data, scrolling in languages none of them had studied yet each of them understood. The system wasn't just awakening. It was *adapting,* learning their languages, their technology, their minds.

Marcus froze as one thermal signature drifted close. The air grew brittle with cold, each breath crystallizing instantly. In the wavering shimmer, the faint suggestion of a face appeared ancient, formidable, and unmistakably aware of him.

"We're not just observing it," Marcus whispered. "It's observing us. Testing us."

The hum grew louder. Around them, devices began to swivel and shift, aligning themselves toward the cave like compass needles snapping to true north. The Watchers loomed closer, their forms growing less translucent, more substantial with every passing second.

The mountain's pulse quickened. They felt it in their bones. Something vast and ancient had turned its full attention upon them.

The test had begun.

Dazzling shadows flared within the crystalline mist that veiled the cave's threshold. The sweeping beams of headlamps fractured into shifting symbols, glyphs writ large across vapor. Marcus led the descent. Each step echoed like a heartbeat, deliberate and weighted, as he moved into the living stone.

The air thickened. Denser. Charged. Every breath buzzed with static, every hair on their bodies prickling in warning.

"Spacing!" Ghost barked, scanning his proximity sensors. "Magnetic interference's killing feeds. Keep sight contact, don't rely on comms."

One of Sofia's drones floated ahead, its modified sensors cutting deeper than human eyes. "Architecture is shifting again," she reported, frustration tightening her voice. "The walls are reorganizing molecular structure realigning on the fly."

Maya froze mid step, scribbling furiously in her journal before her pen sputtered out. She switched to her camera, capturing symbols glowing faintly across the rock. "They're not static," she said, trembling with excitement. "These symbols are *writing themselves.* They're recording this moment reacting to us telling a story as we walk."

A rumble thundered through the tunnel, dust cascading from the ceiling. Pebbles bounced like drumbeats.

"That's the third tremor in ten minutes," Leo said, checking a half functioning monitor. "They're stronger. And..." He faltered, voice low. "They feel... intentional."

The passage widened, giving way to a cavern vast and unnatural. Its immensity stole breath from their lungs. The ceiling vanished into darkness, while the floor stretched into a hall ringed with pedestals. Upon each pedestal floated artifacts: metal spheres rippling like mercury, crystalline latticework that thrummed with piercing frequencies, and objects too alien to name.

"Don't touch anything," Marcus ordered, though even he felt the pull an attraction more psychic than physical.

Sofia's fingers flew over her controls. "I'm trying to get clean readings, but the signatures won't lock. Every time I focus on one, it changes like it's actively *dodging* analysis."

Ghost moved in careful circles along the perimeter, sidearm low, eyes darting. "Multiple contacts," he muttered. His thermal scanner filled with movement in every adjoining passage. "Could be rival teams. Could be…"

"Watchers," Maya finished, snapping photos of new glyphs spiraling up the chamber walls. "The texts spoke of guardians. They arrive when the Gate awakens fully."

The unspoken tension thickened. Leo's eyes lingered on Ghost's rifle, calculating. Sofia shifted her stance so her helmet cam tracked everyone in the chamber. Maya hugged her journal to her chest. Ghost's hand hovered close to his sidearm.

The ground heaved. Artifacts lifted higher above their pedestals, humming louder, weaving into complex orbits. The chamber became a resonant cathedral of sound, a rising symphony of alien music.

"These markings," Maya said breathlessly, her tablet glowing with unstable translations. "They're not just warnings. They're instructions ritual sequences. But…" She stopped, blinking at her screen. "Each person sees something different."

Leo stepped closer to the wall. "I see numbers equations, like math problems."

"I see tactical data," Ghost said, his gaze locked on shifting diagrams. "Entry points. Defensive positions."

Sofia's brow furrowed. "My screens are showing schematics engineering blueprints."

Maya clutched her journal tighter. "And I see… myths. Stories of the Divine Treasury. Of gateways."

Marcus exhaled, the weight of realization heavy. "It's showing each of us what it thinks we'll understand. Tailoring the test to the operator."

The artifacts hummed louder, orbiting faster. Shadows stretched impossibly long. The chamber trembled like the lungs of a god taking its first breath in millennia.

The test was no longer just beginning. It was personal.

"They're showing each of us what we understand," Marcus realized aloud. "What we're trained to see."

Urgent beeps screamed from Sofia's monitors. "Energy spike incoming… something big is…"

The chamber plunged into absolute darkness. Every light headlamps, drones, consoles died in the same breath. For a heartbeat, there was nothing but silence and the sound of their own breaths.

Then the artifacts ignited. They glowed with an otherworldly brilliance, casting shifting patterns across the walls, shadows dancing into impossible shapes. The air grew heavy, alive with static. It tasted metallic on their tongues, buzzing on their skin.

The lights blinked back on. And the chamber had changed. Passageways once open were now sealed; new corridors had appeared, angled with deliberate design. The artifacts had rearranged themselves into a configuration Maya recognized instantly.

"It's a key," she whispered, awe in her voice. "The artifacts… their arrangement is a key to something deeper in the complex."

Ghost's thermal scanner shrieked warnings. "Multiple contacts closing in. All sides."

The temperature dropped sharply, breath crystallizing mid air. Frost lingered in glyph shapes before dissolving again.

"The tremors aren't random," Sofia said quickly, shoving seismic readouts into a new overlay. "They're a sequence building toward a culmination."

The artifacts flared brighter, their surfaces whirling faster, symbols sliding into new alignments. The markings on the walls liquefied, molten lines rearranging themselves, stretching outward as if reaching for the team.

Marcus felt it then the tablet in his pack warming, pulsing in rhythm with the chamber. The weight of its choice pressed harder on him, heavier than ever. The ancients had marked him as operator. The responsibility was unmistakable.

"We have to move," Marcus said. His eyes scanned the glowing pedestals, then locked on a passage where the artifact pattern pointed like a compass needle. "The system is live. If we hesitate, it may decide we've failed the test."

Another quake tore through the chamber. This one carried a sound, not just a vibration an eerie chant, like voices from far below echoing through stone.

Ghost's scanner howled. Heat signatures converged. The Watchers were closing in, herding them inexorably toward the path Maya had already chosen.

The team exchanged silent looks. Each knew it: they were crossing the line of no return.

With every step into the passage, the ground throbbed beneath their boots. The mountain's pulse was quickening, alive and aware.

Then chaos.

A violent earthquake shook the chamber. Crystal formations exploded from the walls, shattering into shards of radiant light. Instead of falling, the shards froze mid air, hanging in impossible geometric arrays.

"Seismic activity off the charts!" Sofia shouted above the roar. Her displays glitched into nonsense, only one fact clear: "The mountain isn't just moving it's rewriting itself. The entire structural matrix is reconfiguring!"

Ghost swore under his breath, toggling between overwhelmed sensors. "Multiple breach points forming walls opening like doors. The whole complex is unfolding!"

The shards spun into synchrony, their glow intensifying until it hurt to look. A resonance filled the chamber…a rising chorus as if the mountain itself were singing.

Maya's voice cut through, frantic as she scribbled. "The texts… the prophecy…'When the Watchers come together and the stones sing, the Path shall appear unto the worthy!'" New symbols blazed onto the walls, seared in light.

Leo's gear rattled, rising into the air. His ever present deck burst free, each card aligning with precision into the same pattern as the crystal shards, mirroring their spirals. "Uh, guys? Gravity just went sideways!"

True to his words, physics unraveled. Droplets of melting ice floated upward. Metal snapped into alien shapes. The air rippled with luminous waves, bending sight itself.

Marcus's pack throbbed as the tablet surged, humming in resonance with the storm around them.

"Sofia!" he shouted. "What are we seeing?"

She scanned furiously, her face pale. "The energy signature… it matches the tablet's. But amplified thousands of times over. It's like…" She faltered, staring wide eyed. "It's like the tablet was a key and this is the lock turning."

The far wall rippled, solid stone becoming translucent. Behind it pulsed a radiance that seemed to exist everywhere and nowhere at once.

"Portal energy," Maya breathed, half in fear, half in wonder. "Exactly as the ancients described. 'A door between worlds, born from the conjunction of earth and sky.'"

Another quake nearly threw them off their feet. Ghost's perimeter alarms screamed: incoming forces, multiple directions.

"Chinese military. Contractors. Everyone's converging!" he shouted.

"We have seconds!" Marcus barked over the cacophony. "That portal is forming whether we want it or not!"

The shards spun faster, the light spiraling into a vortex aimed at the shimmering wall.

The Watchers appeared in force now, their towering outlines clearer than ever, motion deliberate. They gestured toward the forming portal, their silent intent unmistakable: *Enter.*

Sparks erupted from Sofia's consoles. "The energy pattern is completing itself!" she cried. "This… this is what the tablet has been guiding us to all along!"

Behind them: the thunder of boots, weapons, pursuit. Before them: a portal rippling like liquid mercury, flashing glimpses of somewhere *else.*

"If we don't go now," Maya warned, eyes glued to her glowing translations, "the system resets. The chance is lost."

Leo's cards froze in mid air, fanning into a perfect wedge pointed straight at the portal. He let out a shaky laugh. "Call me crazy, but I think that's our invitation."

The chamber shifted again, corridors sealing like a labyrinth rearranging itself, forcing them toward one inevitable decision.

"Twenty seconds before company!" Ghost barked, rifle raised. "Whatever we do, it's now!"

Marcus clutched the tablet. Power surged through his hands, bypassing space, resonating perfectly with the gateway ahead. And he understood: this wasn't just a door. It was a threshold poised to rewrite the laws of reality itself.

"We go through!" he ordered, his voice absolute. "Sofia…drones first. Ghost…cover our backs. Everyone else, final gear check!"

The portal rippled violently, liquid light peeling open into vistas of impossible space.

Maya's screen blazed with final translation: *The First Gate opens to those who dare to cross.*

The shards exploded into blinding light, coalescing into a corridor lined by Watchers. The mountain itself seemed to hold its breath. They had found the Gate. But what lay beyond was no treasure vault, no simple prize. It was something far greater, and far more dangerous.

And now, the choice was made.

## Chapter 4: First Contact

Dust swirled in shafts of unearthly light as the team staggered upright, still shaken from the cataclysmic upheaval.
The cave they had entered was gone, replaced by something alive. Where solid stone once stood, crystalline formations now jutted outward in impossible geometries facets refracting light into colors no human eye was meant to see.

Marcus brushed the chalky grit from his tactical vest and forced his voice steady. "Status check!"

"Still breathing," Ghost answered, already roping off the perimeter. His visor blinked red, motion sensors pinging anomalies where rock should have been. "But we've got movement. The structure's still shifting."

Sofia knelt among the shattered remains of her monitoring station, coaxing what she could from her salvaged consoles. The surviving screens screamed nonsense spikes, spirals, signatures that mocked every known model. "The energy fields are… evolving," she whispered. "It's not damage. The cave's rewiring itself on a quantum scale."

A few meters away, Maya was transfixed by what the collapse had revealed. The quake had peeled away eons of stone to expose sprawling murals living cave paintings whose figures writhed and morphed in the eerie glow. She raised her tablet with trembling hands, recording every shift. "These aren't just art," she said, voice unsteady with awe. "They're… responsive. They're changing as we watch." Symbols shimmered like liquid mercury, sliding across the rock face to rearrange themselves before her eyes.

Leo edged closer, his scanning rig slung across his shoulder. Sparks jumped from the equipment; screens glitched and went black. "That's the fourth unit fried. The EM field just went orbital." He swallowed, unsettled. "Feels like the air itself is… thinking."

A low hum rose from deep within the earth, a resonance so heavy it rattled their teeth. Sofia's monitors spasmed with cascading anomalies. "Pressure, temperature, even the molecular makeup of the air… it's all shifting. The cave isn't collapsing. It's… *waking up*."

Marcus turned as crystalline spires extruded from the walls in real time, their surfaces dripping with condensation. But instead of falling, droplets floated upward, gathering into spheres of water that orbited the spires in hypnotic arcs. The chamber became a solar system in miniature, each droplet a star pulsing with inner fire.

"Maya," Marcus called, his voice edged with disbelief. "What are we looking at?"

She flipped frantically through her notes, cross checking translations against the shifting murals. "The texts foretold this…'When the bones of the earth crack, the veil grows thin.' This isn't destruction. It's a metamorphosis. The tremor was meant to *start* the process."

Ghost's visor screamed fresh warnings. "Atmosphere's changing. Oxygen's fine for now but I'm reading trace elements I've never seen. Unknown compounds."

Sofia's sensors synchronized with the floating spheres. "Each one has a unique energy profile. Together they're resonating in perfect harmony. It's not random it's a system."

The murals quickened, figures twisting into luminous narratives that blurred myth and science. They showed worlds unraveling and re forming, gateways flaring open, humans transformed into something… other.

Maya's eyes widened as she sketched. "It's a chronicle of change between what we are, and what we might become."

A sudden gust swept through, carrying whispers in languages they couldn't recognize. The crystals quivered in sympathy, sending harmonic waves through the chamber that shimmered like liquid sound.

"New passageways forming," Sofia said, flipping to a live geological feed. Her voice tightened. "Not faults. Growth. The tunnels are *growing*."

Leo's deck of cards stirred again, floating up to mirror the murals in intricate alignment. "Guys… it's running the show now. We're just along for the ride."

The tablet in Marcus's pack flared, its pulse syncing with the crystalline heartbeat of the chamber. He clutched it reflexively, feeling its rhythm bleed into his own chest.

"Document everything," he ordered, forcing steel into his tone. "Sofia, log every reading. Maya, focus on the murals catch them before they shift again. Ghost, update maps every sixty seconds. Leo, shield what gear we can still trust."

The hum climbed into a resonance that bordered on music. The water spheres brightened, flaring from within like captive stars. Their light refracted across the murals, quickening the pace of their stories until they blurred into pure radiance.

"Something's building," Ghost warned, scanning the perimeter. "Massive energy spike, bigger than anything we've seen yet."

Marcus steadied himself as the chamber quaked again, the ground flexing like living muscle beneath his boots. Around them, reality itself seemed to warp and breathe.

Maya's voice came quiet, almost reverent. "This isn't just awakening. It's preparation."

Sofia froze, watching as her sensors auto adjusted into sequences she hadn't programmed. "Preparation for *what?*" she whispered.

The answer loomed in the silence between tremors. The cave wasn't merely alive. It was waiting.

"These aren't just light tricks," Leo called out, his voice wavering between awe and alarm as one sphere fractured into perfect crystalline shards before fusing whole again. He clenched his jaw, focusing. The sphere nearest him rippled, shifting hue until it glowed with the exact shade he'd pictured in his mind. "They're… responding to thought. To intent."

Marcus's gaze drifted to a newly revealed wall where stone and crystal had peeled back like the layers of a wound. What lay exposed beneath wasn't ruin, but design organic crystalline growth fused seamlessly with intricate, technological structures. He reached out with his scanner; the readings scrambled and then pulsed in sync with the wall. The patterns within shifted, exposing deeper layers of complexity like gears within gears.

"These aren't ruins," he said slowly, the words sinking into the chamber's charged air. "They're dormant machines. And now, they're waking up."

Sofia's entire array pulsed as one, all sensors orienting toward the center of the chamber as though drawn by gravity. "Energy spike incoming!" she shouted. "Localized distortion in the spatial fabric."

The air wavered, bending light into concentric rings that rippled outward. Around the disturbance, the floating spheres of light quickened their dance, weaving impossible geometries through the air like a symphony made visible.

"Perimeter status?" Marcus barked.

"Secure, sort of," Ghost replied, his eyes flicking across a tactical readout that seemed to know his moves before he made them. "The field's… anticipating. Like it's operating outside normal time."

Maya darted between glyphs newly carved into exposed walls, her voice breathless as she traced their glowing edges. "The inscriptions are describing this moment. 'When the Watchers' dance aligns with eternal geometry, the Gate begins its awakening.' It's happening exactly as written!"

The light spheres wove faster, folding into fractal spirals that seemed to dip through dimensions they couldn't perceive. Leo's deck of cards rose from his hands, joining the dance, arranging themselves into mirrored lattices that matched the symbols around them. His face drained of color. "This isn't random. They're building a scaffold in spacetime itself."

Sofia's monitors bled cascading streams of alien data. "The energy signature matches the tablet's, but multiplied by thousands. That was just a fragment. This… this is the full system."

At the heart of the chamber, the very air began to crystallize, shimmering into macrostructures that extended beyond three dimensions. Ghost's thermal optics flared with signatures blinking in and out of existence forms like shadows slipping through parallel layers of reality.

"Multiple contacts," he said tightly, though even his hardened tone trembled with awe. "The Watchers are gathering."

Marcus felt the tablet against his chest pulse in perfect harmony with the chamber. It throbbed like a second heart, its ancient circuits eager, almost jubilant. He clenched it, his breath ragged. "Maya what are we seeing?"

Her hands shook as she scrolled through her frantic translations. "It's a bootstrap sequence. The portal isn't just forming it's *teaching itself* how to exist here."

The spheres of light shrieked into overdrive, their patterns so elaborate they physically hurt to watch. Crystalline machinery, once hidden, now hummed in resonance, joining the chorus of awakening.

"Energy levels at critical threshold!" Sofia shouted, her voice rising over the mounting hum. "Whatever is coming it's almost here!"

Reality warped at the chamber's core, folding inward, then unfurling again, as if space itself was learning to breathe. The Watchers' silhouettes coalesced, towering forms now almost visible to the naked eye, their faceless heads tilting toward the team like judges awaiting a verdict.

"Secure everything!" Marcus snapped, his voice sharp with the weight of command. "Document it all this is history breaking open in front of us."

The chamber pulsed, each beat stronger than the last. Their base camp was no longer a camp at all but a crucible, a nexus where the rules of reality bent toward something vast and alien.

Maya's fingers raced across the glowing glyphs that flared brighter under her touch. Her voice trembled as she read. "They're not just warnings… they're terms. 'The Path opens only to those who know the price of crossing.'"

Sofia's instruments displayed raw sequences of quantum fluctuations energy waves that weren't noise but deliberate syntax. "It's forming a language. The whole system is... *talking to itself.*"

Suddenly, the chamber floor ignited with a line of luminous markers. They flickered to life one after the other, creating a path that spiraled deeper into the complex. Each symbol glowed as Marcus stepped near, lighting his way like ancient runway lights leading to something unimaginable.

"They're processional markers," Marcus called, eyes wide. "This is ritual. The ancients walked this path."

Ghost's scanners confirmed it. "Spiral design all leading to a central convergence point sixty meters below."

The team advanced cautiously as the crystalline walls warped into archways and corridors in real time. Each footfall seemed to *summon* new passages into being. The air thickened with whispers, a ghostly litany of ceremonies long past.

Leo's cards fanned out in his hands unbidden, each flipping over until they replicated the spiral itself. His laugh was strained, nervous. "The whole place is remembering."

Maya read aloud from fresh glyphs, her voice echoing strangely as though layered with another tone not her own. "'The Chamber of Crossing lies where earth's veins entwine, where the old powers gather, and the barriers grow thin.'"

Sofia's equipment wailed with sudden spikes. "The energy fluctuations are stabilizing they're locking into coherence. Whatever this place was built to do, it's rearming itself."

The spiral opened into a chamber that took their breath. Vast, circular, carved and grown in equal measure: colossal pillars of living crystal arced upward, their cores alive with flowing currents of radiant light. At the center waited a raised platform forged of alien metal, its surface rippling with symbols that shifted like molten script.

"A ceremonial chamber," Maya breathed, awe and certainty mingling in her tone. "But it's more than ritual it's machinery of transformation."

The towering crystal pillars pulsed in rhythm, each beat channeling torrents of energy into an invisible field that swelled like a living lung. Ghost's sensors flickered erratically as the Watchers began to manifest along the edges of the chamber once mere shadows, now shimmering into nearly tangible forms, their elongated outlines rippling as though woven from the chamber's light itself.

"Multiple energy signatures converging," Sofia reported, her instruments struggling to keep pace with the impossible. "The chamber is concentrating power like a lens focusing sunlight, only it's amplifying spacetime."

Marcus felt the tablet stir against his chest, its etched surface heating with recognition. Machinery embedded in the crystalline walls silent for millennia stirred to life, lending their ancient strength to the gathering power.

"The platform," Leo said, eyes fixed on the raised dais. His cards floated upward again, arranging themselves into a miniature replica of the chamber. "It's not just ceremonial it's the focus. Whatever's trying to manifest, it's happening *there*."

Maya sprinted between the pillars, glyphs flashing to life at her touch. Her translations poured out in rapid bursts: "The texts speak of a gateway but not only through space. 'The Path opens through time and thought, through what was and what *could* be.'"

The air above the platform shimmered as though reality itself were bending, coiling around a point of growing intensity. Energy streamed from the pillars in luminous braids, weaving doorways nested within doorways each one layered like secrets concealed in deeper truths.

"First visible manifestation of portal energy," Sofia shouted, eyes darting across her surviving screens. "The quantum field is stabilizing sorting itself into coherent patterns!"

The Watchers moved now in perfect synchrony, their forms impossibly fluid as they took their positions around the platform. Their choreography mirrored the pulsing symbols crawling across the walls, glyphs that told stories of thresholds and rebirth.

"This is it," Marcus realized, fingers tingling as the tablet pulsed in his grip. "This is what it was leading us to the true threshold."

The surface of the dais rippled like molten metal, and above it, space folded open, spilling forth ripples of light that hinted at depths beyond comprehension.

Maya's voice rose in crescendo as her translations aligned with the moment: "'The Gate awakens to those who dare to see beyond the veil of what is known!'"

The chamber bloomed with light, infinite and merciless, as its ancient machinery fulfilled its timeless purpose. This was no ceremonial hall, it was a nexus where realities bled together, where existence itself grew thin.

The first tremor struck without warning. A deep, resonant thrum rolled through the chamber, shaking it to its foundations. Crystalline towers splintered, only to reassemble into impossible forms, as if the earth itself were obeying some alien command.

"Structural integrity compromised!" Ghost bellowed, his tactical display vomiting distortions as the cave's very architecture warped in real time. "The entire complex is destabilizing!"

Sofia's fingers flew across her half functional console, eyes wide. "The seismic waves they're synchronized with the portal's frequency! The earthquake isn't random it's *part of the process*!"

Above, the ceiling split into four jagged seams, revealing strata of luminous rock that glowed like veins of living fire. Ancient mechanisms stirred within the fissures gears of stone and light meshing for the first time in millennia. Crystal shards rained down, only to hang suspended midair, spinning in geometric constellations.

"Move, now!" Marcus barked as walls folded in on themselves, then unfurled into spirals that defied physics. "Get to higher ground!"

Maya shielded her head as she read frantically from the glowing glyphs streaming across every surface. "The Gate demands sacrifice matter for energy, form for transformation!" Her voice cracked. "This isn't collapse, it's *reconfiguration*!"

Leo's cards whirled in a defensive storm around him, slicing the falling debris into harmless dust. "The portal's feeding on the quake it's using destruction as fuel!"

At the chamber's core, reality bent inward toward a growing point of brilliance, energy devouring itself like a newborn star. Sofia's surviving sensors screamed warnings, each line of data breaking the boundaries of known physics.

"Multiple cascades in progress!" she shouted, clutching her console. "The portal's not just opening it's *building its own rules of reality*!"

The Watchers solidified fully now, towering over the chaos, their liquid shadow bodies sliding into deliberate positions to encircle the portal. Ghost's motion sensors shrieked in panic, every angle blocked. The guardians had arrived.

Another violent tremor ripped through the chamber, and the massive pillars pulsed in perfect sync with the portal. Each rhythmic surge hurled shockwaves across the chamber, reshaping rock and crystal as though the mountain itself were clay.

"The tablet!" Marcus cried as the relic seared with power, glowing hot against his palm. "It's resonating it's syncing with the portal!"

Maya's translations flared across her screen as fresh glyphs erupted in fire across the walls: *When earth's bones break and reality bends, thus shall the path open but only to those who endure the trial.*

The very air crystallized into lattices of living light, weaving the chaos into a luminous web of terrifying precision. Leo's cards fell into formation, sketching the same pattern in miniature a cosmic diagram etched into their world.

"Energy levels surpassing every known parameter!" Sofia screamed, her voice ragged with awe. "The portal is drawing from the quake, but it's more than that it's drawing from *probability itself*! It's rewriting what can and cannot happen!"

The floor yawned open with a roar, splitting to reveal depths bathed in black light, luminous with impossible radiance. From below, ancient mechanisms rose like titans from slumber, crystalline and metallic limbs sliding into alignment. Their dance fed the growing maelstrom of the portal, which now pulsed like the heart of an awakening god.

Ghost's tactical systems flared red with impossible alerts. *"Reality fractures forming across the complex multiple breaches! Whatever's coming through, it's happening now!"*

The Watchers moved with eerie precision, their bodies rippling like shadows caught in liquid glass. They bent the light itself as they circled the chamber, their movements half dance, half rite. With each motion, they guided the chamber's chaos into a singular purpose. The portal's glow intensified, casting shadows in contradictory directions tenebrous shapes that seemed alive.

The tablet in Marcus's grip surged violently, awakening as if to declare its true purpose. Heat seared into his palm. *"Brace yourselves!"* he shouted. *"The threshold opens!"*

Time stuttered. Seconds stretched, then skipped like broken film. The quake's rhythm pulsed like a colossal engine awakening, like the heartbeat of the Watchers themselves. Around them, Maya's voice rose into a frantic crescendo, translations spilling from her lips: *"The Gate opens not into space or time but into transformation itself!"*

The chamber's madness coalesced into perfect geometry. Walls folded, energy streamed, and at last the portal began to *manifest reality* opening in an origami of light and force, revealing layered depths that glimmered between instants of time.

The team held on, breathless, knowing they were watching humanity's understanding of existence burn away before their eyes. The portal offered not a place, but a promise: realms no human had ever dared to see.

Chaos was the crucible; change, the threshold. And now it was open.

The portal blazed into full manifestation a writhing membrane of light and possibility. Space itself bent inward, curving like water spiraling toward a drain. The chamber groaned, transformed into an architecture barely able to contain the strain.

*"Full quantum breach!"* Sofia cried over the deafening roar of reality tearing apart. Her final sensors screamed nonsense: energy patterns that obeyed no law of physics. *"The portal's generating its own gravitational field!"*

The floor fractured beneath them, shattering into floating islands adrift in seas of raw energy. Ancient machinery blazed awake, their mechanisms glowing like veins of fire. The Watchers slid like obsidian titans through the storm, their silhouettes elongating as they rode dimensional currents.

The tablet blazed hotter, dragging at Marcus with invisible chains. He staggered forward as though pulled by a tide none of the others could feel.

*"Marcus!"* Maya's cry tore across the chaos. She lunged, but a swell of energy knocked her back. *"It's the tablet it's acting like a beacon!"*

Ghost's systems scrambled in panic. *"Fractures everywhere I can't get a lock on his position!"* He fired a magnetic line; the cable bent midair, warping like ribbon in water, curling through the twisted space.

Leo's hands shook as his cards whirled into desperate patterns. *"It's too strong it's calling him!"*

Marcus braced his feet against the crystalline floor, but the pull was merciless. The tablet pulsed in perfect rhythm with the portal, each beat hotter, heavier, more insistent. Around him, reality shimmered like glass about to crack, offering fleeting visions: vast alien cities, forgotten ages, skies with too many stars.

*"The translations!"* Maya gasped, scrolling through blazing glyphs. *" 'The Chosen will be drawn to the Path, bound by artifacts of the crossing!' "* Her voice broke. *"It's him. The tablet was never just a key it's a beacon for the chosen!"*

Sofia's remaining systems shrieked. *"Critical convergence! The portal's going to finalize now!"*

The Watchers raised their arms in unison. The air tore with soundless thunder as their power channeled directly into the portal. Energy waves rolled outward, separating the team. Distances warped; meters became miles in an instant.

*"Can't hold formation!"* Ghost yelled as he was shoved back, his voice fragmented by the warping space. *"It's splitting us apart the space between us is growing!"*

Through the veil, Marcus saw them as distorted shadows stretched through stormlight. His teammates' movements slowed, elongated, as though they were trapped in another timeline. The tablet burned in his hand, its surface a living mirror showing the chaos all around. For a heartbeat, knowledge pressed against his mind fractured glimpses of what waited beyond.

*"Stay back!"* he shouted, voice echoing in strange harmonics. *"It's choosing I can feel it. It knows who it wants!"*

Symbols erupted like fire across the walls, blazing brighter with each pulse: *"The Path opens to one but changes all! The crossing point approaches!"*

The portal rippled like molten mercury, revealing geometries that hurt to look at and landscapes that defied imagination.

Its pull became irresistible. Marcus's boots lifted clear of the ground.

Sofia screamed over the static. *"If he goes through, we may not follow! The portal's signature is bound to him alone!"*

Marcus floated, suspended in the tide. Time slowed; the chaos unfolded like a painting his team's desperation etched into his memory: Maya clutching her translations, Sofia fighting to record every datum, Ghost calculating impossible rescues, Leo's cards fanned into lattices of probability.

*"Find me!"* he roared, his voice echoing across dimensions. *"Follow the tablet's signal!"*

The Watchers blazed, their arms raised high. The portal's surface split like a curtain of fire and light, unveiling an abyss of impossible radiance.

*"Marcus!"* Their voices merged into one as he vanished from their grasp.

The tablet flared, flooding the chamber in searing brilliance. For an instant, Marcus glimpsed what lay beyond: clarity, terrible and beautiful. Then the pull consumed him. He was torn across dimensions, stretched through the heart of the portal crossing a boundary no human had ever crossed.

Behind him, the chamber roared with unleashed power. Light devoured shadow, order unraveled into new forms. And Marcus was gone, swallowed by the Path, carried into a realm where no certainty remained.

## Chapter 5: Through the Looking Glass

Marcus tumbled through Between Space, stretched across realities like light through a fractured prism. Time lost coherence; meaning dissolved into a kaleidoscope of alien geometries. The tablet pulsed with violent insistence against his chest, guiding him like a lodestone through chaos.

Colors without names flooded his sight tones no human eye was designed to see. Sound became heavy enough to press against his ribs, thought became tactile as cloth, flavors carried texture and weight. The senses no longer stayed in their lanes; everything bled into everything, collapsing categories.

Fragments of impossible worlds stuttered past like shards of broken film. He saw crystal cities drifting beneath violet skies; oceans woven from threads of living light; mountains that breathed in slow, tectonic rhythm; forests spun from pure mathematics. Each vision stretched into eternity then collapsed into an instant.

The tablet's pulse grew faster, pulling him downward at an angle toward something coherent. Amid the storm of Between Space, a world began to crystallize. First it was an impression, then a certainty.

The smell hit him first strangely metallic, organic, pungent, like blood on copper. Then the hum came, vibrating through every atom of his body, as though the very air sang. Chaos solidified. Spectrum narrowed. And Marcus fell.

He hit hard on a surface that was neither stone nor soil. It rippled like flesh yet rang like struck metal. Crystalline waves spread outward beneath him, the ground alive, calculating his impact as if assigning value to his arrival.

Trees towered into a copper sky, but they were not trees as Earth knew them. Their trunks coiled upward in iridescent spirals of alloy, branches fractal and endless. Instead of leaves, clusters of gems and coins pulsed with inner light, each glowing fruit ripening in seconds before dropping to the ground and melting into the living lattice of currency below.

The land itself breathed wealth. Beneath Marcus's boots, a surface of shifting currency coins fused to bills, metals braided into liquid geometry undulated with his weight, computing worth with each step. Above, constellations of numbers scrolled across the heavens, equations burning like stars.

Marcus staggered upright, his HUD useless, spitting data it could not parse. The tablet in his grip had changed as well: its surface now flowed with molten gold patterns, mirroring the very substance of this world.

The sound of wind became crystalline music. The trees bent, their branches striking harmonies of profit and risk, growth and loss. Marcus's head reeled. This was not metaphor. This was life expressed in the only currency that mattered here *value itself.*

Through the shock, clarity seeped in: this was but one node in a larger network, a facet of some grander economic cosmos. The tablet had not simply led him here it had synchronized him to this world.

One by one, his team arrived scattered across the realm like seeds flung by a storm.

Sofia was the first. She landed hard on a platinum avenue of a floating city suspended in the copper sky, its towers sculpted from wealth itself. Streets paved with living coin shifted beneath her boots. Her surviving instruments shrieked in awe as they recalibrated. *"Quantum coherence…*

*at a planetary scale,"* she whispered. *"The entire ecosystem is financial energy, alive and aware."*

Ghost phased into being in the shadow of juvenile Money Trees. Their crystalline fruits chimed in metallic harmony as his tactical systems scrambled. He swept his visor across the groves, identifying "targets" before catching himself. *"I'm reading... resources as threats,"* he muttered, unsettled. The trees whispered back, their fruits resonating as though mocking his instincts.

Leo arrived in a cascade of golden light, his cards bursting forth in a frantic orbit. They gleamed now like minted coins, their symbols shifting in sync with the surging channels of liquid wealth that carved glowing rivers through the floor of a trading plaza. He exhaled sharply. *"They're not showing probability anymore,"* he murmured. *"They're showing value. Real value. Across dimensions."*

Maya materialized amid towering, ancient Money Trees. Their branches shimmered with constellations of mathematical glyphs. Her translation tablet ignited, decoding streams of formulaic language written in the air itself. *"It's not just another world,"* she cried, voice carried by the harmonics of the grove. *"It's another order of existence. Here, life and language speak only in terms of worth."*

Together, they gazed upon the horizon: floating cities like jewels adrift in copper skies, strung together by bridges woven from economic energy. Towers of precious metal bent like living monuments, half building, half transaction, their forms equal parts architecture and market.

For the first time, the team understood: they had crossed not just into another dimension, but into the embodiment of humanity's oldest obsession.

They stood within the realm of the Money Tree.

Far off, stretching to the horizon, vast forests of Money Trees towered skyward, their metallic canopies shimmering and humming in a hypnotic symphony of growth and relentless accumulation. Colossal giants soared miles high, their uppermost branches dissolving into copper colored clouds. From those clouds rained cascades of alien currency coins and gems from other dimensions, an endless downpour of fortune that glittered as it fell.

"This is… incredible," Sofia whispered, awe stripping away her usual clinical detachment. She froze as the earth ahead split open and a new Money Tree erupted upward, showering golden seeds into the air. "The entire ecosystem is built on economic evolution. Growth isn't symbolic here it's literal."

Ghost's visor pulsed with strange readings. His tactical display mapped restless movement in the crystalline undergrowth. "Life signs multiple but none that match any known biology. It's like… living calculations. As if math itself learned to breathe."

Leo's cards spun outward, forming a luminous three dimensional map of the terrain. Streams of energy lit up beneath the surface, flowing like glowing rivers of potential. "The whole place is one vast market, but alive. Trading isn't a transaction here it's the law of nature."

Maya scribbled furiously in her notebook as equations rippled through the air itself. "These aren't just descriptive symbols. They're active forces. Every equation is *doing* something. The texts we studied hinted at this, but they never captured the scale."

They regrouped on a broad plain of mirrorlike alloys, its surface reflecting them in distorted, coin stamped patterns. Above, flying cities drifted endlessly across the copper skies, their structures shifting and reforming with the ebb and flow of values. Below, the Money Trees sang, their crystalline harmonies vibrating with the pulse of exchange.

"Marcus's signal " Ghost finally announced, locking onto the faint trace. "It's coming from one of those floating cities."

They stood together for a moment, the first human explorers in a realm where wealth was not symbolic but elemental, woven into the very foundation of existence. The Money Tree world breathed with secrets, and they had barely scratched its surface.

The team advanced, every step across the living ground spreading concentric ripples of value. The air glimmered with suspended particles of crystallized potential, turning every breath into a communion with raw worth. Even Ghost's navigation systems flickered as the terrain bent around concentrations of value, warping distance itself.

"The atmosphere isn't just oxygen," Sofia reported, watching her recalibrated readouts. "We're breathing in condensed *potential*. Crystallized opportunity suspended in the air."

Creatures stirred in the undergrowth entities shaped like shifting theorems, their bodies flickering between radiant equations and solid gold. A herd bounded past, flickering like proofs in motion, their bodies collapsing and reforming in rhythmic logic. Overhead, birdlike creatures with wings woven from strands of debt and credit soared between the trees, trailing arcs of compound interest across the sky.

"Look at this," Maya called, kneeling to inspect tiny stock graphs sprouting like mushrooms from the metallic soil. The miniature charts glowed as they shifted. "They're reacting to us. The ecosystem is *measuring* us tracking and calculating our value in real time."

Leo's cards mapped the movements of the creatures. Patterns emerged relationships of exchange instead of predator and prey. "Even survival here is commerce. Every interaction is an exchange of value, not violence."

They entered a grove of young Money Trees, their saplings rising in flawless logarithmic spirals. First fruits appeared as small diamonds, refracting sunlight into copper hued beams before dissolving into the lattice of the soil.

Ghost raised a hand. His sensors pinged something ahead. "Artificial structure. Older than the trees around it. Definitely not organic."

The ruins waited in the grove, silent but alive with residual hums of power. Machines and spires fused technology with value itself architecture that computed through economics, not electricity.

"These aren't ruins in the usual sense," Sofia murmured, tracing a device that still pulsed faintly. "They're engines economic engines. They harvested wealth as a fundamental force of physics."

Screens flickered to life, ancient displays running on reserves of alien energy. Holographic markets spread across the chamber walls, showing transactions not of goods, but of *possibility*.

"This was a trading hub," Maya said, her voice trembling with excitement. Her tablet strained to decode the cascading symbols. "They weren't just trading resources they traded futures. Entire potential realities exchanged like commodities."

Crystalline growths jutted from the walls, each containing preserved flashes of exchange moments of trade frozen in perfect clarity.

Ghost's visor tracked movement above. Shapes slipped across the upper levels like flowing liquidity. "The Watchers," he said tightly. "They've followed us. And here, they're stronger like this world was *made* for them."

Leo's cards clicked into intricate patterns, syncing with circuitry still humming in the walls. "These machines… they're not dead. They're evolving."

Sofia's instruments locked onto a powerful signal emanating from the core of the ruins. "There's something alive down there. A power source unlike anything we've seen even here."

They descended deeper. Roots of gold threaded through ancient machines, grafting biology and technology together until the distinction was meaningless. Living currency pulsed through conduits, the whole structure breathing as one hybrid organism.

Maya translated symbols glowing across the walls: *"The Trees took the machines inside themselves. They adapted."*

At the chamber's heart, a lone console pulsed with steady light. Its display mapped streams of wealth across the entire realm, highlighting nodes like stars. One node pulsed brighter than the rest the same place Ghost had detected Marcus's faint signal.

"It's all one system," Sofia whispered. "The Money Trees, the living currency, the ruins they're fused. And Marcus is somewhere inside that network, calling to us."

Above, the copper sky rippled with equations recalculating. The world itself was adjusting, writing the presence of humans into its endless ledger of value.

Static rasped through their comms. Radio signals warped into streams of market data and broken trading algorithms, as if the realm itself wanted to remind them: here, nothing existed without a price.

"Can't get a clean signal," Ghost grumbled, twisting the dials on his tactical comm unit. His words broke through their earpieces not as language but as fragmented echoes of market chatter commodity futures, fluctuating exchange rates, and dividend tallies.

Sofia cursed under her breath as she clawed at her instruments, recalibrating them for the hundredth time. "The atmosphere's conducting pure value instead of electricity. Our devices are treating wealth itself as data, and it's scrambling everything."

Above, something vast and translucent drifted through the copper sky: a living market trend, its diaphanous body rippling like an index chart come alive. The team instinctively pressed themselves against the metallic trunks of the nearest Money Trees. Their branches shifted with protective grace, weaving a canopy of assets over the intruders.

"We're being watched," Leo whispered. His cards, now alive with local resonance, spun themselves into defensive configurations that echoed the frequencies of the realm's unseen economy. "And not just by the Watchers something native to this place has taken notice."

The air thickened into a dazzling gold, and Maya's translation tablet flared to life with new glyphs, answering presences moving invisibly through them. "They're... curious," she breathed, fingers flying across the tablet. "We're anomalies in their system entities with value they can't calculate."

The ground beneath their boots warped in response: flowers of precious metals unfurled like blossoms of silver, platinum, and diamond. Possibility particles clung to their skin, leaving crystalline traces that sank slowly into their bodies.

"Something's happening to us," Sofia muttered, checking her scanners. The readouts twisted with impossible data. "The atmosphere is rewriting our molecular structures reshaping us to fit their economic biology."

From the underbrush came movement. A herd of native creatures emerged cautiously, drawn by the humans' unfamiliar worth. They resembled deer, but their bodies were woven from flowing currencies, their fractal antlers branching into recursive patterns of investment and yield. Their eyes glowed with curiosity as they tested the strangers' value signatures.

"Hold position," Ghost warned, his hand hovering near his weapon though he dared not raise it. "They're not predators. They're gathering information."

Small, quick creatures scurried between the herd's legs ambulatory credit ratings, chattering streams of market news. Overhead, bird like entities with wings spun from luminous strands of credit circled lower, their flight trails sketching arcs of compound interest across the sky.

Leo's cards began to hum, each one morphing to reflect the traits of the creatures nearby. "They're not just animals," he whispered in awe. "They're financial instruments made flesh each embodying a different economic force."

One of the deer like beings approached, its liquid metal muzzle brushing against Maya's translation tablet. Instantly, streams of new symbols cascaded across the screen like a waterfall of meaning.

"They're offering an exchange," Maya gasped, eyes wide. "Not goods. Not wealth. Knowledge. They want to trade in understanding."

Around them, the air rang with a higher pitch as more wildlife gathered predators, prey, and abstractions alike forming a living amphitheatre of commerce incarnate. The atmosphere shifted, adjusting local concentrations of value to sharpen the humans' comprehension.

"They're teaching us," Sofia realized, watching her readings stabilize into patterns. "Deliberately altering conditions so we can grasp their world."

Ghost's visor mapped the gathering into a vast, coordinated structure. "They're building a demonstration a model in motion."

And then it began: the deer like beings moved with balletic grace, their antlers inscribing geometric arcs as they danced. The smaller creatures swirled among them in counterpoint, while the airborne beings traced luminous spirals overhead. Together, the symphony of motion embodied a living theorem: economy as ecosystem, value as biology, transaction as breath.

"It's… beautiful," Leo whispered, his cards joining in the rhythm, mimicking the creatures' every motion. "They're showing us their truth. Here, life and worth are one and the same."

Maya's tablet filled with glowing translations, symbols pulsing in time with the dance. "They know Marcus," she breathed, stunned. "They're telling us he's part of this now that he's changed, and they're showing us where to find him."

The copper sky rippled with fresh equations as if the entire realm recognized this moment: the first exchange between humans and the native intelligences of the Money Tree.

The team followed the procession into a vast clearing where several ancient Money Trees had grown in communion, their trunks braided into a natural amphitheatre of radiant wealth. At its center stood Marcus.

His presence was transformed. Crystalline veins of value shimmered beneath his skin, and his eyes glowed with the precise cold fire of calculation. He radiated the energy of the realm itself, as though he were both man and equation.

"You made it," Marcus said, his voice vibrating with the resonance of market forces. "Though I imagine the journey was… less than straightforward."

Sofia scanned him, her devices struggling to keep up. "The adaptation is more advanced in you. You've been here longer, and the realm's energy has rewritten you more deeply."

Before anyone could reply, movement stirred at the edge of the amphitheatre. Tall, luminous beings emerged from the forest of Money Trees. Their bodies were fluid streams of value sometimes solid, sometimes liquid, sometimes little more than radiant fields of wealth given shape.

"They're not just advanced," Maya whispered, clutching her tablet as it struggled to translate. "They *are* the culmination of everything we've seen the living embodiment of economic evolution."

The beings moved with liquid grace, every gesture bending the financial currents of reality. As they stepped forward, the air thickened with fluctuations of localized value, the space itself shimmering with their attention. For the first time, the true denizens of the Money Tree civilization regarded humanity and weighed their worth.

"They've been watching us since we arrived," Ghost reported at last, his tactical systems locking onto the patterns that had eluded him. His visor displayed converging threads of surveillance woven into every phenomenon they'd experienced. "The wildlife encounters, the atmospheric changes, even the storms it was all observed, monitored, recorded."

Leo's cards clicked into formation in his hands, falling like puzzle pieces into a greater pattern. His eyes widened as he saw the truth written in their dance. "They're not just observers," he murmured, voice tinged with awe. "They're assessors evaluating us, calculating our worth in ways that go beyond wealth. Value here is measured in potential, not possession."

Marcus stepped forward, the tablet burning in his palms. Its glow throbbed in perfect synchrony with the luminous beings who encircled them, its surface alive with shifting symbols that mirrored their movements. "They brought us here," he said, his voice low but certain. "All of us. The tablet, the Watchers, the portal, it wasn't chance. It was part of their equation, and we're the unknown variables."

The citizens of the Money Tree drew closer, their forms radiant streams of living currency and flowing light. They moved like equations made flesh, weaving great arcs of meaning in the air. Symbols manifested above them, overlapping and reforming like the shifting tides of an eternal market.

Maya's tablet shook in her hands as she raced to keep up with the flood of information. Her breath came fast, her words urgent. "They're facing… a crisis," she translated. "A dimensional imbalance, a collapse of value across realities. Their system can't stabilize it alone. They need intervention." She looked up, her eyes alight with fear and exhilaration. "They need *us*."

Sofia's mind whirred at the implications, her scientific detachment fighting with awe. "Of course. Their system is too perfect balanced, predictable, efficient. But perfection is brittle. They've never accounted for chaos, for human irrationality, for the very thing we embody."

Above them, the copper sky thickened as equations scrawled themselves across the heavens. Whole constellations of symbols flared to life, reconfiguring the architecture of the floating cities as they drifted into new alignments. It was as if the entire world was preparing for a moment of decision.

The beings arranged themselves in flawless formation, their pulsing bodies casting waves of harmonic energy across the amphitheatre. The ancient Money Trees behind them swayed as if moved by the same rhythm, their branches chiming in resonant counterpoint a living orchestra of value.

"We have a choice," Marcus said, turning to his team. His gaze lingered on each of them, Maya clutching her translations, Sofia surrounded by her impossible data, Ghost bristling with disciplined wariness, Leo's cards flickering like omens. "They're offering us knowledge in return for help. Knowledge that could rewrite everything we think we know about reality."

Ghost's voice was taut with calculation, each word measured. "This goes beyond archaeology, beyond espionage, beyond anything in human experience. If we engage, we're stepping into forces that don't just shape economies, they reshape entire dimensions. The risks are incalculable."

Leo gave a crooked smile, though his eyes betrayed unease. His cards spun faster, forming echoes of the beings' equations. "Look at how they live. Every trade, every exchange, every movement feeds into a larger system, an engine of purpose we can't even begin to fathom. We're specks in their design and yet, somehow, we're necessary."

The Money Tree beings stood silent, but their silence was full rich with expectation, the hum of value resonating through the glade. The trees behind them thrummed in unison, their harmonic voices joining the song of decision.

Maya's voice cut through the charged air as her translations surged to their peak. "They're ready. This is formal contact. Whatever happens next, the exchange begins now."

The team exchanged quick nods, united not by certainty but by the weight of inevitability. They had crossed dimensions, survived the impossible, and now stood face to face with a civilization that embodied the very principle of worth.

Marcus lifted the tablet. Its surface had become a living mirror of the beings, flowing symbols linking human and Money Tree alike. His voice was steady, though his chest burned with the tablet's pulse.

"I think we all know why we came here," he said. "The real question is, are we ready to pay the price for what follows?"

Overhead, the copper sky brightened with equations written in fire. The amphitheatre of ancient trees swayed with precise rhythm. And the Money Tree civilization, luminous and eternal, prepared to welcome Earth's first ambassadors into their inexhaustible equation.

## Chapter 6: Welcome to Wonderland

First light unfurled in waves of copper and gold over the Money Tree world, washing across a panorama unreadable by earthly minds. From their crystalline observation platform, the team beheld the full majesty of this economic ecosystem for the very first time.

Cities drifted across the equation etched sky, vast constellations of raw, undistilled wealth. Towering forms defied gravity, suspended by calculations of value so precise they made markets into architecture. Each was a masterpiece of economic genius rising like compound interest incarnate, flowing upward toward a copper hued heaven. Streets glimmered with rivers of living currency, while buildings shifted and morphed, their outlines reshaped by the tides of unseen markets.

"It's like watching the whole history of commerce evolve into a living thing," Sofia breathed. Her instruments whirred, desperate to record data that would upend entire scientific disciplines. The cities didn't drift aimlessly; they moved in flawless harmony, their paths charting economic theories far beyond human comprehension.

Below them sprawled the forests of the Money Trees, stretching to infinity. Ancient titans rose with trunks spiraling for miles into the sky columns of metals unknown to Earth. Their branches braided into webs of exchange, bearing flowers and fruits of crystal that pulsed with inner light.

"Look at the integration," Ghost said, his tactical display tracing luminous strands running through bark and branch. "Circuits of pure value woven into living trunks. No boundary between what's natural and what's engineered it's all one continuous system."

Clusters of younger Money Trees huddled around their elders, experimenting with new manifestations of wealth. Some birthed fruits of condensed potential, others sprouted branches that calculated market trends in real time.

Leo's deck fluttered in his hands, cards spinning like they were part of the ecosystem itself. Each one shimmered with facets drawn from their surroundings. "The whole place is a trading floor that's alive," he said, almost reverent. "Every transaction feeds back into the system  fueling it, evolving it."

They watched as a new Money Tree erupted from the soil, scattering golden spores into the copper dawn. Its growth was furious, relentless; within minutes, clusters of precious metal fruit emerged, each stamped with a unique calculation.

"The symbols are everywhere," Maya said, her translation tablet nearly overwhelmed. "They don't just describe this reality they *build* it. Language here is infrastructure."

Between trees, wildlife embodied theories. Bird flocks swooped and cried profit margins into the forest canopy. Herds of market trend beings flowed like mercury across plains of metal, shifting with uncanny synchronicity. The sky cities above cast rippling shadows, each specializing in domains of value human minds could barely imagine raw potential, distilled worth, futures unnamed by any language of Earth.

"I've never seen anything so perfectly weighted," Sofia whispered, staring at the balance of ecosystem and economy. "It's like evolution and economics finally merged into one."

Advanced technology sprouted like foliage. Crystalline computers thrummed inside tree cores, calculating cosmic worth. Collectors harvested excess value from the air, channeling it back into the system an endless cycle of renewal.

Marcus stepped forward, the tablet in his hands vibrating in resonance with the world itself. "This is what the ancient texts were pointing toward. Not just a different world, but a different way of existing altogether."

As they spoke, another city assembled itself overhead from crystallized wealth, rising from a cluster of mature trees. Equations scrolled across the sky in fire bright arcs, recording and tallying every human movement.

"And somewhere in all this," Ghost muttered, eyes narrowing at incoming signals, "are answers to why we were chosen."

Around them, the Money Tree world pulsed with endless value and transformation, each ripple adding a new variable to the vast equation. Their very presence was already changing the calculus.

From the forests came the scouts. They streamed together from trickles of pure value, coalescing into forms like liquid assets given consciousness. Three approached, flowing with radiant equations and the fluid grace of living wealth. Each step rippled through the economic fabric of the world.

"They're scanning us," Ghost reported, his display filling with complex metrics. "Not weapons, not biology, they're measuring our *potential worth.*"

The scouts' bodies pulsed, casting waterfalls of symbols into the air mathematics that glowed, cascaded, then re formed. Maya's translation tablet nearly sparked from the effort of processing so much at once.

"It's not just language," she realized, her voice sharp with wonder. "Every gesture is a transaction. They communicate by exchanging value itself." Her fingers blurred across the tablet, aligning the flowing signs with fragments of the ancient texts.

The lead scout extended a crystalline appendage, part energy, part substance. Symbols poured from it like liquid light, hovering in the air between them in equations of daunting complexity.

Sofia's instruments surged with new readings. "They're setting a benchmark," she said. "An exchange rate between their reality and ours."

Then Maya's tablet chimed with success. "I've got it, three layers: mathematical value, energy exchange, and conceptual worth. That's their communication system." She tapped out a sequence, and the tablet projected human aligned symbols back at the scouts.

The scouts glowed brighter, approval radiating from their forms. But when Leo instinctively stepped forward, their light shifted to harsh crimson symbols of warning flashing across their bodies.

"Don't move!" Maya shouted, eyes locked on her screen. "Unaccounted action reads as unauthorized trade. Everything here has to be pre calculated, valued before it occurs."

Leo froze, cards fluttering nervously. The scouts corrected his stance, guiding his gestures into a ritualized exchange. Each motion layered meaning upon meaning hierarchies of worth, permissions of interaction, acknowledgments of balance.

"It's like a stock market crossed with a state dinner," Leo muttered, his cards rearranging to echo their rhythm. "Every step's a transaction, every breath has to be valued first."

The team stood very still, realizing in this moment that first contact wasn't merely conversation. It was commerce and their worth was on trial.

The team sat in stunned silence as Maya translated the foundational rules of this society: **all exchanges must balance; everything holds value; value must be conserved; unauthorized transactions threaten the system itself.**

"They're not just rules," Marcus said, his voice low but steady as he traced the deeper structures in the scouts' demonstrations. "They're the *laws of physics* here but physics built on worth instead of force."

A sudden misunderstanding rippled through the clearing. Ghost's tactical systems automatically tracked the movement of one scout. The beings flared, their forms rippling in agitation. Unauthorized observation, Maya realized, was an *unbalanced transaction* a theft of information without exchange.

"Quick show them your worth calculations!" she urged.

Ghost immediately projected his tactical data into the air. Hard metrics and cold probabilities unfolded in luminous equations, and the scouts calmed, their distress melting into resonance with the mathematics. Balance restored.

The indoctrination began. The scouts wove a ritual of light and value, teaching the fundamentals of their civilization: how to move without disturbing delicate flows of worth, how to open dialogue through calibrated exchange, how to exist in their world without destabilizing it.

"Everything has an account," Sofia murmured, scribbling furiously. "Even *thoughts* carry value here. If they aren't exchanged correctly, they create imbalance."

The lead scout formed a lattice of cascading symbols. Maya's tablet captured it instantly. "They're offering us temporary value signatures," she explained breathlessly.

"Like diplomatic passports identities calibrated to their economy."

Streams of living currency flowed from the scouts, wrapping each team member in unique, glowing sigils that sank into their very molecules. Marcus felt it settle in his chest like a second heartbeat.

"We're being calibrated," he said, watching his team glow with their new identities. "We can exist inside their system now without breaking it."

The scouts shifted into solemn forms, a formal acknowledgment that the first exchange was complete. Above, the copper sky thickened with fresh equations, vast and intricate, heralding the dawn of official dialogue.

"Remember," Maya warned, steadying her hands on her tablet, "from this point forward, *every word is a barter.* Choose carefully."

The scouts turned and led them along a crystallized pathway, the ground pulsing beneath each step as it recalibrated their value signatures. Subtle bursts of economic energy radiated outward, adjusting the environment to their presence.

They paused at the foot of a towering, mature Money Tree, its trunk spiraling skyward in a double helix of precious metals. Up close, it was staggering veins of pure platinum glowed beneath bark alive with constant calculations.

"Incredible," Sofia whispered, her instruments unspooling layer after layer of quantum data. "It's processing value the way Earth trees process sunlight on a scale that defies physics."

Above, harvest beings moved with delicate grace. They touched crystalline fruits, releasing concentrated bursts of worth into multidimensional vessels.

"It's not just harvesting," Maya translated, eyes darting over streaming glyphs. "They're cultivating different *types* of value. Each fruit holds a unique strain of economic energy."

"Look at the precision," Ghost said, tactical overlays mapping the harvest. "Perfect balance never more than the system can sustain. It's integrity woven into biology."

They followed the flow as harvested value funneled into the city's foundations, strengthening both tree and civilization in a perfect, symbiotic cycle. Everywhere they turned, new devices appeared grown rather than built. Some filtered surplus worth from the air, others refined raw potential into crystalline streams of usable force.

The scale of wealth was overwhelming. Leo, entranced, let his cards spin in shimmering harmony with the patterns of the system. "It's like watching the birth of currency itself," he murmured, as a crystalline fruit formed before his eyes.

Sofia fought to keep her composure, her hands trembling as she documented processes that annihilated known science. "They're conjuring *concepts* into tangible value. The conversion rates impossible. And yet..."

Ghost's mind raced ahead, assessing applications. His enhanced vision traced flows across dimensions. "Transaction integrity like this... It's perfect security. No corruption, no breach."

Maya's tablet blazed with translation, glyphs spilling across the screen. "Every exchange is recorded, not just as data but as *culture.* They're building history through commerce."

Only Marcus remained unsettled. His eyes narrowed at currents beneath the surface. "They're not showing us everything," he muttered. "There are deeper calculations we're part of whether we agreed or not."

The scouts guided them onward, through groves of experimental Money Trees. Saplings bore fruits of probability, or branches that stretched into unseen dimensions to trade with parallel realms.

"The diversity is staggering," Sofia whispered, circling one sapling. "Each tree evolves its own strategy for processing value."

They passed under a verification gate an arch of living force that read and confirmed their new signatures. Beyond lay the city proper, its structures shifting like conscious investments, growing and folding as if compounding themselves for return.

"Remember," Maya warned again, her voice low and urgent, "*everything* is a transaction. Even standing here has already been factored into their calculus."

The scouts blurred, symbols rewriting their forms into sharper glyphs. Maya translated: "*The Central Exchange. That's where they'll induct us where our presence joins their economic network.*"

Above them, the floating city stirred, its structures realigning to prepare for the first human visitors. The copper sky erupted with equations, vast and searing, as the Money Tree civilization calculated the implications of this unprecedented transfer of value across dimensions.

Marcus rested a hand on the cool surface of the tablet at his side, feeling its steady pulse beat in rhythm with the city around                                                                            him.
"We're about to see what real wealth looks like," he said softly. "Let's just hope we're ready for it."

Before them, the transportation hub crystallized into a vast, prismatic algorithm of trade architecture that was both immutable and mercurial, as though logic itself had been frozen mid thought. Viscous currents of distilled economic energy coursed through translucent veins, weaving pathways that casually defied the axioms of known physics. The scouts, moving like echoes of a vanished future, guided them onto what seemed less a platform than a precarious lattice of equilibria market forces stilled into a fragile truce beneath their feet.

"It's a value current system," Maya translated as her tablet filled with symbols. "They move along streams of condensed value, using economic momentum for propulsion."

Sofia was already scanning. Scientific curiosity overrode protocol. "The energy conversion is unlike anything we've theorized. They're transforming abstract value directly into kinetic force."

A transport vessel coalesced around them, its walls writhing with calculations and market predictions. The interior shifted in real time, reshaping itself to provide interfaces that bridged human comprehension with the civilization's advanced economic systems.

"The ship itself is a trader," Ghost observed, his tactical overlays parsing the details. "It's in constant exchange with the infrastructure millions of microtransactions per second to maintain balance."

The scouts performed the boarding ritual: a complex cascade of acknowledgments, each motion registering their existence in the transport network's ledger. Every step mattered, maintaining equilibrium in a system where imbalance was an existential threat.

"Even their public transit runs on perfect market principles," Leo said, watching his cards resonate with the vessel's energy. "No waste, no excess pure efficiency."

The vessel lurched forward, sliding into a current of liquid assets that carried them deeper into the city. Through the transparent walls, the team glimpsed the civilization's defensive layers: vast fields of economic force regulating every flow of value in and out of the city.

"Their defense isn't weapons," Ghost said, eyes narrowed. "It's authentication. Anything that doesn't belong anything outside their patterns of worth they erase from reality."

Sofia's voice trembled with awe as she recorded. "They've erased the line between biology and economy. Between natural and artificial. Everything fits seamlessly."

The transport glided across branching streams, each junction resolved through instantaneous calculations preserving the balance between divergent currencies of worth. The scouts moved fluidly alongside, translating the luminous ciphers that shimmered in the currents traffic signals in this vast mercurial highway.

"These aren't just directions," Maya murmured as her tablet strained to keep up. "They're live market updates. The whole transport system adjusts in real time, based on supply and demand of movement itself."

At each checkpoint, Leo noticed something new. "They're layering more onto our signatures," he whispered. "Every gate adds detail to our profile. They're trying to build a complete picture of our worth."

The vessel slowed as it approached a nexus where streams of value converged in a dazzling spectacle of fiscal power. Other transports moved like constellations of cost and calculation, their passengers rendered not as bodies but as patterns of abstract accounting.

"This whole society," Ghost muttered, watching the intricate dance, "is one secure transaction. Every interaction verified, every move logged."

Sofia's instruments pulsed in agreement. "It's all connected Money Trees, floating cities, transport systems. One vast economic organism."

The scouts guided them into a deeper current. Around them, architecture unfurled like a living equation, buildings rising, dissolving, and reshaping themselves in response to tides of worth. The city revealed itself not as a construct but as a living calculus of value.

"Remember," Maya warned, scanning fresh glyphs. "Every movement matters here. We need to master their protocols fast, or risk disrupting their entire system."

The vessel docked at a terminal woven from pure potential energy, stabilized into a platform that recognized their physicality. The scouts indicated their first destination: a cultural integration center, where they would learn how to properly interact with the civilization's advanced systems.

As they prepared to disembark, Marcus glimpsed through the walls: vast calculation chambers, worth refineries, and halls where reality itself was traded like a commodity. The enormity of their mission pressed heavier on him.

The city itself was alive, its structures in endless flux growing, reconfiguring, recalculating. Stepping from the vessel into a vast atrium where value streams converged from every direction, they found themselves at the heart of a radiant symphony of commerce.

Their temporary quarters formed instantly, morphing from the city's fabric as algorithms analyzed and responded to their unique worth signatures. The walls crystallized into place, sculpted with the precision of a well managed investment.

"The architecture is responding to us," Sofia noted, her voice hushed. "It's building according to our potential."

Then came the delegation. Unlike the fluid scouts, these forms were rigid, precise embodiments of bureaucracy. Their bodies were composed of regulatory equations and compliance protocols, every movement a balance sheet made flesh.

"They're administrative functions, given consciousness," Maya whispered, translating symbols as they streamed between officials. "Each one represents a branch of governance."

The officials initiated the entry ritual, a lattice of light and value unfolding around them. Maya translated quickly: "We're being granted temporary trading rights within designated city sectors."

But Ghost's tactical systems caught subtle undercurrents in the officials' movements. "They're divided," he said grimly. "Some calculate opportunity. Others see only risk."

Leo's cards shifted restlessly, picking up the same tension. "They keep recalculating us. They don't know where we belong in their system."

The team was fitted with value markers crystalline instruments designed to trace the economic interactions of every citizen in the city. Marcus studied his intently as it pulsed with measured precision, each flicker syncing seamlessly with the rhythm of his tablet, both devices calibrated to the heartbeat of the marketplace itself.

"These aren't just monitoring devices," he whispered to the others. "They're restrictions. They've already limited our freedom of access to certain types of transactions."

As the officials continued their orientation procedures, the team exchanged uneasy glances, each member interpreting their new reality in starkly different ways.

Sofia saw, in a rush, the boundless expanse of research potential unfurling before her…her scientific mind already forming questions with the quiet urgency of a storm gathering at sea. Ghost, ever vigilant, scanned the environment with a tactician's eye, mapping advantages and vulnerabilities woven into the city's design. Leo, still and watchful, traced the rhythms beneath the surface, perceiving patterns that whispered of concealed motives and unspoken agendas.

Maya's translations revealed increasingly complex layers of meaning. "There are factions here," she murmured during a pause in the proceedings. "Some want to expand trade across dimensions. Others fear contamination of their perfect system."

Their quarters shifted subtly as their comprehension of the civilization deepened. Walls grew translucent, revealing glimpses of the city's inner workings vast calculation chambers where reality itself was quantified and traded as though it were no more than currency.

"Imagine what this could mean for Earth," Sofia whispered during a private moment, her excitement barely contained. "Their technology could revolutionize every field of science."

Ghost's reply was measured, his expression wary. "Or destabilize everything we know. One wrong calculation here could ripple across dimensions."

With a final exchange of value promises binding agreements governing the team's activities in the city the officials concluded the welcome ceremony. As they departed, their forms trailed glowing regulatory symbols that lingered like afterimages in the air.

The team gathered close.

"We're being tested," Marcus said, eyes fixed on the shifting patterns flowing across his tablet. "Everything we do is being measured against some larger calculation we can't yet see."

Leo fanned his cards open, their shimmering alignments suggesting possible futures. "The opportunities here are immense. But so are the risks. One wrong turn in their algorithms, and the consequences might be catastrophic."

Maya's tablet pulsed as new background symbols revealed themselves. "Some officials already see us as catalysts for change," she said quietly. "Others view us as threats. We've caused ripples in their perfect system just by existing here."

Around them, the city pulsed with a sentient rhythm. Structures reconfigured subtly in response to their presence, as if recalibrating themselves around these new anomalies. Beyond the translucent walls, silhouettes of other beings lingered watchful, assessing, measuring the humans against metrics unspoken but absolute. Above, the floating city made a minute orbital adjustment, recalibrating its course to account for the new variables they had become.

"Whatever their true intentions," Sofia said, unpacking her instruments, "we're here. And we need to learn everything we can."

As night fell, painting the copper sky in deeper shades of wealth, the team settled into their quarters. Unseen, subtle calculations were being etched into the city's very fabric equations that, in time, would force the humans to choose between their mission and the perfection of balance in the Money Tree civilization.

Marcus rested his hand on the tablet one last time before sleep. Beneath his fingertips, unfamiliar patterns stirred, their meanings concealed but urgent. The real calculations had only just begun.

## Chapter 7: The Dawn of The Possibilities

Morning sunlight pierced through the tall canopies of Money Tree City, flooding the world in waves of copper and gold. In an instant, the city came alive with color. Glimmering rays danced across verdant foliage, casting playful shadows on the ground. It was a new day one that promised discovery for the team now set to journey deeper into this extraordinary place.

They gathered beneath the vast canopy of an open air hall, where architecture and nature breathed in seamless harmony. The walls bore intricate carvings of legendary trees, etched with such reverence that the very spirit of the Money Tree seemed to pulse within their grain. The air carried the delicate perfume of blooming flowers, while the gentle murmur of leaves created a hushed lullaby, a serenity so fragile it felt like a secret whispered by the wind.

At the front of the hall stood Zara, exuding confidence, warmth, and approachability. She smiled as her gaze swept the group, sunlight catching in her long, flowing hair. Before she could begin, Tom leaned forward with a grin.

"So, are you going to tell us the secret of this magical city, or do we have to figure it out ourselves?"

Zara chuckled, her bright, inquisitive eyes resting on him. "Patience, Tom. You'll have your answers soon enough."

She raised her voice, clear and steady. "Welcome, everyone, to Money Tree City! Today you step into a world where nature and growth are one. Here, we don't just grow trees we cultivate wealth, knowledge, and connection."

Sarah raised her hand, half joking but curious. "When you say *cultivate wealth*, do you mean literal money grows on trees?"

"In a way, yes," Zara replied with a smile. "But it's more than that you'll see soon enough." She gestured for the group to settle. "Let me explain how it all works."

Her passion was unmistakable as she spoke of the ecosystem. "Each tree is unique almost like it has a personality. And understanding that personality is the key to prosperity here."

Tom raised an eyebrow. "Wait, you mean moods? Like they get cranky or something?"

"Not moods," Zara laughed lightly. "Traits. Some trees are better at producing fruit, others at providing materials. Think of them as partners in growth."

Ava nodded thoughtfully. "So it's about recognizing potential and working with it?"

"Exactly," Zara said, smiling in approval.

She paced slowly as she explained further. "Money Tree City runs on sustainability. The more you nurture your tree, the more it rewards you. But with great power comes great responsibility."

"What kind of responsibility?" Raj asked, his tone serious.

Zara turned to him with a nod. "Rules that ensure balance. Ignore them, and you harm not just the trees, but the whole ecosystem."

Tom leaned forward. "What kind of rules?"

"Rules about harvesting," she said firmly. "When, how much, and where. Respecting these guidelines is crucial. Without them, the city wouldn't exist as it does now."

Raj pressed further. "So the economy here is entirely tree based? No other industries?"

"Exactly," Zara confirmed. "Our trees provide everything resources, wealth, and even energy for our portals."

Sarah's brow furrowed. "Portals? You mean, actual portals?"

"Yes," Zara replied gravely. "They allow rapid travel across the city. But they rely on the trees for power, and misuse can destabilize the entire system. That's why portal use carries strict guidelines."

"What happens if someone misuses one?" Ava asked.

Zara's expression darkened. "Disruption. The system strains, and balance falters. It's rare, but when it happens, the consequences ripple through everything."

When the orientation ended, Zara released them into the heart of the city, urging them to explore. Money Tree City waited with its marvels an awakening unlike anything they had ever known.

Tom, the practical adventurer, was first into the winding pathways lined with blossoms of every hue. He watched residents demonstrate harvesting techniques, their movements fluid and respectful, in perfect harmony with their trees. Enchanted, he was already making mental notes for when he would begin cultivating his own.

Sarah, the team's creative soul, wandered toward an art installation crafted entirely from natural elements. Its colors whispered secrets; its designs seemed alive with stories. Inspiration surged within her. She spent hours gathering materials, weaving the essence of the city into her own creation.

Raj immersed himself in conversation with a local farmer, absorbing every detail about the properties of different trees some yielding riches, others materials for building and craft. He listened intently, determined not to miss a single insight.

Ava, ever the strategist, found herself drawn to the central plaza where the great Heart Tree stood the oldest and most revered in the city, a symbol of unity and prosperity. She felt its energy radiating outward and paused to reflect. Here, in this place of power, she thought about her team's purpose and what they might contribute to the city's growth.

As the day waned, they reunited in the orientation hall. Their faces glowed with excitement, their voices interweaving as they shared discoveries unique experiences woven into the tapestry of a single, shared journey through this new world.

"I saw how the harvest demonstration works," Tom said, eager to share, his enthusiasm infectious. "The way they tend to the trees it's amazing. Every gesture shows respect, carefully aligned with the rhythm of the seasons."

Sarah's eyes glowed as she chimed in. "And look at this wonderful place I found to create art! The inspiration just flows from the environment here. I can hardly wait to start my project."

Raj, thoughtful as always, spoke with precision. "I spent time with the farmers, learning details of cultivation. Every tree has its own balance, and every process requires care. It's a lot to master, but with practice, we'll get it."

Ava nodded, her tone steady and reflective. "The Heart Tree has a lot to teach us about unity, about collaboration. If we can harness its energy, I believe we can strengthen not only ourselves but also our connection to this city."

Zara listened with pride, her heart swelling at their discoveries. "You're beginning to understand the essence of Money Tree City," she said warmly. "Every step you take here is an investment in your future. The more you give to this world, the more it gives back."

As the sun dipped low, painting the city in hues of amber and gold, the team gathered beneath the sprawling branches of the Heart Tree. Their faces glowed with camaraderie, their spirits bound together by past trials and the promise of future hopes. With quiet solemnity, Zara urged them to pledge to safeguard the trees, to honor the city, and to carry kindness into the heart of the community.

It was only the beginning, but a solid foundation had been laid. They were ready to dig deeper into the mysteries of Money Tree City, embracing the responsibilities that came with nurturing wealth and wisdom in this strange and wondrous place.

That night, the stars shone like jeweled fruits in the copper sky a reminder that anything was possible. The morning had revealed a glimpse of the city's infinite potential; now they longed to plunge into its depths and discover all it held. As a team, they would grow trees and futures together in this dreamlike realm.

Each new sunrise was a silent herald of fortunes waiting to be claimed and secrets yet to unfold. Subtle threads of energy wove through the city's air, binding the team ever closer, entwining their lives with the vibrant destiny of this world. To navigate the intricate dance of cultural integration, roles were assigned each member entrusted with a vital task in the stewardship of the sacred trees.

Maya, with her passion for history, became the team's researcher. She immersed herself in archives that resembled living manuscripts scrolls, stories, and artifacts woven into the very fabric of the city. She uncovered tales of the founders, the struggles of early settlers, and the rituals that honored the trees.

"Did you know," she said one evening, her eyes shining, "that the first settlers believed each tree had a spirit? When treated with respect, the spirits would bless them with prosperity. It was a beautiful, mutual bond."

Sofia, with her technical brilliance, devoted herself to the city's advanced technology. She marveled at how seamlessly machines were interwoven with nature, from tree health monitors to crystalline communicators that kept residents connected.

"Look at this!" she exclaimed one afternoon, showing the group a shimmering holographic interface. "It tells us everything growth, nutrients, even weather impact. It's like the tree is speaking directly to us!"

Ghost, ever the strategist, focused on the city's defenses. He spent his days observing patrols and studying the security around the plazas and portals. His instincts told him danger was never far.

"There's more here than meets the eye," he told the group quietly one evening. "Patrols have increased near the central plaza. We need to understand the local power structure. This isn't just about harvesting it's about staying safe."

Leo immersed himself in the city's traditions and culture. He attended festivals and ceremonies, eager to understand the values that bound this society together.

"Today I witnessed the Heart Tree ceremony," he told the team later, his face alight with wonder. "The people sang songs of gratitude, told stories of unity. It reminded me their relationship with the trees is living, not transactional."

As the team settled into their roles, the moment of their first harvest drew near a pivotal milestone. Zara gathered them with a solemn air, her tone soft yet commanding.

"Harvesting is not just a task," she said. "It's a bond of respect, a promise. You must understand your tree and work with it, honoring the spirit within it and the generations who cared for it before. Only then will the tree reward you."

The day of the harvest dawned, and the team stood before their chosen tree a healthy, flourishing specimen that yielded more than most. Excitement shimmered in their voices, but so did a nervous undercurrent. Each brought their own methods, their own experience, and with it, the risk of friction.

Sofia stepped forward first, her technological tools already humming. "I'll scan the tree to determine the best points for harvesting," she said, voice steady and precise.

Eager to prove himself, Tom pushed forward. "Let's not waste time," he countered. "We should maximize our yield! Start with the lower branches they're easier to reach." His competitive spirit was palpable, his movements brisk with urgency as he prepared to climb.

Maya frowned, her caution cutting through his enthusiasm. "Tom, wait. We can't just strip it bare. If we take too much, the tree will weaken. History has taught us that balance is everything."

The air thickened with tension as their differing approaches clashed. Sofia and Tom's ambitions collided, while Maya's voice carried warnings rooted in ancient lessons. Ghost, ever the sentinel, broke the silence.

"We're losing focus," he said, his gaze sharp as he studied the shifting dynamics. "This isn't just about the harvest. It's about relationships ours, and with the trees. Forget that, and we'll fail."

Leo lifted his deck of cards, letting them scatter and reform in gentle patterns. His tone was calm, bridging the divide.

"Let's pause. Each of us has something to offer. What if we combine our approaches work with the tree instead of against each other?"

Zara, sensing the strain rise like heat from the ground, intervened. Her voice was quiet but carried authority. "Enough. We move as one. Each of you has a perspective worth hearing, but if we don't listen, we'll destroy the very thing we're here to honor. Our success lies in collaboration, not competition."

The group drew a collective breath, and the mood shifted still fragile, but leaning toward unity. For Zara, it was more than a lesson in harvesting; it was a glimpse of how hard true integration would be. Beneath the surface, tensions still ran deep, a subtle reminder that culture and ego did not bend easily.

Amid this challenge, another current tugged at her heart. Marcus, the local guide assigned to their group, moved with quiet authority among the trees. Knowledgeable and charismatic, he carried a reverence for the land that stirred something within her. His presence was both grounding and inspiring, a reminder that connection went beyond knowledge it was about respect.

One afternoon, Marcus spoke to her as they worked side by side. "I admire your zeal for the trees," he said, his voice low and thoughtful. "But remember it's a partnership. Trees respond to respect and gratitude, just like we do."

His words lodged deep in Zara's chest. She found herself opening to him in return, sharing her hopes for her team and her dreams of building a bridge between her people and his. Their laughter came easily, and with each passing day, the bond between them grew stronger.

Weeks passed, the group slowly adjusting to the relentless demands of their roles. The memory of their first harvest attempt lingered, sharp as a scar, but it gave birth to a new determination. They gathered once more at their tree, this time armed with lessons learned.

Sofia took the lead again, scanning the trunk with her instruments. "Let's combine our strengths," she said, her tone inclusive now. "We'll use the data as a guide and balance it with care for the tree."

Tom nodded, his earlier brashness tempered by humility. "I'll handle the pruning take only what's needed. We'll leave the tree stronger than before."

Relief softened Maya's face. "That's what I hoped for. We honor its history, and it will keep giving."

As they harvested, harmony replaced discord. Each action felt deliberate, respectful, woven together like notes in a song. Zara's pride swelled as she watched them work not just as a team, but as something more. They had learned openness, the art of balancing difference, and the strength of weaving disparate voices into one chorus.

And through it all, Marcus's presence was never far. He joined them often, sharing stories of the city and of the trees, tales laced with wisdom and care. Zara felt herself drawn not only to his knowledge but to the man himself his calm, his laughter, the way he spoke as if rooted in the soil beneath their feet.

One evening, under a canopy of stars, Zara admitted softly, "I never expected to feel such a connection here especially to its people. Thank you for helping me see it."

Marcus's smile glowed in the starlight, his eyes warm with understanding. "You've got a gift, Zara. You connect. That's what your team needs most and what this city will remember."

Weeks melted into months. The harvests grew more successful, the bonds more resilient. Through conflict and reconciliation, through labor and laughter, the team discovered that their strength did not lie only in what they could take from Money Tree City, but in the respect they gave back to it. Together with each other, with the trees, and with this place they were weaving something enduring.

A foundation had been laid, one that would carry them through trials yet unseen.

With each new attempt at a harvest, the team learned more about the delicate balance required in cultivating wealth and the responsibility that came with it. Their efforts bore fruit, literally and figuratively. They tended the trees with care, and their standing in the community shifted. No longer were they mysterious outsiders; step by step, they became valued neighbors. What might once have unraveled their unity instead released its tension, weaving them into something stronger.

One evening, beneath a starlit sky, Zara sat with her team, their laughter mingling with stories of the day. Pride welled in her heart. They had come far since their uncertain arrival, but she knew this was only the beginning. The real journey lay ahead in cultivating deeper relationships and seeking true understanding of Money Tree City.

As the sun dipped low, painting the city in amber light, the group gathered in their open air pavilion. Surrounded by blossoming trees and the music of rustling leaves, it was here they held their end of day assessments a sanctuary for reflection, learning, and planning.

Zara stood at the front, her expression poised between pride and concern. "Today was big," she began, her voice steady. "We've made progress, but we've also uncovered complications complications we'll need to resolve together."

The team leaned in, anticipation written across their faces. Each carried discoveries, and each was eager to share.

Maya spoke first, her eyes glowing with excitement. "I've been digging deeper into the historical archives. The city's founders believed the trees were not only providers but guardians of their treasures. They had rituals for every stage of a tree's life cycle. It's extraordinary the respect they gave shaped everything about this place."

Sofia leaned forward, intrigued. "That makes sense, Maya. The trees are the center of all this. But today I uncovered something unusual. Some monitoring devices aren't just for health they regulate and control resource distribution. It's as if the city itself breathes through these instruments, a living artery of wealth."

Ghost broke the silence, his tone grave. "I've been watching the guards. They're not just maintaining order they're regulating who gets what. Surveillance here feels… heavy. Prosperity isn't free. The trees are as much about control as they are about growth."

The air thickened with his words. The team exchanged uneasy glances. Then Leo, usually quiet, spoke up. "I joined a community event. It was beautiful songs, rituals, people united. But under it, I sensed tension. Some whispered about the harsh punishments for breaking harvesting rules. They fear retribution. Beneath the beauty, there's… something else."

Zara nodded slowly, weighing their words. "We're peeling back layers," she said. "On one hand, Money Tree City is breathtaking almost utopian. On the other, there's a shadow beneath the surface. We can't ignore it."

The team fell into strategy.

"We'll need to tread carefully," Zara advised. "Our mission is to build trust, not stir fear. We gather information. We listen. We learn."

"Long time residents might give perspective," Maya suggested. "If we understand how these rules evolved, maybe we'll see the bigger picture."

Sofia added, "And I'll keep tracking the technology. If the systems control resources, then understanding how they work could be crucial for our future here."

Ideas wove together as they spoke of transparency, of trust, of staying vigilant. The weight of their discoveries lingered, but so did their resolve.

Finally, Zara brought their attention to what lay ahead. "Tomorrow, we've been granted an audience with the Elder." Her voice softened with both reverence and determination. "This is our chance. We listen. We learn. And maybe we begin to understand the core of this civilization."

Leo's eyes brightened with anticipation. "The Elder is central to all of this. If anyone can clarify the contradictions we've found, it's them."

Ghost's expression remained sober. "We must be careful. The Elder's decisions ripple across the community. Every word we speak matters."

Zara agreed. "We'll present ourselves as allies concerned for the people, invested in their future. Our questions must reflect both what we admire and what we fear."

As evening deepened, they sharpened their focus, preparing for the meeting that could shape everything. What were the Elder's true views of the trees? Why such strict regulations? What were the consequences of imbalance? Each member offered insights, weaving strategy from their diverse strengths.

Maya's voice carried the final note of the night: "We should ask about the rituals of the trees their meaning. It might be the key to opening dialogue, to showing respect."

The pavilion fell into quiet reflection. Overhead, the copper sky faded into stars, each one glowing like fruit in a cosmic orchard. Tomorrow, they would face the Elder and perhaps the truth at the heart of Money Tree City.

Sofia added thoughtfully, "And what about the technological systems? If they influence the running of the city, we should ask how open and accessible they are to the citizens."

As the discussion unfolded, a profound sense of unity blossomed within the team. No longer just a collection of disparate voices with separate aims, they felt themselves becoming a single, cohesive force committed to unraveling the mysteries of Money Tree City and navigating its delicate complexities together.

When the meeting drew to a close, Zara looked around at her companions, pride welling within her. "We've accomplished so much already, but tomorrow's meeting must be approached without closed minds or hardened hearts. What we've discovered so far is only the tip of the iceberg. We have to be ready for more."

With renewed focus, the team dispersed for the night, each retreating into their own quiet reflections. The revelations of the day still pressed on their minds hints of beauty shadowed by control, of prosperity tinged with fear. Yet alongside that unease was a deeper determination: to seek truth, to foster understanding, and to honor their solemn pledge to the city and to one another.

Above them, the stars glittered softly, their light spilling across Money Tree City like a quiet blessing. Tomorrow carried the weight of reckoning: an audience with the Elder, the chance to illuminate the hidden truths woven into the city's fabric.

As dawn's promise stirred faintly on the horizon, one by one they drifted into sleep fitful, restless, yet resolute. Their dreams were filled with visions of trees whispering secrets, of equations swirling in the skies, of doors half opened to truths yet unseen. Tests of will, unity, and allegiance lay ahead, but the team was ready. The Elder awaited, and with them, the answers that could change everything.

## Chapter 8: The City of Gold

Morning sunlight crept over Money Tree City, casting a gilt overlay across the landscape and seeming to illuminate every leaf and pathway. Today would be a day of moments: the team was to attend a formal procession to the central citadel, a grand event that would introduce them to the city's leadership and its intricate power dynamics.

They gathered in the plaza, anticipation crackling between them. The air was thick with flowers in bloom, and the electric hush of expectation clung to every breath. Dressed in garments that reflected the city's vibrant stories, they stood united, though each carried the weight of looming challenges.

With great fanfare, the procession began. Money Tree City thrummed with life streets alive with radiant faces, their pride stitched into the very air. Golden pathways stretched outward from floating structures, gleaming beneath the sun. It was a breathtaking union of past and future, where ancient artistry intertwined seamlessly with innovation. Towers spiraled skyward, alive with carvings that pulsed in rhythm with the surrounding trees.

"Look at that!" Sofia gasped, pointing toward a cluster of shimmering spires. "It's extraordinary the integration of nature into their design. It's alive."

Yet as they moved deeper into the city, contrasts emerged. Opulence flourished in some quarters mansions crowned with verdant lawns and overflowing with wealth while in others, people scraped by with little more than necessity. The team exchanged uneasy glances.

"This place is dazzling," Maya murmured, her brow furrowed. "But also… uneven. How can such abundance coexist with such obvious inequality?"

Ghost's gaze sharpened as his instincts flared. "We need to tread carefully. Something darker may be woven into the roots of all this wealth."

The citadel loomed ahead, an immense monument of spiraling spires etched with symbolic carvings that chronicled the city's history. Its sheer presence exuded power. Here, at the seat of governance, the councilors shaped the fate of every citizen.

Zara's heart pounded as they stepped inside. The hall stretched vast and resplendent, its golden walls gleaming like sunlight captured in stone. But it wasn't the architecture that pressed on them most it was the council. Rows of figures watched with a blend of curiosity, skepticism, and calculation. Some eyes glimmered with interest, while others hid cool suspicion. This was no mere ceremony it was a trial of balance, where one misstep could shift alliances or expose fault lines.

At the head sat Elder Aurelia. Majestic and commanding, she carried the kind of presence that filled the chamber with a single word. "Welcome," she intoned, her voice resonant. "Representatives of the Outside, you enter the City of Gold, where affluence and tradition are bound as one."

A shiver traced Zara's spine. Aurelia's words were measured and strong, but beneath them pulsed a taut undercurrent of tension. The council exchanged subtle glances some nodding in accord, others rigid with doubt. Clearly, the outsiders were not embraced equally among these leaders.

The Elder continued, her voice smooth as polished stone. "Today, we celebrate a bond between our city and your team. But first, you must understand the council's divisions." She gestured to the rows flanking her factions revealed through subtle gestures, the smallest flicker of agreement or scorn.

Zara's keen eyes caught the delicate web of loyalties and rivalries, the fragile equilibrium holding the council together. Their presence here was already a disruption, and every word spoken would echo across that balance.

The welcoming ritual began. Councilors rose, encircling the team, their voices rising in chant. The air vibrated with resonance, weaving ceremony and suspicion into the same moment. Zara felt her chest tighten as if the harmony could fracture at any instant. One by one, the team was asked to rise and state their purpose.

Maya went first. Standing tall, her voice steady, she declared, "Our mission is to learn the history and traditions of this city." The words rang clear, drawing the Elder's narrowed gaze her eyes weighing the statement on an inner scale known only to her.

Sofia followed, brimming with enthusiasm. "I have studied your technology, and I'm in awe of how seamlessly it merges with nature. There is common ground here opportunities for collaboration that could benefit both our worlds." Her voice lifted with conviction, but the room remained still. Only a handful of councilors nodded faintly; others remained stone faced, skepticism radiating from their silence.

Then it was Ghost's turn. He rose deliberately, his words chosen with precision.

"We understand that in every community there is security and governance, and for that, we must learn and respect the systems in place." Ghost's voice carried steady weight, his eyes moving across the chamber. Zara caught the faint flicker of interest from one of the councilors but it was quickly lost beneath the tension that clung to the room.

Finally, Leo stepped forward. His tone was calm, his voice rich with empathy. "We know our presence raises questions.

But our commitment is simple: to nurture relationships built on trust and respect." His words seemed to soften the air, and Zara prayed they had struck true.

When all had spoken, murmurs rippled through the chamber. Zara watched carefully as subtle alliances shifted and divisions flared beneath the surface. Tension pressed down like a storm about to break. And then her gaze caught on something crystalline ornate columns, gleaming walls and behind them, the unmistakable glint of surveillance devices. A chill raced down her spine. They weren't just being heard; they were being measured every gesture, every flicker of expression, recorded and analyzed.

Elder Aurelia's voice cut through the hall with finality. "Your being here is both opportunity and challenge. Your intentions will be weighed against your contribution to the prosperity of Money Tree City. But hear this: our community rests on trust, and any breach will not go lightly."

The ritual ended, and the council dispersed with calculated grace. The team stepped out of the golden hall with heavy minds. The beauty of Money Tree City was intact, but now it seemed veiled its perfection layered over fractures of power, control, and surveillance.

Zara led them to a quiet alcove within the citadel. "We have a lot to unpack," she said in hushed tones. "Today showed us possibility, but it also revealed how fragile the balance of power really is. One wrong move, and we're caught in a conflict far bigger than us."

Maya's expression was grave. "We can't pretend ignorance anymore. The Elder's words were clear we're under their eye, part of their dynamics now."

Sofia folded her arms, nodding. "And everything we do is scrutinized. Even how we talk among ourselves. We need to be very deliberate."

Ghost's voice was sharp. "We need intelligence. Factions exist inside that council. If we split up and study them, maybe we can see where the fault lines are."

Leo, softer, added, "And the people the residents. They'll tell us what really happens when the council makes its decisions."

The team felt the weight of the mission anew. No longer observers they were inside the web, their every move pulling on threads they couldn't yet see.

Outside, the golden pathways gleamed under late sunlight, glittering like promises beautiful and treacherous.

Immediately after the meeting, a shift occurred. Money Tree City itself seemed different, every shimmer of wealth underlaid with something sharper. Their official guide, Councilor Talia, arrived to lead them on a tour of the administrative heart.

With practiced ease, Zara ushered the team along the thoroughfares. Their footsteps echoed on golden pathways that shone with arpeggios of captured sunlight. Above them, floating structures drifted like vast ships, delicate in motion yet immense in scale. Around them, the city thrummed with prosperity the laughter of merchants, the rhythm of trade, the hum of machines. Yet beneath it all was a dissonance, as though the perfection were carefully orchestrated, each note tuned to mask the fractures beneath.

"Welcome to the heart of Money Tree City," Talia said proudly. "This is where decisions are made every thread of our community is woven here. You'll see the technologies that sustain us, and the systems that keep balance."

They entered a vast open hub, its walls alive with displays. Information surged across them resource allocation charts, atmospheric and climate data, needs from the grassroots all updating in real time. Along the murals, history unfurled: the city's founding etched in luminous strokes, stories of "unity" flowing seamlessly into depictions of "wealth."

Sofia's eyes lit up like fire. "This is... incredible." She reached toward one of the displays, resisting the urge to touch. "It's not just data. It's integration. The city breathes through this system. It listens to its people, and the feedback loops create balance."

As Talia continued explaining the systems of Money Tree City, Sofia's focus began to drift. Her eyes caught the faint shimmer of nearly invisible devices embedded in the walls silent sentinels of surveillance disguised as ornamentation. A chill ran down her spine as the realization settled: this wasn't just governance. This was control.

Meanwhile, Ghost's gaze roamed with mounting unease. The system was efficient, yes but the hairs at the back of his neck refused to lie flat. Something here, he sensed, was profoundly wrong.

As they passed a cluster of three figures near the entrance uniforms unlike any worn by the citizens, armed, unsmiling, and alert Ghost leaned in toward Zara, lowering his voice. "Have you noticed the military presence?" he murmured. "This isn't for show. Something's churning in these waters, and I don't like it."

Zara nodded slightly, her expression mirroring the concern etched into the faces of her team. The air itself seemed electric, and she realized that with all this prosperity came an underbelly: a tension so taut it felt like a thin wire they'd have to walk carefully.

Their next stop showcased the city's agricultural marvels. Talia led them into a vast greenhouse facility where trees flourished in a breathtaking synthesis of traditional farming practices and high end science. Automated drones hovered in silence, tending the plants. Above the foliage, holographic displays floated in midair, flashing real time health metrics and projecting future growth in cascading light.

"This is where we harvest the symbiotic relationship between nature and technology," Talia explained, her voice reverent. "We maintain the highest oversight watching every detail to ensure prime yields and the continued health of our trees."

Sofia's eyes sparkled as she studied the systems at work. "This is extraordinary," she breathed, ambition flickering in her gaze. "If we could adapt even a fraction of this back home, it would revolutionize sustainable agriculture."

Yet even as she marveled, a small voice whispered in the back of her mind. The systems designed to monitor the trees, she realized, also monitored the city's inhabitants. The price of such grand advancement was the quiet erosion of personal freedom. The thought settled heavily in her chest.

Deeper into the complex, Maya found herself drawn to the historical archives an entire room lined with ancient scrolls and tomes chronicling the city's past. The air smelled faintly of aged paper, a living echo of history in a place where everything else felt meticulously new.

"This is where the story of Money Tree City is kept," Talia said, sweeping her arm across the shelves. "We believe knowledge of our history is key to preserving our identity."

Maya took an eager step forward, her heart racing. "I have to go in," she murmured under her breath. Even the few glimpses she caught of the texts stirred something like fire in her belly. This could illuminate their current situation give shape to what lay hidden beneath the city's glittering surface.

As the tour drew to a close, Talia gathered them for an announcement. "Each of you will be attached to a section within the running of this great city," she said. "Your contributions will add value to our operation divisions."

Zara's pulse quickened. "What positions will we hold?" she asked.

Talia smiled faintly, her eyes glinting. "Maya, you will work within the historical archives to help preserve and interpret our history. Sofia, you will join the technology department to enhance agricultural systems. Ghost, your instincts will serve within the security division to observe and ensure safety. Leo, you will take part in community outreach, building bridges between the council and our residents."

The team exchanged glances, digesting their new roles. This was their chance to be part of the city's fabric to influence its growth. But even as excitement flickered, a lingering apprehension took root: they were stepping into roles that carried privilege and power, but such gifts often came shackled with unseen restraints.

"Your housing will be assigned in different districts," Talia continued. "This will help you learn and understand the diverse dimensions of our community. Every district has its own culture and challenges."

As she outlined the city's structure, it became clear they would be scattered across vastly different worlds. Zara was assigned to the affluent district of grand buildings and abundant resources. Maya would live in a middle class neighborhood steeped in history and tradition. Ghost would reside in the security district, close to the city's military heart, while Sofia and Leo were placed in a cutting edge technological enclave.

"Enjoy the privileges of your posts," Talia said, her tone edged with warning. "But remember every privilege carries great responsibility. You are ambassadors beyond these walls. Your character must reflect that, or the consequences will ripple far beyond yourselves."

As they left the administrative district, the opportunities ahead glimmered like gold, but so did the weight of unseen eyes. Every decision they made, every word they spoke, would be measured not only by the council but by the hidden forces shaping the city's future.

"What do you think happens if we push too hard for change?" Maya asked quietly as they walked the golden pathways, her brow furrowed.

"Let's not forget we're being watched," Ghost muttered, his voice a low growl. "One ill move, and the consequences could be more than we've bargained for."

Sofia nodded gravely. "And the military aspect is no small thing. We can't disregard it. We have to move intelligently cautiously."

Subtle hues of beauty tinted Money Tree City, but beneath that beauty the truth was beginning to reveal itself piece by piece. What had once felt like an enchanting floating utopia now seemed like a cloak brilliant, dazzling, but hiding something deeper. The team, prepared to investigate, could feel the shift. Evening drew them back to their quarters, each member retreating into their own inner world. They were no longer visitors to Money Tree City; they had become players in a carefully choreographed game of power and privilege, set against a backdrop of boundless opportunity and quiet peril.

Maya immersed herself in the city's historical archives, unraveling the founding principles etched into its past. Sofia delved into technological breakthroughs innovations poised to redefine farming itself. Ghost poured his focus into security protocols, learning exactly how movement and dissent were monitored. Leo continued cultivating contact with the residents, trying to understand their attitudes and unspoken frustrations. As the sun set over the City of Gold, one realization grew stronger: their mission was no longer simply to gather knowledge. They were now stakeholders in a society brimming with promise but riddled with problems.

That night, as twilight deepened, the team convened in their new quarters a sleek, modern apartment at the heart of the tech district. The space was understated but beautiful: soft couches, a large table, and vast windows overlooking the glittering city below. Yet the air was heavy with tension as they settled into their first private team meeting amidst the beauty surrounding them.

Zara took a steadying breath, the weight of the day's revelations pressing on her shoulders. "Alright, everyone," she said, her voice calm but edged with fatigue, "let's talk. What are your thoughts? What concerns you most?"

"I can't shake the feeling that we're being watched more closely than we even realize," Maya began, her brow furrowed. "Those surveillance systems are everywhere. It feels like every step we take is being recorded. It gives me chills."

Sofia nodded, her fingers drumming against the table as her mind raced. "And the military presence it's not just for show. They're preparing for something. The atmosphere is tense. If anyone but Elder Aurelia approached those guards right now, I doubt it would end well. It's unnerving."

Ghost leaned back in his chair, arms folded, eyes narrowed. "We have to be careful about our positioning. These opportunities aren't all roses. Every privilege here comes at a price. Push too hard, ask for too much, and we'll find ourselves in real trouble."

Leo finally spoke, his tone softer but edged with worry. "I've been talking to residents. Many are disenchanted with the council's rulings. There's mistrust between the wealthy and those barely scraping by. People whisper about punishments for breaking harvesting rules. It's like loyalty and faith are as tightly monitored as resources."

His words settled over them like a heavy curtain. An ocean of silence filled the room speaking louder than any voice. Divided loyalties, they realized, might be the unspoken currency of this place. The very fabric of Money Tree City was woven far deeper than they could yet grasp.

A knock at the door cut through the silence. Zara rose to open it and found Marcus standing there, his warm smile a contrast to the tension inside.

"Hey," he said smoothly, his voice easy. "I hope I'm not interrupting."

"Not at all," Zara replied, steadying herself. "We were just having a team meeting. Care to join us?"

Marcus stepped inside, his presence shifting the room. He moved with effortless confidence, his eyes holding hers for a heartbeat longer than necessary. Zara felt the dynamic tilt Marcus's interest in her was becoming harder to ignore, and the timing couldn't have been more complicated.

"We're discussing what we've seen of the council," she said, guiding the conversation back to task. "There's a lot to navigate."

Marcus nodded solemnly. "I understand. Money Tree City shines with affluence, but there's always an undertow. Things here can become more complicated than they look. You think the cameras and the military are overwhelming? You're not alone."

As the meeting wore on, Marcus added his own observations rich with insight into the way the council operated. "This council is divided, to say the least," he said. "Some members stand firmly beside Elder Aurelia, while others hold very different viewpoints. And then, of course, there's the unpleasant fact of military involvement in nearly every council decision."

Sofia leaned forward, her curiosity sparked. "What do you mean, 'divided'? Is there a faction working against the Elder?"

Marcus chose his words carefully. "Let's just say there are those who believe the wealth of the city should be more widely shared not concentrated among a select few. They quietly win the confidence of the people, gathering support in shadows. It's a tightrope, and the wrong step could light the fuse."

Ghost's face hardened. "That means we have to be very careful who we align ourselves with. In a power struggle like this, it's too easy to get caught in the crossfire."

Zara felt the weight of Marcus's presence his insight illuminating but unsettling. It bound them together with shared understanding, yet made everything more precarious. "We need to keep our focus," she said firmly, though unease flickered in her eyes. "It's not just about the rules we see on the surface it's the hidden currents of power beneath them. One wrong move, and we'll be swept away by forces we don't fully understand."

The discussion shifted to strategy. Each of them considered their new assignments archives, technology, security, and community outreach as potential channels for information. "We need a careful plan," Ghost muttered. "We have to move around this city without anyone realizing how much we're learning."

Marcus leaned in, his voice lowering conspiratorially. "If you're serious about understanding the dynamics here, I can help. I have connections among the residents who see things differently from the council. They can give you perspective."

Maya raised a cautious eyebrow. "What kind of connections? Are these factions or people outright opposed to the council?"

Marcus lifted his hands in a gesture of defense. "Not necessarily. I'm just saying, I can help you see the lay of the land. Who to trust, who not to. But you must tread carefully there are eyes everywhere."

Zara's pulse quickened. The offer was tempting, but dangerous. "We can't afford to get dragged into conflicts we don't fully understand," she said firmly. "It's delicate. We need to be cautious."

As the night dragged on, she became increasingly aware of Marcus's darting glances, each lingering moment charged with something unspoken. His interest unsettled her as much as it intrigued her, for his knowledge was invaluable, but his presence carried shadows of danger she couldn't ignore.

At last, the meeting wound down. As the team rose, Marcus lingered by Zara's side. His voice was low, carrying a quiet intensity. "I know this is a lot to take in. But I believe in what you're trying to accomplish. If you need me, I'll be around."

A flutter of uncertainty stirred in Zara's chest, though she masked it with composure. "Thank you, Marcus. Your insights mean a great deal. Just be careful. This city is more dangerous than it looks."

When he left, the room seemed to exhale, and the team turned on Zara with a mix of curiosity and concern.

"Anyone else feel that?" Maya asked softly. "There's something happening between you and Marcus it's hard to ignore."

"I did," Ghost admitted, discomfort in his voice. "We need to keep our guard up. Divided loyalties could complicate everything."

Leo, ever the peacemaker, lifted his hands slightly. "Let's stay focused. Personal dynamics can't distract us. Our mission is too important. We have to learn the rules of this society and navigate them carefully."

Zara swallowed hard, feeling the scrutiny but nodding. "You're right. Our priority must be to understand where the balances of power truly lie and how to move within them."

As night fell, unease churned in her gut: anxiety, determination, and something deeper she dared not name. The line between the personal and the political was blurring fast, and the stakes had grown sharper than ever.

In the days to come, they would need one another more than ever. Money Tree City was fraught with tension that mirrored their own, and survival would mean stepping gingerly, eyes open, through a labyrinth of beauty and shadow. Familiarity with the rules was only the first step. The real test would be surviving the divisions running beneath the golden veneer.

Burdened with the weight of their mission and the unshakable knowledge that their every move was being measured, the team steeled themselves. The journey had only begun but already the cost was rising higher than any of them had ever faced before.

## Chapter 9: Rules and Regulations

Early morning sunlight streamed through the high set windows of the central education hall, scattering in golden patterns across the varnished floor. Zara and her team sat in a semicircle, their faces a mix of curiosity and apprehension. This was the beginning of their formal training their first lesson in the laws and governance of Money Tree City.

The air buzzed with anticipation as the room filled with council members and citizens those who enforced the city's intricate regulations surrounding portals, resource flow, and the transport of wealth. Zara felt the heavy weight of expectation settle upon her shoulders. They were no longer observers. They were ambassadors of their own world, and the eyes of this civilization were upon them.

At the front of the hall, Talia the same council member who had guided them through the administrative district stood with a grave expression. The low murmur of conversation fell away as she began to speak.

"Welcome to today's lesson in formal education," she said, her voice clear and commanding. "In Money Tree City, harmony is sustained by law. Every rule exists to preserve balance. Today, we will explore the regulations governing the transportation of wealth and the severe consequences of violating those sacred rules."

Zara glanced at her team. This wasn't a lesson it was a warning.

Talia continued, stepping forward. "Let me be clear: the transportation of wealth in Money Tree City does not refer to the movement of physical goods. It is about the flow of energy and vitality our city's lifeblood into the trees. Every resource must be accounted for, logged, and tracked. To neglect this duty is to threaten the foundation of our community."

Maya leaned forward, her curiosity piqued. "What happens if someone doesn't follow the rules?"

Talia's gaze darkened. "The consequences," she said, pausing for effect, "are severe. Rule breakers face public reprimand, the loss of their resources, or " she hesitated, her voice dropping into a lower register, "in the gravest cases, exile."

A hush fell over the room. Zara felt a chill creep down her spine.

Talia gestured toward a low platform at the back of the hall. Her expression was unreadable. "Now," she said, "to demonstrate what it means to breach our wealth transport laws, we will conduct a live example."

Zara stiffened. "A demonstration?" she whispered to Ghost. He gave a terse nod, eyes narrowing.

The doors opened, and a disheveled man was led to the platform by two guards. His shoulders were hunched, his eyes wide and darting with fear. Talia's voice rang through the hall, cold and precise. "This man attempted to smuggle resources through a portal without authorization. Today, he will face public reprimand a reminder of what happens when trust is broken."

The air grew thick, pulsing with silent dread. Zara's heartbeat quickened as she watched the man take his place. Talia recited the charges, her tone clinical and detached. The man's trembling form seemed to shrink under the collective gaze of the audience.

No silence had ever felt so heavy. To Zara, this wasn't simply a warning it was a performance of power.

The punishment was swift: public shaming. The man stood before the assembly while his offense was read aloud, every word etching itself into the uneasy air. Zara's pity warred with unease. This was a human being, not merely an example. Yet here, he was both a symbol of control disguised as justice.

When it ended, a murmur rippled through the hall a low, restless tide of whispered voices. Talia raised her hand for silence.

"This," she said sharply, "is why we must adhere to the rules. Our city thrives on mutual trust, and even the smallest breach weakens the foundation of that trust. One fracture can bring down the whole."

Her gaze swept the crowd before she continued. "Our monitoring system ensures transparency and accountability. Every transaction, every movement of resources, is recorded and analyzed. This is not mere precaution it is survival. Each citizen's duty is to preserve that integrity."

Sofia tilted her head, intrigued. "How does the system track everything? Is it automated?"

Talia's expression softened slightly. "It is both technology and tradition," she explained. "Sensors embedded in the portals log every transfer. Council members review the data, while the trees themselves provide feedback. When energy flows irregularly, the trees alert us. It is a delicate balance but it works."

As the presentation continued, the team took careful notes. With every word, the truth became clearer: these laws were not just bureaucratic measures. They were the very heartbeat of the city the mechanism through which power, control, and survival intertwined.

And as Zara glanced around the hall, she couldn't shake the feeling that the lesson had been meant for them most of all.

The team gathered in the quiet of their quarters, the events of the day weighing heavily on them.

"That was brutal," Maya said, breaking the silence. Her voice trembled slightly. "That wasn't just a punishment it was a warning. They wanted us to see what happens if we step out of line."

Ghost leaned back in his chair, his expression grim. "It's not just about the rules," he said. "It's about control. Did you notice the council members during the demonstration? Some looked disturbed but others seemed almost… satisfied."

Zara nodded slowly, her mind still racing. "It's clear those rules aren't just guidelines. They're tools of control. We need to be careful very careful about how we navigate this system."

Sofia frowned, her tone measured. "You can tell how the council views rebellion. Even curiosity is dangerous here. We'll have to be cautious in everything we do."

Ghost leaned forward, his voice low but firm. "I noticed something else during the demonstration the council's division. Some of them were clearly uncomfortable, but others were… detached. Maybe even approving. There are fractures within their ranks. We need to be mindful of that."

A knot twisted in Zara's stomach. "We need to understand what these laws really mean. They aren't just for order they define how the entire city functions. If we're going to make a difference, we need to know the rules inside out."

The team spoke long into the night, carefully strategizing their next steps. They knew that mastering both the written and unwritten rules of Money Tree City would be essential to surviving here.

The next day began with their first hands on session training in harvesting, the foundation of Money Tree City's prosperity.

They stood beneath the sprawling canopy of trees near the central district, where golden fruit glimmered like lanterns. The air was warm and heavy with the scent of blossoms. An elderly instructor approached, her hands calloused, her voice steady yet kind.

"Harvesting isn't just about taking," she said, her tone imbued with quiet reverence. "It's a dialogue with the trees. Each cut, each touch, must be done with respect. If you take too much, or harm the tree, it will stop giving. And remember every harvest is logged and reviewed. There is no room for greed here."

Zara watched the sunlight filter through the leaves, casting dappled light across the group. Something inside her stirred a deep respect for this system that seemed to blend economy and spirituality into one. "It's not just an economy," she murmured softly. "It's a way of life."

The instructor smiled faintly, overhearing her. "Exactly," she said. "Harvesting is about care, not collection. Learn to listen to the land it will tell you what it needs."

When practice began, Zara found herself in rhythm with the trees. It wasn't mere labor; it was communion a pulse shared between herself and the city.

Sofia, ever the technologist, caught on quickly. "These devices are remarkable!" she said, studying the hovering tools that pruned and measured simultaneously. "If we could adapt this kind of sustainable system back home, it would change everything."

Ghost, too, moved with ease. His precision and discipline translated naturally to the delicate balance required. For once, his guarded expression softened, his actions guided more by instinct than protocol.

As the training sessions progressed, Zara noticed a subtle change in Leo. At first, he was captivated by the elegance of the city's economic system the way every resource was counted and valued. But soon, that curiosity deepened into something else, something sharper.

His eyes gleamed whenever instructors explained the valuation metrics or showed them the tracking screens. "Do you see how efficient this is?" he whispered to Sofia during one session, his voice alight with excitement. "If we could implement something like this back home, we could control everything resources, trade, even governance."

Zara overheard him, a frown tugging at her brow. "Leo," she said gently but firmly, "this isn't about control. We're here to understand, not to exploit."

Leo gave a small shrug, his gaze still fixed on the glowing data screens. "Why not both?"

Her unease deepened. Something in his tone almost reverent unsettled her. "Leo, we're here to learn," she insisted quietly. "Not to let greed drive us."

He waved her off, still lost in the calculations flickering across the monitors. "All I'm saying is if we understood their wealth systems, we could adapt them. Imagine what we could build."

Their second session delved deeper into how wealth was quantified and monitored. The team was escorted to a vast facility an intricate hub of energy and data where every movement of value was logged.

Banks of holographic screens covered the walls, streaming live figures that danced and shifted like liquid light. "All transactions are quantified and recorded," explained their instructor. "This ensures transparency and enforces integrity across the community."

Sofia's eyes widened with awe. "This is genius," she breathed. "The precision, the interconnectedness it's beyond anything I've seen. If we could replicate this kind of efficiency..." She trailed off, her voice filled with wonder.

Zara turned to her, uneasy. The thrill in Sofia's voice mirrored the glint of obsession she'd seen earlier in Leo's eyes. The allure of this system its promise of perfection was beginning to pull at them all.

"Remember why we're here," Zara said quietly, her gaze steady. "We came to learn, not to take. There's power in understanding, yes but even more in restraint."

No one answered immediately. Around them, the screens flickered, their numbers shifting like tides. The hum of the city's heartbeat surrounded them beautiful, relentless, and alive.

And as Zara watched her team, she couldn't shake the thought that Money Tree City was already working its subtle magic on them all.

Leo straightened, his expression hardening. "I know why we're here, Zara," he said, his voice edged with frustration. "But can we really just dismiss the possibility of using what we've learned? This is a learning curve, yes but what's the harm in taking it back with us? Why not?"

A knot pulled tight in Zara's stomach. She saw it clearly now the glint of ambition in Leo's eyes, the dangerous curiosity spreading through the team like wildfire. They were diverging, drawn down paths that shimmered with promise but led into peril. The pursuit of wealth and power could cost them everything their mission, their unity, perhaps even their humanity.

By the time the day ended, tension lingered like static in the air.

That evening, they gathered in their quarters to debrief. As each shared their observations, the undercurrent of unease became impossible to ignore. Every voice carried the same conflict curiosity against conscience, discovery against danger.

Maya spoke first, her tone thoughtful but strained. "Today opened my eyes," she admitted. "I see the potential for cooperation here, but these rules they're not guidelines. They're leashes. Tools for control."

Sofia nodded, the fire that had once driven her dimmed by the day's events. "We have to remember our purpose," she said softly. "If we lose sight of that, we stop being learners and become part of the problem."

Zara listened, her heart heavy. The temptation surrounding them was immense, but she sensed that their strength would have to come from unity from holding one another accountable when the lure of power grew too strong.

When the discussion ended, she looked around at her team faces resolute, eyes shadowed with doubt and made herself a silent promise: she would keep them grounded, whatever the cost.

As they settled for the night, hope and apprehension tangled in her chest. They were standing on the threshold of something immense, their choices soon to decide not only their fate but the fate of Money Tree City itself.

The following days passed in a blur of study, observation, and cautious experimentation. Each new session revealed more about the city's systems its beauty, its brilliance, and its suffocating rigidity.

The more they learned, the clearer it became: behind the golden order of Money Tree City lay a web of loopholes tiny cracks in perfection, waiting for anyone daring enough to exploit them.

Evenings found the team back in their quarters, the air thick with whispered theories and the hum of digital interfaces.

"The system has blind surveillance spots," Sofia said one night, her voice trembling between excitement and caution. She projected a holographic map across the table. "Here see? The lesser districts have unmonitored zones during specific hourly rotations. Especially near the portal access points."

Her eyes gleamed with equal parts fear and exhilaration. "If we moved carefully, we could pass through those blind spots. It's risky, but it's possible. We'd just have to time it perfectly."

Ghost's fingers swept over his own display, overlaying the guard rotations. "I've been tracking patrol shifts," he added. "They change every two hours. There's a ten minute lull between transitions a perfect window. If we move then, no one will notice."

Maya's brow furrowed as she listened, unease deepening. "This feels dangerous," she said quietly. "We're already being watched. If we're caught..." She trailed off, the memory of the punishment demonstration flashing vividly in her mind. "I don't want to end up like that man."

Marcus, silent until now, exhaled heavily. His expression was torn, eyes shadowed with conflict. "I understand the temptation," he said at last. "But if we start bending the rules if we exploit their system what does that make us? We came here to learn, not to manipulate."

A heavy silence followed. The question hung in the air like the weight of judgment itself.

Zara felt the pressure of every eye, the burden of every choice pressing down on her. They were walking a knife's edge ambition on one side, morality on the other and the drop beneath them grew deeper with each passing day.

Yet the thrill of discovery was intoxicating. The city's systems were complex, elegant almost inviting. Each revelation pulled them deeper, and soon, curiosity blurred into compulsion.

Then, one night, it happened.

Leo, restless and exhilarated by their findings, decided to act. "Just a small test," he insisted, eyes gleaming. "There's a grove that hasn't been logged into the system yet. We take a few samples nothing major. We'll be in and out before anyone notices."

Zara's pulse spiked. "Leo, no. We've talked about this. It's too risky if we're caught "

He cut her off, brushing aside her concern. "What's the worst that could happen? It's a few trees, that's all. We'll test Sofia's analysis, Ghost's timing. It's the perfect opportunity."

Her protest faltered. The conviction in his voice was infectious, and the others were watching her waiting for her to decide. Finally, with a reluctant nod, she whispered, "Fine. But we do this carefully. One mistake, and it's over."

The plan unfolded under the copper light of dusk. Ghost led the way through narrow alleys, his movements fluid and deliberate. Sofia monitored the feeds from her handheld device, heart hammering as she watched the surveillance grid flicker across her screen.

They slipped through the unmonitored zones silent, efficient, invisible. Every heartbeat, every breath, measured against the ticking rhythm of the city's security system.

And as Zara followed close behind, the gleam of the Money Trees ahead reflecting in her eyes, a single thought echoed in her mind  They had crossed a line.

There would be no going back.

All were exhilarated as they approached the grove. The trees stood tall and proud, their colorful fruits glistening in the sun. Leo's eyes shone with excitement as he hurried forward. "This will prove we can work around the system!" he exclaimed triumphantly.

But before anyone could respond, a sharp alarm split the air an ear splitting shriek that echoed through the grove. The sound reverberated off the metallic bark, a chilling reminder of just how alive the city's surveillance truly was.

Sofia's face drained of color. She glanced at her device, her voice trembling. "The monitoring system reacted! We've triggered something!"

Panic surged through the team. They scrambled to gather the few samples they had taken, but the blaring alarm shattered any sense of order. From the distance came the unmistakable rhythm of boots pounding the ground the guards were closing in fast.

"Move! We need to get out of here!" Maya shouted, her voice cutting through the chaos.

They ran, hearts pounding, their footsteps echoing through the gleaming pathways of the grove. Zara's chest burned as adrenaline flooded her veins. The realization hit her hard they had crossed a line, and now the city's watchful eyes were upon them.

They didn't stop until they were a safe distance away. The group collapsed against a cluster of trees, panting and wide eyed.

"What just happened?" Ghost gasped between breaths. "I thought we had it all worked out!"

"Clearly we didn't account for the system's response," Sofia said, shaking her head. "It's more advanced than we realized. It reacted in real time. We need to analyze what went wrong."

Zara's voice trembled with a mixture of anger and fear. "This was reckless! We shouldn't have done it, Leo. Do you realize what could've happened if we were caught? The consequences could've been catastrophic not just for us, but for everything we've been working toward."

Leo raised his hands defensively. "We learned something, didn't we? Now we know how the system reacts. We can plan better next time."

"Next time?" Maya's tone was sharp, incredulous. "Leo, this isn't a game! Those laws aren't arbitrary they're tied to the survival of this entire community. We can't afford to toy with them."

The adrenaline faded, leaving a heavy stillness in its wake. The thrill of defiance gave way to a gnawing sense of dread. They had gambled and survived for now but the cost of their choices loomed darkly over them.

Leo, still high on adrenaline, shrugged off the tension. "We'll be fine," he said with forced confidence. "We got away, didn't we? We just need to be smarter next time."

"This isn't about getting caught," Maya replied, her voice tight with worry. "If the council investigates this incident, they'll find us. They don't take rule violations lightly we could face serious punishment."

Marcus, who had been silent until now, finally spoke. His expression was strained, caught between loyalty and unease. "I get the appeal of testing the limits," he said quietly, "but we need to ask ourselves what that makes us. We came here to learn and understand, not manipulate."

A heavy silence settled over them. The weight of Marcus's words pressed on everyone like gravity itself.

Zara exhaled, trying to steady herself. "We have to stay united," she said, her voice calm but resolute. "If we're going to survive here if we're going to do what we came for we need to depend on each other. We can't let greed or ambition break us apart."

Ghost's brow furrowed as he considered her words. "But what if understanding the system means using it? We've seen how it works and where it's weak. Isn't that knowledge valuable?"

Zara clenched her jaw, frustration flickering in her eyes. "There's a difference between understanding and exploiting. We have to find balance learn from this world without corrupting what makes it work."

The air in the room grew thick with tension, each member lost in their own battle between curiosity and conscience.

"I just wanted to prove we could do something," Leo said, defensive but subdued now. "I thought we were here to make an impact."

"And without getting ourselves killed," Maya replied firmly. "If we want to be part of this world, we need to earn its trust, not betray it."

Zara looked around at them all exhausted, divided, but still together. She drew a deep breath, steadying her resolve. "We'll regroup," she said finally. "We've made mistakes, but we can learn from them. From now on, we find ways to function within the system, not against it."

A pensive silence fell over the group. One by one, their expressions softened not in defeat, but in acceptance. The path ahead would be hard, but they understood what had to be done.

As their discussion turned from blame to purpose, a fragile sense of unity began to return. They spoke in quiet voices, charting a new course one guided by patience, not impulse.

By the time night deepened, the air between them had shifted. The earlier rift had not vanished, but it had been tempered by understanding. They would face whatever came next as a team, grounded by a shared resolve to respect the city they had so nearly provoked.

The road ahead was uncertain, the challenges immense but in that moment, they found renewed strength. For all its dangers, Money Tree City still shimmered with possibility and as long as they remained true to one another, there was hope they could master both its beauty and its peril.

The moon hung high above, casting its silvery sheen upon Money Tree City. Inside their quarters, tension coiled thick as wire. Zara and her crew had gathered for a late night strategy meeting one that could change everything. The events of the past few days weighed heavily on them, and a quiet urgency filled the air. Tonight, decisions had to be made.

Sofia was the first to break the silence. Her tone was steady, though the gleam in her eyes betrayed her excitement. "Alright," she said, spreading out her notes. "Loopholes and security protocols analyzed. Now we start planning the operation FX, the heist. If we time it right, we could secure enough resources to actually make a difference."

Zara's gaze swept across the room, gauging each reaction. Leo's eyes blazed with ambition. Ghost leaned forward, analytical and calculating. Only Maya looked uneasy, her brow furrowed.

"I don't know if we should call it a heist," Maya said, frowning. "We're supposed to gain their trust, not their suspicion. This sounds like theft, not diplomacy."

Marcus nodded slowly. "Maya's right," he said, his voice calm but firm. "If we do this, we need to remember our mission. It's not about resources it's about who we are. What we stand for."

Leo leaned back in his chair, arms crossed, a faint smirk tugging at his lips. "Come on. We're not stealing from anyone. We're redistributing. The elites have more wealth than they can even account for. They won't miss what we take. It's a victimless act."

Sofia frowned, tapping her pen against the table. "If we're caught, that won't be how they see it," she warned. "You've seen how fast the council acts on rule breakers. We need a plan that minimizes risk and keeps us out of sight."

Ghost's voice cut in, low and deliberate. "I agree. We need to treat this like a tactical mission. There are blind spots in their patrol patterns, shift rotations we can use. We hit during the transition window, minimize exposure, and stay unseen."

Zara felt the tension rising like a tide. "So what are we saying?" she asked quietly. "We obey the letter of the rules while bending their spirit just far enough to help ourselves? Because I'm not entirely comfortable with that."

Leo's expression hardened. "What's your alternative, Zara? We just sit here while the elite hoard everything? We have the chance to act to make a difference and you want to play it safe?"

Maya's voice rose, sharp and desperate. "It's not about playing safe it's about staying true! We represent our home. If we cross that line, we lose our credibility, our integrity everything."

Voices overlapped, growing louder. The argument spiraled, each voice pressing against the others ambition clashing with caution, principle against impulse. Zara's heart pounded as she tried to rein them in.

"Enough!" she snapped. "Everyone, stop. We all want to make a difference but not at the cost of who we are. If we can't do this without betraying our purpose, then we've already failed."

Leo shook his head, frustration flashing in his eyes. "You're all being naive," he said bitterly. "This is reality. Change doesn't happen by waiting it happens by taking risks. If we let this chance slip away, it might be our last."

As he spoke, Zara felt something break a hairline fracture in the unity that had once held them together. The rift was growing, and she could almost hear it, like a crack spreading through glass. Marcus watched quietly, his expression thoughtful and heavy.

Finally, Sofia raised her hands. "Everyone, breathe," she said, trying to steady the room. "We're not getting anywhere like this. Let's each share our approach, then decide together."

Zara nodded, grateful for the reprieve. "Alright. One at a time. Let's hear it."

Leo spoke first, his tone loud and confident. "We go in fast and hard. One strike, grab what we can, and vanish before anyone even realizes we were there. Hesitation will only get us caught."

Maya followed, her voice quieter but resolute. "We start small," she countered. "Gather information first. Maybe negotiate. We can work with the community instead of taking from them. We don't have to break trust to get what we need."

Ghost leaned forward, offering a middle ground. "Recon first. Find the weakest points. We can collect minimal resources and test the system's response. Low risk, high information yield."

Zara listened to each in turn, weighing their words. The tension in the room thickened until it felt almost physical, a pulse of conflicting ideals that refused to sync. Beneath it, she sensed something deeper an invisible shift in loyalties, quiet seeds of betrayal being sown in silence.

Marcus broke it at last, his voice calm and steady as stone. "We need to remember who we are," he said. "We didn't come here for a single victory. We came to build something lasting a future. If we manipulate their system for our gain, we become exactly what we came to challenge."

His words fell like a stone into still water, sending ripples through the room. Silence followed uneasy, fragile, heavy.

Zara clung to that silence, hoping it might hold them together a little longer. But when she met Leo's eyes, the hope faltered. His face was clouded, frustration simmering just below the surface.

"So what then?" he demanded. "We do nothing? Sit here and watch the elites drain this city dry while we pretend we're above it all? You preach restraint, Marcus, but restraint doesn't change anything. This" he pointed to the holographic plans glowing between them "this is our chance."

His words hung there, sharp and dangerous, as the moonlight pooled across the table casting each of their faces in stark relief.
Zara saw it clearly now: the first real fracture in their unity, and the storm waiting beyond it.

The argument ignited again, fiercer than before. Voices rose and clashed, the air thick with anger and frustration. Zara could feel the tension spiral out of control, emotion coiling around them like a living thing. The cracks in their unity were widening hairline fractures that, left untended, would soon split them apart. Beneath it all, she could sense it: the quiet sprouting of betrayal.

"Enough!" Zara's voice cut through the noise like a blade. "That's enough! We can't afford this division. We are stronger together, and unless we find a way to unite, everything we've built will fall apart!"

Her words hung in the air, heavy and unmoving. Silence rippled through the room, broken only by the sound of their uneven breathing. Each of them knew she was right, but the damage had been done the argument had left its mark, and the air still trembled with unspoken resentment.

They stood at a crossroads. The decisions made this night would not only shape the mission ahead but decide the fate of the fragile bonds between them.

Maya was the first to speak, her voice soft yet steady, cutting gently through the lingering tension.

"Zara's right," she said. "We have to find a way forward even if we don't all agree on how. Let's step back for a while. Clear our heads. When we meet again, we'll bring our proposals but with respect. We can't let our differences blind us to what's important."

Leo crossed his arms, his face tight with stubborn resolve. "Fine," he muttered, his tone edged with defiance. "But I'm not backing down. We need to act, not just talk."

The tension lingered, taut and unresolved, as the meeting drew to a reluctant close. One by one, they filed out, each carrying the weight of uncertainty like a shadow.

Zara stayed behind, sitting alone beneath the mellow glow of the city's lights filtering through the window. The night hummed softly outside, but within her chest, unease pulsed like a drumbeat. Their unity once their greatest strength was unraveling thread by thread. The path ahead had never looked so uncertain.

Later, lying awake in the darkness, the weight of their mission pressed down on her mind. Images flashed behind her closed eyes: Leo's defiance, Maya's worry, Ghost's guarded silence, Marcus's quiet disappointment. And beneath it all, the echo of her own fear the sense that something within their group had shifted irrevocably.

A seed of betrayal had been planted, and no matter how she tried to banish the thought, it lingered cold and insistent. Their path to success was twisting into peril, their loyalties fraying under the pull of ambition and distrust.

In that sleepless silence, Zara made a vow. Whatever came, she would hold them together. She would not let greed or division destroy what they had fought so hard to build.

But as she finally drifted into uneasy sleep, one thought refused to leave her.

Would they triumph over their differences or would the shadows of betrayal consume them all?

Only time would tell.

## Chapter 10: Hidden Agendas

Zara nodded, her gaze skimming the plaza's intricate carvings as if searching for answers in the stone. "Yes. It's beautiful." She let her fingertips trail along a mural that told the city's history in layered relief. "But it's a reminder of how fragile civilizations are. One crack in the foundation and everything can fall."

Marcus tilted his head, reading the elders' faces frozen in the mural. "And yet this city stands. Maybe they learned to patch the cracks early before they could spread."

Zara smiled, small and private. She didn't answer; her thoughts had already wandered back to the fissures in their own group.

They threaded deeper into the heart of the city where human noise rose vendors calling, musicians tuning, children shrieking with play. Night softened the edges of the buildings; lantern light made the market stalls glow. Marcus stopped at a fountain and watched the water ripple, his reflection breaking into fractured fragments. "What makes a civilization thrive?" he asked, dipping a hand into the cool stream. "Is it technology, stability, or something less tangible?"

Zara watched the children dart and laugh. "All of it," she said at last. "But mostly it's values the habits of people. Trust, cooperation, a respect for the living things that sustain you. Those are the things that last."

Marcus's question hung in the air. "And what of those values when they are betrayed? Can a civilization survive when its own foundations have been sold out?"

The question struck her like cold. "I've seen it happen. Societies choosing power over people. It starts slowly and then there's never any turning back."

A flicker of something vulnerable crossed Marcus's face. "My past isn't clean," he confessed quietly. "I was part of systems that put growth ahead of decency. I saw people used as tools."

Zara's chest tightened with empathy. "You don't have to tell me more than you want. But if you do if you want to talk I'm here."

He looked away, voice thin. "There are choices I regret. I've watched ambition swallow people whole."

They held each other's gaze, the moment warming into something close to confession. A thread of attraction hummed between them tentative, complicated until a burst of children's laughter ruptured the intimacy and pulled them back into the street. "We should rejoin the others," Zara said, breath steadying. "There's still much to discuss."

A quiet hope unfurled in her chest: maybe, even with their fractures, they could build something better.

Later, the team split to follow their threads through the city. Zara and Marcus drifted through the market's close lanes while Sofia and Ghost slipped toward the tech hub, moving through clean architecture pulsing with holographic light.

"I want to see what's under all this polish," Sofia said as they reached the tech district. Her fingers hovered over the bright panels. "A city that perfect must be hiding something."

Ghost scanned the rooftops and the patrolling guards. "Be careful. If they catch you digging, it won't be a polite conversation."

Sofia's grin was all teeth and focus. "I'm already in the main node. If I can get deeper, I can see their military manifests."

They moved inside a building rimmed with the city emblem; screens streamed market analytics, resource flows, and hidden beneath the public dashboards layers of classified entries. Sofia froze. "Look at this," she breathed, pointing. "They're not just a trading civ. They've been developing weaponry and portal logistics."

Maya's voice crackled over their comms. "Weapons? This place is built on trade, not war."

Sofia kept typing, urgency sharpening her voice. "That's what we believed. But these logs show portal capable logistics, armaments, stockpiles. If that's true if they're preparing this isn't just a city problem."

Ghost's jaw clenched. "If they're prepping for conflict, everyone's at risk. Not just here."

Sofia's expression hardened. "We need to know who and why. Are they building defenses against something or weapons to project force?"

The unease in Zara's gut tightened into a knot. "We must be careful," she said when they rejoined. "If we pry too aggressively, we draw attention. Lives are at stake."

Sofia hesitated only a beat before diving back into her data streams, fingers skating across glass. The room's tension rose with each blocked access and bubbling notification. Outside, Money Tree City hummed its gilded arteries still beautiful, still dangerous.

Zara paced the market district, her communicator buzzing intermittently with updates from the team. Every step felt like a balancing act a tightrope walk over invisible peril, with no safety net below. The weight of their choices pressed hard against her ribs.

"Sofia, don't push too hard," she said into her comm, her voice edged with worry. "We can't afford attention. Not now."

"Got it!" came Sofia's quick reply. Static crackled in the line, followed by a low whistle. "I'm in. Let's see what secrets this city's been hiding."

Back at the quarters, the team gathered around Sofia's workstation. The screen bathed their faces in cold light, its shifting data painting the room in uneasy hues.

Zara leaned in, breath catching as file after file scrolled across the display. "What is this?" she murmured. "Advanced weaponry... portal based strategy models. This isn't defense it's preparation for something bigger."

"Here," Sofia said, pointing at a cluster of entries labeled *Military Operations*. "Training exercises, weapons systems, logistics... this is full scale mobilization."

Marcus's eyes widened as he scrolled further. "They're not defending themselves they're positioning for expansion. Why would a city built on trade need an army this powerful?"

Maya frowned, the crease between her brows deepening. "If they perceive us as a threat, we could become targets. You saw how fast they act when someone breaks the rules."

Ghost crossed his arms, gaze cold and analytical. "If we're going to survive here, we need to understand the flow of power. Knowledge is our only real weapon."

The air thickened around them as they delved deeper. Each new revelation felt heavier than the last evidence of a system thriving not through peace, but through quiet conquest.

"Wait," Maya said suddenly, pointing to another file buried in the archives. "Here *Historical Records*. Let's see how deep this goes."

Sofia opened it, and silence fell like a curtain.

Across the screen, images and text flickered battle maps, accounts of invasions, annexed territories marked with precise coordinates. Zara's stomach twisted. "This city didn't just survive war," she whispered. "It *prospered* through it. They built their empire by taking what they needed."

Marcus exhaled slowly. "If they've done it before, they'll do it again. Maybe they already are."

Zara nodded grimly. "Then we have to tread carefully. If the council thinks we're spies or interlopers, they'll erase us before we can even explain."

The group exchanged tense glances, absorbing the magnitude of what they'd uncovered. The line between observer and participant was gone they were entangled now, part of something vast and dangerous.

Leo, who had been silent until then, shifted against the wall. "Maybe we need allies," he said quietly. "People who know what's really happening here. There are factions in this city we've seen signs. If we can make contact, we might gain some leverage."

"Contacts?" Maya echoed, suspicion in her voice. "That's a huge risk. We can't know who to trust."

"Sometimes risk is the only way forward," Leo countered, tone sharp. "Information doesn't come from the surface. We need to deal with those who operate beneath it."

Zara narrowed her eyes. "What kind of factions are you talking about?"

Leo's smirk was faint but unmistakable. "Let's just say I've been paying attention. There are people who don't agree with the council's control. They could be useful."

"Leo," Marcus cut in, his tone clipped, "this isn't a game. We're not here to manipulate anyone. The moment we start using people, we become no better than the system we're criticizing."

The tension surged again, invisible sparks leaping between them.

"I'm just trying to keep us alive," Leo shot back. "If that means making a few connections, so be it. You can stay idealistic I'll handle reality."

Maya stepped forward, her calm voice slicing through the argument. "Stop. This is exactly what will destroy us secrets and divided loyalties. We need to be unified or we're done."

Zara drew a slow breath, forcing steadiness into her voice. "Enough. We've learned more today than we were ready for. Let's take a break think about what this means. When we regroup, no hidden motives, no side deals. We face this together."

Reluctantly, they dispersed. The room felt heavier as they left, the hum of the console lingering like an unspoken warning.

Zara stepped out into the street. The sun had dipped low, casting long shadows through the golden towers of Money Tree City. Warm light kissed her skin, but the shadows told another story one of power, secrecy, and silent unrest.

They had uncovered dangerous truths. Yet, as Zara looked toward the glowing horizon, she knew the greater danger lay not in the city's secrets, but in the fractures forming within their own ranks.

Hidden agendas moved like ghosts among them, and one haunting question refused to leave her mind:

Could they stay united long enough to face what was coming?

As the days unfolded in Money Tree City, the team scattered in purpose but not in proximity. Each member pursued their own goals with fierce determination, the air around them thrumming with ambition. Yet beneath that ambition ran an unspoken current of secrecy thin, sharp, and ever tightening. The bonds that had once united them now strained under the weight of hidden motives and half truths.

Marcus found himself gravitating toward Zara more often. Their conversations had become a quiet refuge from the chaos, a space where words flowed freely and laughter softened the growing distance between them. But with every shared glance, Marcus sensed the precariousness of it all the way affection and danger so often intertwined.

Meanwhile, Sofia buried herself in her research. Her mind burned with the possibilities offered by the city's advanced systems, each discovery more astonishing than the last. "Look at this," she exclaimed one afternoon, summoning everyone to her workstation. Her eyes gleamed with feverish excitement. "I've gained access to their central database and their technology is far beyond anything we've ever encountered. They're developing weapons systems that could rival our own!"

Zara leaned closer, her brow furrowing. "Weapons? But why? This city seems so… peaceful."

Sofia nodded, her enthusiasm dimming. "That's exactly what I'm trying to understand. If they're preparing for something, it means they're anticipating a threat or creating one."

While Sofia chased patterns in the city's code, Ghost focused on what he did best: contingency. His digital map was an intricate lattice of escape routes and blind zones, each one a potential lifeline. "If things go south, we'll need these," he explained, tracing glowing lines across the screen. "There are gaps in surveillance near the outskirts narrow windows, but they're there."

"Good work, Ghost," Marcus said, his tone steady but grave. "The more we learn, the clearer it becomes we can't assume we're safe."

Maya, meanwhile, spent her hours in the archives, her hands ink stained from the ancient texts she studied. "These scrolls speak of past wars," she told them one night, her voice hushed. "Entire civilizations destroyed when greed outweighed wisdom. I can't shake the feeling history's repeating itself here."

Each of them was consumed by purpose, but their growing silence spoke louder than words. Zara sensed it first the glances exchanged when they thought she wasn't looking, the sudden pauses when she entered a room. The mission was splintering into secrets.

One evening, as twilight bled across the city, Zara and Marcus walked along the edge of the central park. The distant hum of the portal towers filled the air, a mechanical heartbeat beneath the soft rustle of leaves.

"Do you think we can stop this?" Marcus asked quietly.

Zara hesitated, her gaze on the skyline's shimmering gold. "I don't know," she admitted. "But we have to try. If we don't, no one will."

He studied her face, and she, in turn, searched his. Something heavy passed between them an unspoken truth.

"You've been spending a lot of time with Sofia," Zara said lightly, though her tone betrayed a flicker of curiosity.

Marcus's expression shifted. "We're just working on the tech findings. There's a lot to analyze, especially the military data."

"Right." Zara's lips pressed into a thin line. "I just want to make sure we're aligned. We can't afford division, not now."

"I know," he said softly. "But trust goes both ways, Zara. We have to hold that line even when it feels impossible."

They walked in silence after that, the city glowing around them, its lights reflecting off the water. Their connection felt stronger, yet shadowed by something darker. Every secret they unearthed seemed to birth new ones, each more dangerous than the last.

In the days that followed, the discoveries grew even more disturbing. Sofia unearthed not only weapons data but entire networks traces of contact with off world entities. "There are records here," she whispered one morning, "showing interactions with Earth. This isn't new. They've been preparing for something for years."

Ghost's eyes narrowed. "If they were expecting an invasion, why build an army and then wait? There's no imminent threat here unless they plan to *make* one."

Maya looked up from her translations, realization dawning. "What if it's expansion, not defense? If they control the portals, they can reach anywhere other dimensions, other civilizations."

The room went still. The hum of Sofia's console was the only sound.

Zara's voice broke the silence. "They've turned their city into a weapon," she said, her words trembling. "And we're standing in the middle of it."

Sofia's screen glowed with intricate diagrams the interlinked portals forming a vast web across the city. "If they can move resources or troops through these gateways, they can strike anywhere. No borders, no warning."

Marcus exhaled sharply. "That's not defense. That's dominance. They're not protecting themselves they're planning to expand their reach."

"Then we need to learn everything we can about this technology," he added. "If we understand how it works, maybe we can stop it."

But understanding came with a cost. The deeper they dug, the more mistrust took root. Leo had grown secretive, disappearing for hours at a time and taking hushed calls when he thought no one noticed.

Zara confronted him one night. "Leo, what's going on? You've been distant, and you keep vanishing without explanation."

He didn't meet her eyes. "I'm just keeping up with our contacts," he said briskly. "Don't worry about it."

"Contacts?" she pressed, her unease growing. "Who exactly are you talking to?"

"People who know more than we do," he snapped, irritation flashing across his face. "If we want to survive this, we can't just sit around analyzing data. We need allies."

Zara felt a chill run through her. His tone was confident too confident. "Leo," she said quietly, "just be careful who you call an ally. In this city, the wrong trust could destroy us."

But Leo only smiled faintly and turned away.

For the first time since their arrival, Zara realized that danger wasn't just closing in from the outside it was growing from within. The true threat wasn't the city's hidden armies or its portals of power. It was the fractures forming between them the quiet betrayals already taking shape in the shadows of their hearts.

"Are you sure those contacts are trustworthy?" Zara pressed, her voice low and deliberate. "We need to be cautious about who we align ourselves with."

Leo's expression hardened. "I can handle it, Zara. You don't need to worry about me. Just focus on your own tasks."

The confrontation left her deeply unsettled. One by one, her teammates withdrew into silence, their unity unraveling thread by thread. The air between them thickened, heavy with tension and the unspoken fear that something within their fragile alliance was breaking apart.

That night, as the team gathered for their debrief, the unease reached a breaking point.

Sofia had uncovered more disturbing data about the city's military capabilities, and Ghost had finalized his network of escape routes. "We need to prepare for the worst," he said, his voice calm but weighted. "If they're planning something, we can't be caught off guard."

Maya's tone was grave as she laid out her findings. "The historical records I've translated warn of civilizations that ignored the signs those who overreached and were destroyed. We can't underestimate what we're facing."

Marcus leaned forward, frustration flashing in his eyes. "But we can't panic, either. We need to act strategically, not reactively. Understanding what we're up against is the only way to survive this."

Zara looked around the table, her pulse quickening as the air seemed to hum with tension. "We're all on edge," she said, her voice steady but urgent. "But we can't let fear divide us. We have to communicate openly, share what we know no more secrets."

Leo scoffed, crossing his arms. "And what, you want everyone to lay their cards on the table? That's how you get people killed. Some things are better kept quiet."

The room erupted accusations, counterarguments, raised voices all colliding at once. Suspicion and frustration boiled over until every word felt like a weapon.

Zara's heart hammered. "Enough!" she shouted, her voice slicing through the chaos. "This infighting is exactly what they want. We're handing them our downfall. If we don't stand together, we're already lost!"

Her words struck the room into silence. For a moment, the only sound was the low hum of the city beyond their walls.

Marcus met her gaze, and something in his expression softened an understanding, a promise. But even as that brief flicker of connection passed between them, the storm clouds of mistrust lingered overhead, gathering strength.

They all knew it: the danger wasn't only outside. It was within them now.

Each member retreated into uneasy silence, wrestling with private fears and ambitions that no longer aligned. The path ahead was perilous, and the cost of failure had never loomed so high.

Zara realized with a pang that the greatest battle they faced wasn't against the forces of Money Tree City it was against the slow, corrosive pull of suspicion eating away at their unity.

## Marcus and Zara's Connection

As the sun set, casting long, honeyed light across the city, the air inside their quarters grew heavier with every passing day. The team had become a collection of solitary ambitions five people chasing separate purposes under the guise of one mission.

Marcus, though, found himself drawn more and more to Zara. In her strength and quiet certainty, he found something rare: clarity amidst the chaos. Their early morning walks had become small sanctuaries from the suffocating tension of their lives.

One morning, as they wandered through a park bathed in golden light, Marcus spoke softly. "Do you ever wonder what it really means to belong?"

Zara paused beneath the shifting canopy of leaves. "Belonging," she said, "is about connection finding those who share your values and see the world as you do. But in a place like this, it's hard to tell who anyone really is anymore."

He nodded, a shadow crossing his face. "I've spent most of my life chasing ambition. It cost me more than I'd like to admit. But being here, with you… it feels different. Like it actually matters."

Zara's heartbeat quickened. "I feel it too. This place this mission it's changed us. But I can't shake the feeling there are things we're not saying to each other. Secrets we're not sharing."

Their eyes met, and for a moment, time seemed to still. The air between them was charged an unspoken understanding, fragile and dangerous. Before either could say another word, a distant shout broke through the quiet, pulling them back to the present.

The moment was gone, but its echo lingered.

**Sofia's Discoveries**

Back at their quarters, Sofia was deep in her work. Her fingers moved across the keyboard with focused intensity, the glow of the monitor illuminating her face in pale blue light. "I've got something," she announced suddenly, her voice laced with both triumph and fear.

The team crowded around.

"What did you find?" Zara asked, stepping closer.

Sofia's expression flickered between awe and dread. "The technology here it's extraordinary, but terrifying. I've uncovered plans for advanced military systems drones, weapons, even something tied to portal manipulation."

Ghost leaned forward, his interest sharpening. "Portal technology? What kind of application?"

"They've built a network capable of transporting resources and potentially troops across different dimensions," Sofia explained quietly. "If they ever choose to launch an offensive, they could strike anywhere, instantly. No warnings, no defenses."

Maya looked up from her ancient texts, her brow knitted. "If that's true, it changes everything. We have to understand this system its purpose, its limits before it's too late."

Zara felt a cold tremor run through her. The team was unraveling, the city's secrets growing darker by the day, and the shadow of war seemed to stretch longer with every discovery.

She knew, with sinking certainty, that the real test had only just begun.

**Ghost's Escape Routes**

Meanwhile, Ghost had been meticulously charting potential escape routes throughout Money Tree City.

"If things go south, we need to know how to get out quickly," he said, projecting a digital map across the screen. "I've found several paths that are less monitored particularly near the outskirts. These can serve as fallback routes if necessary."

Zara studied the glowing map, feeling the weight of their situation settle heavily on her shoulders.

"This is good work, Ghost," she said. "But we also need to think about how to use this against them. If they're planning something, we can't just react we have to be proactive."

As the team sank deeper into their individual work, the air thickened with unspoken fears. Though each member was absorbed in their tasks, a quiet paranoia pulsed beneath the surface, subtle yet inescapable. Zara felt it creeping closer a shadow hovering at the edge of her awareness, waiting for the perfect moment to consume them all.

**Maya's Translations**

Maya, buried in her translations, began uncovering increasingly ominous passages.

"These texts talk about civilizations that ignored ancient warnings," she said, her voice heavy with unease. "It seems those who disregarded the elders faced dire consequences. We can't afford to make the same mistake."

Sofia's excitement faded as she absorbed the meaning behind Maya's words.

"We have to take this seriously," she murmured. "If this city's past is filled with conflict and invasion, it might mean they're preparing for something similar again."

"Or anticipating retaliation," Marcus added, his brow furrowed. "Either way, we need to understand the full scope of what we're dealing with."

As the evening wore on, silence replaced conversation. Each of them was trapped within their thoughts, wrestling with fears they dared not voice. Zara could feel the secrets weighing on them all. The more truth they uncovered, the more fragmented they became.

## Leo's Secretive Contacts

Amid the growing unease, Leo became increasingly guarded. Zara noticed his frequent disappearances and the hushed calls that always ended with a cautious glance over his shoulder.

One evening, she finally confronted him. "Why are you always disappearing?" she demanded, her voice taut. "What aren't you telling us?"

"I'm just keeping tabs on our contacts," Leo replied, dismissive but defensive. "This isn't a game, Zara. We need allies if we're going to survive what's coming."

Frustration flared in her chest. "We can't afford to put our trust in people we don't know," she shot back. "You need to share what you're doing with the rest of us. We're supposed to be a team."

Leo's expression hardened. "You don't understand. Sometimes, to survive, you have to make deals in the shadows. I can handle it."

He turned and walked away, leaving Zara staring after him. A knot of dread tightened in her stomach. The secrets were multiplying, and the distance between them was becoming irreparable. Trust, once their greatest strength, was slipping through her fingers like sand.

## Revelation of Invasion Plans

The next day, the team gathered once more to piece together their discoveries. Sofia stood before them, her face pale but composed.

"We need to talk about the military capabilities we've uncovered," she began. "They're not just building weapons they're preparing for an invasion."

Maya's eyes widened. "If they already have a plan, we need to counter it. We can't just sit and wait."

Marcus nodded grimly. "Agreed. We need to understand their timeline and their intent. If we can gather enough intel, we might stop their plans before they move."

Zara felt her pulse quicken as the implications set in. "But how? We can't exactly waltz into their operations and expect to make it out alive."

Ghost leaned forward, tapping a sequence on his device. "We use the portal network. If we can breach their systems, we might find a way to disrupt their plans from the inside."

"Disrupting them could expose us," Maya warned. "If they catch wind of this, it's over."

The discussion spiraled into uneasy murmurs. Each person wrestled with their own doubts, their ambitions clashing silently beneath the surface. Paranoia hung in the air like a thick fog every breath heavy with tension.

## The Breaking Point

The inevitable fracture came when suspicion finally broke the surface.

"I can't shake the feeling that not everyone here is being honest," Zara said, her voice calm but firm. "We need to come clean about what we're hiding. Secrets will destroy us faster than any invasion."

Leo's eyes narrowed. "And what about you, Zara? You've been getting close to Marcus. What exactly are you after?"

The accusation cut deep, sharp as a blade. Zara felt her cheeks burn, but she refused to falter. "This isn't about personal feelings, Leo," she said evenly. "It's about trust and without it, we're doomed."

Sofia stepped in before the argument could erupt. "Enough," she snapped. "We're all under pressure, but turning on each other isn't going to solve anything. The real threat is out there, not in here."

Ghost nodded, his tone calm but edged with urgency. "Let's take a breath. We're still a team. We can't afford to forget that."

But it was too late. The words that had been spoken couldn't be taken back. The cracks had widened into chasms, and distrust now coursed through every interaction. The group that had once been united by purpose was now divided by fear.

**The Aftermath**

When the meeting ended, silence lingered in their quarters like smoke after a fire. Each member drifted away, lost in their private thoughts. The team that once felt like a family was now nothing more than scattered fragments of ambition and suspicion.

Zara sat alone in her room, staring out at the city's gleaming skyline. For all its beauty, it pulsed with quiet menace a reflection of the turmoil inside her own team.

The threat of invasion loomed large, but it was the fractures within that terrified her most. If they couldn't trust one another, how could they hope to confront what was coming?

As the night deepened, she made a silent promise to herself. She would not let them fall apart not without a fight. Tomorrow, she would reach out to Marcus. They needed to rebuild the trust that was slipping away before it was lost entirely.

In the heart of Money Tree City, beneath the shimmer of golden light, the storm was gathering. Secrets were unraveling, alliances crumbling, and Zara knew that the days ahead would test not only their mission but the very core of who they were.

Only by confronting the darkness within could they hope to stand against the darkness ahead.

## Chapter 11: The Test

Morning finally arrived in Money Tree City. The first rays of sunlight slipped between the towering skyscrapers, stretching long shadows across the polished streets. Inside the team's quarters, anticipation mixed uneasily with anxiety the air almost electric. Today marked their **first authorized harvest**, a critical step to gather resources and test the intricate systems sustaining the city.

Zara stood at the center of the room, her pulse racing as she surveyed her teammates. Before she could speak, the sharp chime of Sofia's device broke the stillness.

"Hold on," Sofia muttered, her eyes narrowing as lines of data streamed across her screen. "The city's monitoring systems are flagging unusual activity near the harvesting site."

"Unusual?" Marcus stepped closer. "Could it affect the operation?"

"I can't be sure," Sofia replied, tension threading her voice. "It could be system maintenance or maybe a change in patrol routes. Either way, we shouldn't assume everything will go as planned."

Zara's stomach tightened, but her tone stayed steady. "Then we adapt. If there's even a hint of trouble, we abort. No risks. Understood?"

Sofia nodded but then froze mid motion, her brow furrowing deeply. "Wait," she said, fingers flying over the controls. "This doesn't make sense. There's a **new monitoring node** near the site it wasn't there yesterday."

Ghost straightened from where he leaned against the wall. "What kind of node? Surveillance?"

"Possibly," Sofia said tightly. "Either way, it's not on the standard grid. They're updating their systems faster than I anticipated."

Marcus groaned, rubbing his temples. "This isn't just a test anymore it's a trap waiting to spring."

Zara stepped forward, her voice firm. "Then we move carefully. Sofia, monitor the node's activity. If it shifts, we abort. Everyone else stick to your roles."

Ghost nodded. "We've mapped our escape routes, but we'll need to move fast. If anything goes wrong, there's no time for hesitation."

Maya, who had been unusually quiet, finally spoke, her voice low but steady. "I've been reading more about past harvest attempts," she said, her eyes flicking between them. "One team failed not because of the system but because they turned on each other. Greed tore them apart."

Ghost frowned. "You think that's going to happen to us?"

"I think we need to be careful," Maya replied. "These treasures they're meant to tempt us. To distract us. If we lose sight of our mission, we'll fail before we even begin."

Zara nodded, her jaw tight. "She's right. This isn't just a harvest it's a **test of our resolve**."

Marcus added quietly, his voice like steel. "Maya's right. We're here to gather information and resources for our mission, not to fall to temptation. We can't afford distractions."

The air thickened with unspoken tension as they reviewed their assignments.

"Ghost, you're on extraction monitoring," Marcus said briskly. "Sofia, handle the tech. Maya, oversee collection. I'll coordinate movement."

Zara's gaze swept across the room. "And I'll make sure we stay on task. But one thing needs to be clear if anything feels off, we pull out. I don't care how much we've gathered."

"Understood," Ghost said, though his eyes lingered on the gear, fingers twitching slightly. Zara noticed and the unease in her chest deepened.

"Any last minute changes?" Marcus asked, scanning the room.

Zara exhaled slowly. "Just remember communication. If something feels wrong, speak up. We stay in sync, or we don't move at all."

With one final nod, they gathered their gear and set off.

The path wound through narrow trails, dense with vegetation that pressed close on all sides. Strange, luminous leaves brushed their shoulders as they moved. The hum of energy grew stronger with each step, vibrating through the ground like a pulse.

"Do you feel that?" Zara whispered.

Marcus nodded, scanning the trees. "It's the energy field. The closer we get, the stronger it gets."

Ghost glanced back over his shoulder. "Let's just hope it doesn't get any stronger. I'm not a fan of surprises."

When they finally broke through the foliage, the sight that met them stole their breath.

The **harvesting site** spread out before them like a vision fields of golden flora swaying in the morning light. The plants shimmered as if made of liquid metal, their leaves rippling with faint luminescence. Strange fruits hung low, each one pulsing gently as though alive.

"This is it," Marcus whispered.

Zara's gaze darted to the edge of the clearing. A faint glint caught her eye metal, half hidden in the brush. Her stomach twisted. "Someone's watching," she murmured under her breath.

But there was no turning back now. The air thrummed with expectation as the team prepared their equipment.

"All right," Zara said, forcing calm into her tone. "Sofia, start the extraction."

Sofia powered up her device, the screen flaring to life. Her fingers moved quickly, hacking into the city's systems with practiced precision. A low vibration rolled through the earth, and the plants responded, glowing brighter as if awakening.

"We're live," she said, unable to hide the tremor of exhilaration in her voice. "Extraction has begun."

The ground shimmered. Light pulsed from beneath the roots, coalescing into streams of glittering energy that twisted upward like threads of gold. Slowly, the true wealth of Money Tree City emerged **coins**, **gemstones**, and delicate **artifacts** that reflected sunlight in prismatic flashes.

The team stood transfixed.

"Marvelous!" Ghost breathed, eyes wide with awe. "Just look at it imagine what we could do with all this!"

As the treasures continued to surface, Zara's unease grew heavier. The dazzling beauty of it all felt wrong too easy, too alluring.

Her gaze shifted to Maya, who stood motionless beside a mound of radiant trinkets. Her fingers hovered above them, trembling slightly.

And in that fragile, shimmering silence, Zara understood exactly what Maya had meant.

The harvest wasn't merely a test of skill or courage. It was a **test of integrity** and the true danger wasn't in what the city hid… but in what it revealed within them.

"Stay focused," Zara snapped, her voice cutting through the rising tension like a blade. "This isn't about the treasures. We're here for the mission information, resources, and nothing more."

But even as she spoke, she caught Ghost out of the corner of her eye, his fingers brushing against a glittering gemstone. The shimmering light reflected in his eyes, and she saw it the creeping allure beginning to take hold.

And just like that, the delicate balance started to slip.

As the two women pressed deeper into the extraction, the first signs of corruption began to reveal themselves. Greed crept in like a silent current. Ghost's gaze fixed on an ornate jewel an intricate stone that pulsed faintly in the sunlight. He lifted it to his face, marveling.

"Just think of what we could do with this!" he breathed, his voice filled with awe.

Maya's expression darkened, the furrow in her brow deepening. "We have to be careful. It's through temptation like this that civilizations fall. We can't lose ourselves we're here for a purpose."

Marcus stepped in, his tone firm, commanding. "Everyone, remember why we're doing this. Greed can break even the strongest team. We cannot let it divide us."

Despite his words, Zara could see it in their faces the struggle. The wealth glittering at their feet was intoxicating, and the promise of power shimmered like a dangerous dream.

As the extraction continued, excitement curdled into unease. The hum of the energy field seemed to deepen, vibrating through the soil, through their bones. Then Zara's instincts flared. Her peripheral vision caught a flicker of motion at the treeline.

She turned sharply.

A group of city officials was approaching, their silver robes gleaming beneath the filtered sunlight. Their faces were masks of authority emotionless, unreadable.

"We've got to move now!" Zara barked, adrenaline flooding her veins.

"Everybody, grab what you can!" Marcus shouted, urgency lacing his tone.

The team sprang into motion, scrambling to gather their yield. The sound of their rushed movements filled the clearing, mingling with the low hum of the harvest systems.

"Ghost, what's the status on our exit routes?" Zara called, her voice tight with fear.

"They're still clear for now!" he yelled back. But his voice faltered. Zara saw his gaze flick from the data display to the glittering artifact still in his hand. His breathing quickened, torn between reason and desire.

"Just one more," he whispered, almost pleading, reaching toward a golden trinket glowing faintly in the sunlight.

"Ghost, leave it!" Zara shouted. "We don't have time for this!"

His hand hovered, trembling, caught between impulse and command. The footsteps behind them grew louder an unrelenting chorus closing in.

"Just one more!" he cried, fingers stretching toward the artifact.

"No!" Maya's voice cracked with panic. "We can't risk it let's go!"

Zara's heart pounded. With one last glance at the treasures glinting on the ground, she forced herself to turn away. "Move out! Now!"

The team bolted for the tree line, adrenaline coursing through their veins. The forest swallowed them whole branches slapping against their arms as they raced through the dense foliage. Every heartbeat was a drum of survival.

Behind them, the rhythmic footsteps of the officials echoed closer.

Zara ran faster, lungs burning, every sense screaming. They had succeeded in the harvest but the price of their greed had already begun to show.

They burst through the trees into open light. Before them stretched the sprawling city alive, radiant, and pulsing with energy. But behind, the figures of the officials closed in, their intentions veiled in silence.

Zara knew then: this was no longer a test of skill. It was a trial of **unity**, and the first cracks were already spreading.

A heavy stillness blanketed their quarters that evening. The air felt thick, suffocating, the echoes of the chaotic harvest still ringing in their minds. Each of them sat in silence, haunted by the choices they'd made and the consequences they couldn't yet see.

They had tasted fortune's sweetness, but the shadow of greed now loomed over them dark, inevitable, unforgiving.

Ghost fidgeted at the table, unable to meet Zara's eyes. His movements were restless, his guilt palpable.

"We need to regroup," Zara said firmly, her tone steady despite the turmoil within her. "We can't let what happened define us. We have to learn from it."

Before anyone could respond, a sharp, blaring alarm shattered the silence. Red warning lights flared across the ceiling, bathing the room in crimson.

"What the hell is happening?" Sofia shouted, fingers flying over her device.

A cold, mechanical voice echoed through the intercom: **"Unauthorized collection detected. Lockdown procedures initiated. All team members are to vacate immediately."**

Marcus slammed his palm against the table. "Unauthorized collection?! That's impossible we followed the protocols!"

And then Zara understood. Her stomach dropped like stone. "Ghost," she whispered. "You took more than we were cleared for."

Ghost's face went pale. He opened his mouth, but no words came.

"We have to find him," Zara ordered, already moving for the door. "If the system's flagged him, the city won't show mercy."

They sprinted down the corridor, alarms shrieking in their ears, the walls pulsing with red light.

Zara's mind raced. She could see it clearly now the officials, the punishment, the reckoning that awaited anyone who dared defy the city's rules.

"We can't let him face this alone!" she shouted over the din.

They reached the access door to the harvesting sector, the metallic hum of lockdown gates reverberating through the air. Time was running out.

Zara's pulse thundered as her hand hovered over the control panel. One thought consumed her they had crossed a line, and now the city was closing in.

They burst through the door to find Ghost crouched amid a chaotic sprawl of treasures, his hands reaching greedily for shimmering artifacts that hummed with living energy.

"Ghost, stop!" Marcus shouted, his voice straining over the blaring alarms.

"I'm not stopping now!" Ghost's voice was wild, frenzied, his eyes wide with delirium. "Look at all of this! We could change everything with it!"

"Don't you see?" Maya cried, desperation breaking through the noise. "This isn't about us anymore! The city is responding we have to get out!"

The ground trembled beneath them, a low rumble booming through the harvest field. The portal shimmered violently, its edges flickering like an unstable flame. Zara felt a chill run through her spine.

"We need to go now!" she yelled, her voice nearly lost in the chaos.

But Ghost stood frozen, entranced by the dazzling wealth surrounding him. His hands shook, torn between awe and obsession.

"Just one more!" he shouted, stretching toward a jewel that glowed like a captured star.

"No!" Zara screamed, lunging forward. Her fingers brushed his arm then came the blinding flash.

The portal erupted. The air crackled, the world itself seeming to twist as a surge of dark energy broke free. Tendrils of light and shadow coiled outward like living chains.

"Ghost!" Marcus shouted, surging forward, but it was too late. The portal's energy lashed out, ensnaring Ghost in its radiant grasp.

His scream tore through the air, raw and human, before the energy yanked him into the churning void. His form vanished in an instant swallowed whole by the storm of light.

And then, silence.

The alarms wailed, yet the team stood paralyzed shock etched into their faces.

"We have to get out of here!" Sofia cried, trembling as the ground quaked again.

The earth split and folded, the energy field collapsing inward. The team turned and ran, lungs burning, the taste of fear thick in the air. Zara's mind reeled as they stumbled through the exit tunnel every step haunted by Ghost's last scream.

They burst out into the open, collapsing onto the safe pathways outside the harvest zone. The alarms faded behind them, replaced by the sound of their ragged breathing.

"We lost him," Maya whispered, tears streaking her cheeks. "It's my fault I should have stopped him."

Zara shook her head, swallowing hard. "No. We all knew the risks. He made his choice. We have to focus on surviving now."

Even as she spoke, she could feel the unity between them fraying like torn thread. The silence that followed was heavy, their shared guilt a weight none of them could bear to name.

Days passed, each one heavier than the last. The city's vigilance tightened around them like a noose. Officials now shadowed their every move; their freedom what little of it remained was gone.

Zara fought to restore some semblance of order, but the ghost of their failure lingered everywhere. Ghost's loss hung over them not just as tragedy, but as judgment.

Sofia withdrew into herself, her usual spark dimmed. "I should have seen it coming," she whispered one night, staring blankly at her screen. "I should have known what he would do."

Maya, however, hardened. Her grief transformed into cold resolve. "We can't afford to dwell on what happened," she said firmly. "We need to understand the rules of this city and use them. We must learn from his mistakes."

Her tone was iron. It silenced the room.

Marcus, though, couldn't contain his turmoil. "We were supposed to be a team," he snapped, frustration breaking through his composure. "We were supposed to have each other's backs and we lost him! Because of one reckless moment!"

The silence that followed was suffocating. Every breath was laced with unspoken blame.

Zara could see it clearly now: the fractures spreading among them like cracks through glass. What once felt like family had withered into suspicion, grief, and shame.

One evening, as they gathered in the dim light of their quarters, the tension finally boiled over.

"We can't live in fear," Maya said, her voice rising. "We need to take control. We can't let Ghost's mistake define us."

"But we can't ignore the rules," Zara countered, her heartbeat quickening. "We've already lost one of our own. We can't afford to lose anyone else."

Arguments flared, voices overlapping in frustration and grief. Marcus slammed his fist against the table. Sofia looked away, trembling. The air crackled not with energy this time, but with barely restrained anger.

Zara forced herself to her feet. "Enough!" she shouted. "We need to remember why we're here. We are in this together and we can't let fear destroy us!"

Her voice echoed through the room, but even as she said it, she knew the truth clawing at the back of her mind.

The team had crossed a line one they could never return from. And though they were still together, Zara could feel it deep down…

The real war had only just begun.

The city would not forgive them.

And neither, perhaps, would they forgive themselves.

Standing amid the aftermath of their failure, Zara knew they had reached a point where decisions could no longer be delayed. The coming days would determine their survival and perhaps the very destiny of the team itself. Money Tree

City had flexed its strength before them, and now they stood to face the consequences. The lessons carved into their hearts would remain like scars.

The fluorescent lights above flickered, casting uneven shadows that seemed to mirror the turmoil inside them. For the first time since the catastrophe, the team had gathered behind closed doors, the silence between them heavy and taut. Fear clung to the air like static.

Zara stood at the head of the table, her heart fluttering as she faced the weary, hollow eyes of her team. Ghost's absence loomed over them like a specter dark, accusing, and inescapable.

"Thank you all for being here," she began, her voice steady but strained. "We need to reconsider our mission goals. After what's happened, we can't just go on as if nothing has changed."

From the far end of the table, Marcus leaned forward, his brow furrowed. "We've got to redefine what we're trying to achieve. The original plan was about gathering resources and intelligence. Now we have to consider the risks. Ghost's actions put everyone in danger."

Maya crossed her arms, her tone unyielding. "We can't live in fear of them. We still have a mission and we owe it to Ghost to see it through."

"At what cost?" Sofia's voice broke, trembling with emotion. "We've already lost one of us. What good is continuing if we refuse to learn from that?"

A suffocating silence fell over the room. Every breath felt heavy. The team's unity had thinned to a fragile thread, stretched nearly to breaking. The weight of guilt and grief sat with them like an unwanted guest, unrelenting and real.

At last, Marcus spoke again, his tone firmer this time. "We need new protocols. We can't operate under the same assumptions we did before. If we're going to continue, we have to be sharper smarter."

Zara nodded slowly, her thoughts already racing. "Then we go back to basics. Focus on intelligence on understanding the systems of this city. We'll analyze the repercussions of every move before we make it. No more unauthorized actions."

The discussion pressed on, but with each word, Zara felt herself sinking deeper into the dark gravity of their situation. Their path forward was uncertain, the waters treacherous. Internal tensions threatened to pull them apart even as they tried to chart a way through.

Then, Marcus's voice broke through the din quiet, deliberate. "Zara, may I speak with you in private?"

She hesitated, then nodded. They stepped aside into a dim corner of the room, where the hum of the lights seemed to fade. The weight of unspoken words hung between them.

"What's on your mind?" she asked softly.

Marcus exhaled, his eyes searching hers. "I'm worried about the team. Losing Ghost shook us all. I can feel the fractures forming, and I don't know how to hold us together."

Zara felt the sharp pang of empathy. "I know. We're all feeling it. But we have to turn that pain into something productive. If we let it divide us, everything we've done will have been for nothing."

He nodded slowly, though doubt flickered behind his eyes. "Then maybe we dig deeper. We need to understand this city what holds it together, and where it's vulnerable. If we can uncover what lies behind that portal, maybe even harness that energy, we might find an advantage."

Zara's heart quickened. "You're suggesting we investigate it directly?"

"The risks are enormous," he admitted. "But if we don't understand what we're up against, we'll always be one step behind. We need to know what we're fighting and we do this together. No secrets. No lone heroics."

For a fleeting moment, something sparked in Zara's chest a fragile flicker of hope amidst the chaos. "Then we do this together," she said firmly. "But we need everyone on board. Total transparency. Total trust."

"Agreed," Marcus replied, his jaw tightening with resolve. "We owe it to Ghost and to ourselves. Let's set up a framework for this investigation and bring the others in."

When they stepped back into the meeting room, Zara felt the faintest sense of renewal a spark beneath the ashes. The stakes had never been higher, but for the first time since the tragedy, there was direction.

Whatever awaited them in the shadows of Money Tree City, they would face it together.

The path ahead was lined with peril, yet they stepped toward it nonetheless one deliberate, defiant step at a time.

## Chapter 12: Unearthed Truths

Flickering fluorescent lights cast a ghostly pallor over the ancient archives, illuminating drifting motes of dust like suspended stars. Maya sat hunched over a weathered table, surrounded by towers of brittle documents and fragments of forgotten history. The air was thick with the scent of paper and time an atmosphere so heavy with age it seemed to breathe on its own.

It was late. The silence was suffocating, broken only by the soft rustle of parchment and the faint, rhythmic scratch of her pen. Her heart thudded in her chest, caught between the thrill of discovery and the chill of dread. The deeper she dug into the labyrinth of the past, the more she felt its weight pressing upon her soul.

With trembling fingers, she turned page after page, desperate to unveil the secrets that had haunted her since their arrival in the shadowed city of the Money Tree. Then, among the crumbling stacks, something caught her eye a smaller document bound by an almost fraying leather strap. Carefully, reverently, she unfastened it. The parchment unfurled with a whisper, its faint ink alive with complex, interlocking symbols.

Maya's pulse quickened. *This might be it the breakthrough.*

Hours bled away as she bent over the document, painstakingly translating each faded line. The message that emerged was chilling a history not of peace, but of recurrence. A civilization that rose and fell in a repeating cycle of greed, invasion, and consumption.

And then, with one passage, her breath stopped cold.

The portals were no mere gateways.

They were **weapons** instruments of conquest.

The text told of an ancient civilization that had crossed dimensions, systematically draining worlds including Earth of energy and life. Each invasion followed the same merciless pattern: a fleeting age of prosperity before the inevitable storm of exploitation and ruin.

Maya's hands trembled as the truth settled over her like a shroud. *They've done this before.* The Money Tree's beauty was built on ashes its wealth carved from worlds that had already fallen. And now, the cycle had returned.

Hours later, the team assembled in their quarters. Maya stood before them, clutching the weathered document as though it might vanish if she loosened her grip. Her voice wavered but did not break.

"I've found something," she said. "And it changes everything."

The room stilled. Zara leaned forward, her expression tightening. "What did you find?"

Maya laid the parchment on the table, its symbols flickering faintly in the light. "The portals they've been used to invade Earth. Over and over again. Every few decades they return, extract resources, devastate civilizations, and vanish only to start the cycle anew."

Sofia's face went pale. "You're saying this isn't just history… this is happening again?"

Maya nodded. "Yes. And if we don't act, we'll become the next victims of their design."

Her words fell like stones into deep water, sending ripples of dread through the group. Zara's jaw clenched, her eyes narrowing as she tried to process the enormity of it. Marcus's face darkened, his thoughts already racing ahead.

Within Maya's mind, the pattern became horrifyingly clear every recorded invasion aligned with turning points in Earth's own history: unexplained collapses, mass migrations, technological leaps born from desperation. The Money Tree's influence was there, woven into humanity's darkest hours.

She wanted to gather more proof before sounding the alarm further but every instinct screamed that the evidence was undeniable. The portals were not humanity's opportunity. They were its undoing.

Elsewhere in the quarters, Sofia worked furiously. Her fingers flew across the keyboard, the glow of her device illuminating the hard set of her jaw. Each keystroke was a battle; each bypassed firewall a small victory. Layers upon layers of encryption guarded the city's most guarded archives and she was tearing through them one by one.

The rest of the team crowded behind her, tense and silent. The hum of machinery filled the room, broken only by Sofia's muttered curses.

"Almost there," she breathed, eyes fixed on the screen. "Come on…"

A sharp *beep* echoed, and the display flared to life. **Access Granted.**

"Yes!" she exclaimed, adrenaline rushing through her veins. "We're in!"

The others leaned close as streams of data cascaded across the screen schematics, blueprints, and technical readouts written in a hybrid of alien and human notation. The designs were staggering.

"Look at this," Sofia whispered, pointing to a diagram. "These portals aren't just gateways. They're power conduits massive energy transfer systems. Capable of moving not just people, but entire reserves of matter across dimensions."

Maya's eyes widened. "That explains it. They're harvesting more than resources they're draining vitality itself."

As they scrolled further, a timeline appeared a sequence of dates that sent a chill through the room. Each one aligned with catastrophic events in Earth's history: mass blackouts, unexplained climate anomalies, collapses of empires.

"This is it," Maya murmured, her voice barely audible. "It's a pattern. Every few decades, they strike and every time, they leave behind devastation that rewrites history."

Marcus's fists tightened. "If they've done this before," he said slowly, "what's to stop them from doing it again? What if we're not here by chance at all?"

He looked around at his teammates, the realization dawning in his eyes.

"What if we're *part* of the setup?"

Ghost's fist slammed onto the table, the sharp crack echoing through the room like a gunshot. The team jolted to attention, their shared silence shattered.

"Then we stop them," he growled, fierce and unyielding. "We can't let Earth keep falling into this trap. If they see us as pawns, we'll make damn sure they're dead wrong."

"But how?" Sofia demanded, her hands gripping the back of a chair. "We're not soldiers, Ghost. We're barely holding ourselves together as it is. This isn't just about stopping them it's about surviving long enough to figure *how*."

Zara raised her hands, cutting through the tension with firm authority. "Enough. This revelation doesn't just change the stakes it raises them. If we're going to stand a chance, we need unity. No doubts. No distractions."

Sofia's face hardened. "Then we find their next move. This might be our only chance to anticipate them." She turned back to her screen, eyes darting as lines of data cascaded past. "Their archives have detailed reports after action records of every invasion they've ever carried out. Each one precise, deliberate… *methodical.*"

The silence that followed was suffocating. Maya's voice trembled as she broke it. "They've done this before," she whispered. "And if we don't move fast, it'll be us next."

Marcus leaned forward, his voice low but steady. "Then we don't wait. We use what we've learned *against* them. Find their weaknesses, disrupt their cycle, and end it once and for all."

Maya nodded, though unease clouded her features. "This knowledge comes with a price. If they realize how much we know… they'll come for us. And they won't stop."

Zara met her gaze, resolve hardening her tone. "Then we prepare. No more hesitation. We fight back together."

For a long, heavy moment, no one spoke. The air pressed in around them, thick with fear and defiance. Each team member was caught in their own tempest anger, guilt, hope. The room felt smaller, the stakes enormous.

Finally, Zara broke the silence. "This is bigger than any of us imagined. But paralysis is no longer an option. We're the only ones who know the truth and that makes us responsible for what happens next."

Marcus leaned back, frustration carved deep into his face. "Knowing isn't the same as winning. They've been doing this for centuries. What makes us think we're any different?"

"Because we *are* different," Sofia shot back. "We have their plans, their technology, their timelines. For the first time, we're ahead of them. That's our advantage."

Marcus's expression darkened, but he nodded. "Then we use it. If we don't, no one will."

Sofia's fingers flew over the keyboard once more, her focus razor sharp. "If we can find their next scheduled invasion," she muttered, "we'll know when they plan to strike."

The room dimmed as data flooded the holographic display, casting a pale glow across their faces. Code flickered, decrypted lines replacing encrypted ones then, at last, a pulsing alert.

"I've got something," Sofia whispered.

They crowded around the screen as a new file unfolded before them: a timeline. Rows of cryptic coordinates, energy surges, and planetary alignments all mapped to future dates.

"Here it is," Sofia breathed. "Their next invasion cycle."

Maya's heart hammered as she scanned the data. "It's close," she said, her voice tightening. "Too close. We need to warn the others we have to prepare before it starts."

Determined glances flashed between them. In that moment, something unspoken united the team: they were no longer explorers or researchers. They were a line of defense against an ancient, relentless enemy.

The shadows of Money Tree City loomed closer with every heartbeat. They had the knowledge but it had made them targets.

The air was thick with incense and authority. Marcus stood before the massive carved door that led to Elder Valeria's office, his pulse pounding in his ears. The ornate frame told stories of conquest and creation legends of power that no longer felt mythical, but menacingly real.

He took a breath and stepped inside.

Elder Valeria sat behind a grand marble desk, her presence commanding and still. The room was dim, its light filtered through patterned glass that painted strange symbols across the walls. Her eyes gleamed as she looked up at him.

"Marcus," she said smoothly, her tone equal parts warmth and warning. "To what do I owe the pleasure of your visit?"

He stood straighter, swallowing his hesitation. "I need to speak with you about the ancient texts Maya uncovered. They reveal more than we ever imagined details about the portals, the invasion cycles, and how they connect to us."

Valeria's expression didn't change, but the air seemed to grow heavier. "Ah, the archives," she murmured. "A treasure trove of knowledge… and of danger. You understand, of course, that knowledge cuts both ways."

"Precisely," Marcus replied. "That's why I'm here. These documents prove the truth this civilization has used the portals to exploit Earth, time and again. We're part of a cycle that's been repeating for centuries, and we need to understand how to break it."

Valeria leaned back, steepling her fingers. "And what would you have me do, Marcus?" she asked softly. "Declare war on our own systems? Risk the collapse of everything we've built? Perhaps we are pawns in a grander game one beyond your understanding."

Her words carried both irony and warning, but Marcus didn't waver. "No. I believe we can change the course this time. But we need your support. We need the Council's backing to act before the next invasion begins."

Valeria's lips curved in something that wasn't quite a smile. "You speak as though you truly believe you can outwit destiny."

"Maybe not destiny," Marcus said quietly, his gaze unflinching. "But I can damn well try to outwit those who abuse it."

For a long moment, neither moved. The shadows flickered across Valeria's face, unreadable as stone. Then she rose slowly from her chair.

"Be careful, Marcus," she said, her tone velvet and steel. "There are forces in this city older and more patient than you can imagine. They don't take kindly to interference."

He met her gaze without flinching. "Then they'll have to learn to."

"Aid," Valeria repeated, her lips curling into a knowing smile. "Support comes with trust, and trust is *earned*, not given freely. Tell me, Marcus do you believe you have the wisdom to navigate such waters?"

There was a veiled menace beneath her words, and Marcus felt his heart quicken. He knew he was treading dangerous ground, but retreat was no longer an option. "I'm not here to question your authority, Elder," he said evenly. "I'm here to protect my team and the integrity of our mission."

Valeria's eyes narrowed, her gaze slicing through him like a blade. "Integrity is a fragile concept," she said softly. "And knowledge, Marcus… knowledge is the heaviest burden of all. It can drive one to choices that alter the course of history forever."

Each word was a tightening coil of tension. Marcus could almost feel the storm gathering above his head. "If we do nothing," he replied, his tone firm, "then we're doomed to repeat the same cycle as those who came before. We owe it to our people to every world they've touched to fight back."

"Fight back?" Valeria's voice was a silken jeer, though her eyes burned cold. "Be very careful, Marcus. There are forces beyond your comprehension aligned against you. The city watches. And everything you do is weighed in the balance. You would be wise to tread lightly."

Her words slithered through the air like smoke, heavy with implication. The realization struck him like ice: Valeria was not just a guardian of knowledge she was a *player* in a far larger game. One that could swallow them whole.

"I'm not afraid of the truth, Elder," he said finally, forcing his voice steady. "Whatever it takes, we'll uncover it."

"Fear is a fine motivator," Valeria purred. "But true strength lies in knowing when to pause. Take care where your next step leads you."

With that, the conversation was over. She dismissed him with a flicker of her hand, but the warning lingered in the air like an echo of thunder. Marcus stepped out into the dim corridors, his pulse still pounding. Her words were knives dressed as silk and he felt every one of them pressing into his back as he walked away.

Night had fallen by the time Marcus called the emergency meeting. The team assembled in a secure, dimly lit room the flicker of a single overhead light casting uneasy shadows across their faces.

"Maya's discoveries are more critical than we thought," Marcus began, his tone measured but grave. "We're looking at a pattern spanning centuries. It's no longer speculation it's a cycle. And it's closing in on us."

Sofia leaned forward, brow furrowed. "What did Valeria say? Did you get anything useful out of her?"

Marcus exhaled sharply. "She spoke in riddles, as always. But she knows more than she's letting on. She as much as admitted we're dealing with something far bigger something she's either complicit in or terrified of."

Maya's eyes blazed. "We can't let her intimidate us. The documents I've uncovered are explicit. The invasions follow a fixed pattern harvest, drain, withdraw, repeat. If we don't act soon, it'll happen again."

Marcus nodded, his voice hardening. "Then we compile everything every shred of evidence we've found. This isn't just about us anymore. It's about stopping an empire that's been bleeding our world dry for generations."

The room came alive with motion. Charts, maps, and blueprints spread across the table like pieces of a fractured prophecy. The team huddled over them, each line and symbol weaving into a greater truth one more terrifying than they could have imagined.

"This isn't just about Earth," Maya whispered, her voice trembling. "It's about *control*. Every invasion, every resource, every person it's all part of a structure that sustains their dominance. We're just another cog in their machine."

Zara looked up, her eyes fierce. "Then we break the machine. Whatever it takes, we end the cycle here."

Marcus nodded, the steel returning to his tone. "We'll need a plan one that doesn't just react to their moves, but *anticipates* them. We can't afford another mistake."

For the first time in days, the room carried something other than fear. Determination raw, defiant, and electric took hold. They were no longer explorers trapped in the shadows of a strange city. They were soldiers in a quiet war, standing at the edge of history.

The next evening, gray clouds hung low over the skyline. The city's light dimmed to an eerie half glow, painting everything in shades of iron and ash.

From an inconspicuous vantage point overlooking the central training grounds, Marcus and his team watched in silence. Below, rows of soldiers moved in perfect synchrony, their dark armor blending with the deepening dusk. The air was thick with command shouts, the sharp *crack* of rifles, and the thunder of boots against the ground.

"What are they doing?" Sofia whispered. "This doesn't look like a standard drill."

Marcus's stomach twisted as he studied the scene. "It's not," he said. "They're preparing for something big."

Explosions boomed across the field controlled detonations that sent pillars of smoke curling into the night sky. The formations of troops moved with mechanical precision, enacting a scenario that sent a chill through every observer.

Maya's voice was a thin thread. "Those drills… they're simulating an invasion."

The others stared in grim silence as realization dawned. The city wasn't merely preparing for war it was *planning* one.

"They're getting ready," Marcus said darkly. "And we're already in their sights."

A long, tense silence stretched between them as the rhythmic march of soldiers echoed across the distance. Zara's expression hardened. "Then we move faster," she said. "We don't wait for them to make the first move."

Marcus nodded. "Agreed. We don't have time to sit back anymore. If this city wants war " he looked out over the sprawling field, smoke curling like ghosts against the horizon, " then we'll give them something they never expected."

The wind carried the acrid scent of gunpowder and ozone. The city's heartbeat had changed it pulsed now with the rhythm of coming conflict.

The storm was no longer on the horizon.

It was here.

"Are we ready for that?" Maya asked, her eyes wide with unease. "We don't even know how deep this goes much less *who's* involved."

"Trust is a luxury we can't afford," Marcus said, his voice cold and resolute. The steel in his tone cut through the air like a blade. "From this moment forward, we move under new security protocols no exceptions. We protect ourselves, our findings, and our mission by any means necessary."

Urgency rippled through the room. The team withdrew to their secure hideout a dim, reinforced chamber lined with humming servers and flickering monitors. The air buzzed with tension as they reviewed what they had seen: the military exercises, the drills, the unmistakable signs of a city preparing for war.

Marcus stood at the center of it all, pacing. "Effective immediately, we operate on a *need to know* basis," he declared. "No more open data sharing. No transmissions outside this network. No unverified contacts. If information leaks, even by accident, it could mean all our lives."

The team nodded, but unease flickered in their eyes. Every face in the room once a source of comfort now seemed shadowed by uncertainty.

"We'll set up watch rotations," Marcus continued, his voice measured but tight. "All communication channels are to be encrypted. Every piece of intel is logged and double verified. No one works alone."

His words carried the weight of leadership, but underneath the authority was exhaustion a man holding together a crumbling alliance through sheer will.

Around him, silence thickened. The hum of the machines was the only sound, a mechanical heartbeat in the dark. Each person's gaze seemed to linger just a second too long on the others. The unspoken question hung heavy in the air: *Who can we trust?*

As they dispersed to their stations, Zara caught Marcus's eye. For an instant, he thought he saw the same thought reflected in her a flicker of doubt, quickly hidden behind professionalism.

The camaraderie that had once bound them was unraveling thread by thread, replaced by an invisible tension that tightened with every passing hour. Paranoia seeped into every glance, every whisper.

Marcus stared down at the glowing maps and scattered notes before him, his reflection fractured in the screen's cold light. *We're not just fighting them anymore,* he thought. *We're fighting each other.*

The realization chilled him to the core. The greatest threat to their mission wasn't the city's soldiers or the Council's spies it was the slow, creeping erosion of trust from within.

And as Marcus finalized their security plan, one truth echoed louder than the alarms that had once haunted them: **the most dangerous enemy was already in the room.**

## Chapter 13: Shadows of Betrayal

The moon hung low, casting its silvery glow across the secluded alcove where Leo stood waiting. It was a place chosen with care hidden from prying eyes and veiled from curious ears. The air was thick with the scent of damp stone and the silent weight of decisions that could not be undone.

As he waited, Leo's thoughts drifted to his team their laughter, their struggles, the fragile trust they had built together. That trust now felt like a delicate thread fraying in his grasp. The promises whispered by Valeria's agents echoed through his mind enticing, perilous, and laced with deceit.

*Power. Security. Freedom from fear.*

He told himself it wasn't betrayal it was survival. But even as he rehearsed the words, guilt coiled like a serpent in his chest.

When the agents finally emerged from the shadows, their faces were obscured by hoods, their eyes glinting with the sharp intelligence of men accustomed to power.

"Leo," one of them greeted, his voice low and smooth. "We appreciate your discretion."

"Let's get to the point," Leo said. His tone was calm, but his pulse betrayed him. "I have information that could be valuable to both of us."

The taller agent tilted his head, intrigued. "We're listening."

"I can provide insight into my team's operations," Leo said carefully, each word measured. "In exchange, I want resources. Protection. A position within your ranks."

The agent's brow furrowed. "You want to betray your team?"

Leo hesitated, the weight of the question hanging in the air. *Betrayal.* The word struck him like a blow. He forced himself to meet the man's gaze. "It's not betrayal if it means survival. This city will chew us up and spit us out if we're not smart."

"Survival," the agent murmured, almost thoughtfully. "A convenient justification. But survival often comes at a cost."

"I know exactly what it costs," Leo replied, the edge in his voice sharper now. "You want information, and I want security. That's the deal."

The tension in the air was suffocating. Words became weapons, each side testing the other's resolve. Leo offered fragments of intelligence enough to tempt, but never enough to fully expose his team. Still, every word left a deeper scar on his conscience.

When the meeting ended, he stood alone for a moment in the pale light. The thrill of power coursed through him, intoxicating and foul. But underneath the rush, dread simmered. He had crossed a line that could never be uncrossed.

Unbeknownst to Leo, Ghost had followed him.

Something about Leo's recent behavior had set his instincts ablaze the restless eyes, the evasive words, the quiet disappearances. Hidden among the trees, Ghost watched the meeting unfold, the fragments of conversation twisting his stomach into knots.

When Leo's voice carried softly through the still night *"I can provide insight into my team's operations…"* Ghost's blood ran cold.

He had heard enough.

As the agents slipped back into the shadows, Ghost stepped forward, anger burning in his chest. "What the hell do you think you're doing, Leo?"

Leo spun around, startled. For an instant, guilt flickered across his face before hardening into defiance. "Ghost this isn't what it looks like."

"Really?" Ghost's tone was razor sharp. "Because from here, it looks exactly like betrayal."

"I'm not selling anyone out!" Leo shot back, his voice trembling. "You don't understand!"

"Then *make me* understand!" Ghost barked, stepping closer. "Explain how cutting secret deals with Valeria's people is supposed to 'protect' us. Because right now, it looks like you're gambling with our lives!"

"You think I wanted this?" Leo shouted. "You don't know what it's like to live every day wondering if you'll be next if the city will turn on you! I need security!"

Ghost's eyes blazed. "And what about us? The team that trusted you? You think you can just walk away and leave us in the line of fire?"

"I'm not abandoning anyone!" Leo's voice cracked, torn between anger and despair. "I'm trying to survive in a city that's already stacked against us. If I gain leverage if I earn their trust maybe I can use it to help us all!"

Ghost laughed bitterly, disbelief etched across his face. "Help us? You're playing with fire, Leo. You're going to get us all burned."

For a brief, fleeting moment, Leo's expression softened. Their eyes met old friends caught in a storm neither could control. There was still a spark of what once bound them, a trace of shared loyalty flickering in the darkness.

But the moment passed. The shadows reclaimed them both.

Ghost stepped back, his voice low but final. "You've made your choice."

Leo said nothing as Ghost disappeared into the trees. The silence that followed was heavy, suffocating, absolute.

When Leo finally looked up at the moon, its cold light seemed to mock him silver and merciless. The path he'd chosen was set, and every step forward would drag him deeper into the dark.

"I didn't want it to come to this," Leo murmured, his voice breaking under the weight of his choices. "But you don't get it, Ghost. This city it's a machine. It chews people up and spits them out. I'm just trying to survive."

"Then survive *with us*," Ghost said, his tone low and thunderous. "We can still fix this, Leo. But only if you stop now. You're playing with fire, and if you don't pull back, it'll burn all of us alive."

For a fleeting second, something human flickered in Leo's eyes regret, maybe even guilt. But it vanished just as quickly, replaced by weary resignation. "I'll try," he said finally, though the words sounded hollow even to him. "I'll tell them I'm out. But you don't know what they're capable of. This won't be easy."

Ghost's eyes narrowed, his voice firm. "Then do it now. Break those ties before it's too late."

Leo nodded slowly, his breath shallow. "Fine. I'll tell them I'm done. But they won't let me go without a fight."

"Then we'll be ready for that fight together," Ghost said, though the words carried a shadow of doubt. "We just have to be smart. No mistakes."

The uneasy truce that formed between them was thin as glass. Leo knew he was standing on a razor's edge. As he turned away, a chill ran through him a creeping sense that unseen eyes were already watching from the dark. Somewhere, in the depths of the city, the consequences of his choices had begun to stir.

Evening draped the small room in a warm golden light, but the space between Marcus and Zara was cold, filled with unspoken words. The room had once been their refuge from the chaos outside, yet now it felt like a confessional where truth and mistrust stood face to face.

Marcus sat at the edge of the table, head bowed, the silence pressing on his chest. Zara's voice broke through softly. "What's wrong? You've been distant all day."

He hesitated, torn between the need to protect her and the fear of shattering the fragile trust between them. "Everything feels precarious right now," he said finally. "Ghost's suspicions, the military's movements... I don't know who we can trust anymore."

Zara's expression softened. "We *have* to trust each other, Marcus. Whatever happens, you can tell me."

He exhaled slowly, eyes heavy with conflict. "I've been hearing things," he said at last. "About Leo. About meetings with Valeria's agents."

Her eyes widened. "What do you mean? Is Leo in danger?"

"Or are we?" Marcus countered, his voice low. "If he's compromised, then everything we've built everything we're fighting for is exposed."

Zara shifted uncomfortably, the truth cutting through her. "But Leo's one of us. He wouldn't... would he?"

Marcus met her gaze, his tone grave. "People change. Fear changes them faster. I need to know, Zara if it comes down to it, will you stand with me?"

The question lingered like a blade suspended between them. "Of course," she said softly. "But I need to know you're not hiding anything from me either."

Guilt pricked his conscience. "I'm trying to protect you," he whispered. "To protect *us*."

"By keeping secrets?" she snapped, her composure slipping. "That's not protection, Marcus. That's isolation. If we're going to survive this, we have to stand together, not behind walls."

Marcus sighed, his shoulders sinking beneath invisible weight. "I know. I just… I don't want to lose you."

Zara reached across the table, her fingers brushing his hand. "You won't. But only if we start being honest with each other, and with ourselves."

They sat in silence, caught in the fragile balance between love and duty. Outside, the city hummed like a living machine, unaware that the smallest fracture between them could undo everything they'd fought to hold together.

Meanwhile, a different tension coiled through the rest of the team. In the underground war room, the air was thick with unease. Shadows clung to the walls like conspirators, and the faint hum of machinery only amplified the silence.

Sofia's voice broke it first. "I've been monitoring our transmissions," she said, her brow furrowed. "Something feels off. It's like… we're being watched. Our data trails don't add up."

Maya burst through the door, breathless, clutching a bundle of printouts. "You're right," she said, laying them out across the table. "I've intercepted warnings from the city's security archives flags raised about *us*. They know someone's been digging into restricted systems."

Marcus straightened, tension snapping through the room. "How long before they act?"

"Not long," Maya said grimly. "They're tightening surveillance across the sectors. And if Leo's connection to Valeria's agents is real…"

Her voice trailed off, the implication heavy in the air.

Zara exchanged a look with Marcus, the earlier conversation still raw in her mind. "Then we're already exposed."

For a moment, no one spoke. The weight of paranoia settled over them like a suffocating fog.

Outside, the city lights flickered briefly, almost imperceptibly as if the great machine itself were taking notice of their fear.

"They're more sophisticated than we thought," Sofia said, her voice taut with dread. "Anyone could be listening to us."

Hitherto silent, Ghost finally spoke, his tone low and controlled. "I've seen a change in the perimeter. More guards. Patrols are moving erratically as if they're expecting something."

A knot tightened in Marcus's stomach as the implications fell into place. "We can't let fear dictate our moves," he said, forcing steadiness into his voice. "But we also can't ignore it. We strategize carefully every decision counts now."

Sofia's eyes flashed with frustration. "What if Leo's feeding them information? We can't afford a mole in our ranks, Marcus. If he's working with Valeria, everything we've built could collapse overnight."

Marcus's pulse quickened, a cold shiver crawling up his spine. "Then we watch him," he said. "Quietly. We gather proof before we act. If we confront him without evidence, we risk pushing him further or worse, forcing him to sabotage us outright."

Maya shook her head, her tone measured but urgent. "If he's still loyal, suspicion might drive him away. We can't afford to lose another piece of this team. Not now."

Their debate spiraled, each voice laced with tension, fear, and hidden motives. The room felt smaller by the minute crowded not by people, but by doubt.

Marcus rose from his chair and exhaled. "Enough," he said finally. "We can't fracture like this. We either stand together or we fall alone."

But even as he spoke, he could feel the fractures deepening the ghost of betrayal whispering just beneath the surface, gnawing at the fragile ties that still bound them together.

The team gathered in the dim confines of their war room. The air was thick with unease, the low hum of old machinery blending with the anxious rhythm of shallow breaths.

Marcus stood at the head of the table, the flickering light casting sharp lines across his face. Next to him, Zara's eyes darted between her teammates reading every gesture, every silence. Ghost leaned against the far wall, arms crossed, expression blank but tense. Maya scribbled furiously in her notebook, while Sofia's fingers danced over her tablet, her movements more mechanical than focused.

"Thank you all for coming," Marcus began, his voice calm but edged with fatigue. "We need to discuss our next move specifically, everything we've gathered about the troop movements."

He paused, scanning the room. "They're mobilizing. We need eyes inside their compound."

Sofia glanced up, brow furrowed. "Inside? Marcus, that's suicide. We'll never make it past security."

"We will if we're clever," he said, the faintest trace of determination creeping into his tone. "We're pulling a heist."

The word hung in the air like a spark in a room full of fumes.

"A heist?" Maya repeated, leaning forward. "You're serious?"

Marcus nodded. "We need to infiltrate the military's network directly. If we can access their central core, we can uncover their plans maybe even the next phase of their operation."

"And if something goes wrong?" Zara asked softly, her voice trembling just beneath control.

"Then we adapt," Marcus replied. "It's what we've always done."

Ghost shifted his weight, his tone gravelly. "I still don't trust Leo. If he's been working with Valeria's agents, this could all be a setup. We'd be walking straight into their trap."

Marcus met his gaze. "I know the risks. But fear won't save us. Only action will."

The discussion grew heated. Maya proposed gathering intel from surveillance drones. Ghost dismissed the idea, advocating for a more aggressive strike. Sofia argued for caution, warning that their digital footprint was already under scrutiny. Every suggestion carried hidden weight each word sounded less like strategy and more like a test of allegiance.

Marcus could feel the shift, subtle but undeniable. Every voice had an edge. Every glance lasted a fraction too long. Even the air seemed charged with accusation.

He looked from face to face the team he'd built, now splintered by suspicion. What once had been trust now felt like a game of masks.

On the surface, they were unified. But beneath the thin veneer of cooperation, he could feel the truth rising like a cold tide.

They were no longer a team.

They were five people waiting for someone to betray them first.

And somewhere, in the silence between heartbeats, Marcus began to suspect **it might already be too late.**

As the meeting drew to a close, Marcus's gaze swept over his team. Determination flickered in their eyes, but so did something else a quiet trepidation, the unspoken fear that trust itself had become a fragile thing. They stood united in purpose, yet shadowed by doubt, the specter of betrayal hovering just beyond the circle of light, unseen but unmistakably present.

"The night's still young," Marcus said, his voice steady but taut. "Let's keep sharp. We'll regroup before the heist. Remember we're not just fighting for survival. We're fighting for each other."

The words lingered in the air long after they left the room. The silence that followed felt charged, almost electric, as if the city itself were listening. Outside, the wind whispered through the corridors of steel and glass, carrying with it the tension of what was to come.

Marcus could feel it in his bones the gathering storm, heavy and inevitable.

Somewhere in its dark heart, betrayal was waiting.

## Chapter 14: The Plan

The dimly lit conference room buzzed with anticipation as the team gathered around the large table, their faces etched with determination. This was no ordinary briefing it was the culmination of their fears, their hopes, and the fragile burden of trust that bound them together. As Marcus surveyed the group, he could feel the pressure closing in, each of them acutely aware of the stakes that hung over them.

"Okay, everyone," Marcus began, his tone steady but urgent. "We've got a lot to cover, so let's get right to it. We're breaking the heist down into specific roles and a strict timeline. Everyone needs to know their part."

He turned toward the whiteboard, where a rough sketch of the military compound sprawled across its surface. Jagged lines and sharp arrows marked entry points, guard rotations, and possible escape routes.

"Sofia you're on technical prep. We need backdoors into their systems before the operation begins. Can you handle that?"

Sofia nodded, tapping her fingers nervously on the tabletop. "I can reroute their camera feeds and set up a loop. But I'll need at least an hour to install it, and I'll have to access their mainframe to make sure the data manipulation doesn't trigger alarms."

"Good," Marcus replied, confidence flickering in his tone. "Ghost, you're in charge of diversions. We'll need something big noise, confusion, chaos. Nothing lethal."

Ghost leaned back, a smirk playing on his lips. "Smoke bombs, flash triggers, maybe a few timed explosions. Enough to keep the guards guessing while we slip in."

"Perfect," Marcus said, suppressing a grim smile at Ghost's enthusiasm. "Maya, you'll identify key targets inside. We need intelligence anything that'll give us leverage."

Maya leaned forward, scanning the map. "I'll mark the armory, the command center, and any data cores tied to their communications. I'll also need their patrol schedules if we move blind, we're done before we begin."

Marcus nodded. "Understood. Leo you'll build our cover stories. Fake IDs, clean trails, contingency scripts. If anything goes wrong, no one connects this to us."

Leo met his gaze evenly. "I'll make sure our identities are airtight. But if we slip up even once, they'll know someone's working from the inside."

As assignments settled, the tension in the room shifted. Uncertainty gave way to grim purpose. For the first time in weeks, Marcus felt a spark of cohesion returning each of them anchored to a shared mission.

"Now," he continued, "we need a timeline. The compound's next security update rolls out in seven days. That's our window. We strike the night before the drills."

Sofia scribbled notes as Marcus drew a series of intersecting timelines on the board. "We meet daily to review progress," he added. "Every minute counts. We need to be perfectly synchronized."

But even as plans took shape, Marcus couldn't shake the feeling that they were balancing on the edge of a knife. Trust was thinning, stretched taut by paranoia. His gaze drifted to Zara silent, focused, but distant and unease rippled through him. Would loyalty hold when the pressure hit its peak?

Next came the list of resources every tool, gadget, and safeguard they would need.

"We'll need cutting gear, security disablers, comm devices," Marcus said, voice firm. "Nothing that can be traced back to us. Get creative, get discreet."

Sofia rose from her chair, holding up a small metal device no larger than a fist. "This is an EMP disruptor I've been developing. It'll disable surveillance systems for about three minutes." Her voice trembled slightly with excitement. "But it's still untested. I don't want to use it blind."

"Then we test it," Marcus said. He grabbed a nearby chair, climbed up, and positioned the device near the room's security camera. "Everyone, stand by. If this works, we'll see the feed go dark."

Sofia activated it with a soft click. A low hum filled the air, rising to a sharp whine. The monitor flickered once, twice and then the image cut to black.

"It works!" she exclaimed, a rare grin lighting her face.

But the celebration was short lived. A faint acrid smell drifted through the room.

"Uh… is it supposed to smoke like that?" Ghost asked, one eyebrow raised.

Sofia's smile faded. "It overheated. The circuit's not strong enough for extended use." She quickly powered it down. "I'll reinforce the wiring. It'll hold next time."

Marcus nodded, his tone clipped. "Fix it. If this fails in the field, we're finished."

Ghost crossed his arms. "We also need clean escape routes. I'll map one through the outer storage corridors and another through the southern wall in case things go south."

"I'll verify those paths," Maya added. "I'll overlay satellite readings and identify blind zones. No surprises."

As the planning session dragged on, an unspoken dread threaded through the air. The room vibrated with a strange duality precision and paranoia, logic and fear.

Every tool they discussed felt like both salvation and a potential trap. Every exchanged glance carried questions no one dared voice aloud.

Marcus could sense it in the subtle shifts the way Ghost's eyes lingered too long on Leo, the tension in Sofia's shoulders, the faint tremor in Maya's voice when she said "trust." Even Zara, his silent anchor, avoided his gaze.

They looked united.

They sounded ready.

But beneath the surface, Marcus could feel it the quiet hum of betrayal, coiled and waiting to strike.

The plan was solid. The timing was perfect. And yet, as he looked around the room, he couldn't shake the certainty that someone in it was already preparing for a very different kind of mission.

As the meeting drew to a close, Marcus looked around at his team. Determination burned in their eyes, yet unease lingered like a shadow between them. The mission ahead was perilous one mistake could unravel everything. When his gaze met Zara's, he wondered if their fragile trust would withstand the weight of what was to come.

"Let's stay sharp," he said, forcing steadiness into his voice. "We're in this together and together, we'll see it through."

But as the room emptied and shadows lengthened, Marcus couldn't shake the sense that the real battle wasn't against the city's enemies outside, but against the darkness quietly taking root within them.

The hum of fluorescent lights filled the dim laboratory as the team gathered once more. Tools, monitors, and samples littered the workbenches, and the air buzzed with both curiosity and tension. Marcus hadn't called this meeting to review the heist plan he had something far more critical to discuss.

"Alright, everyone," he began, pacing with restless energy. "We need to understand the core of this seed technology. It's not just a tool it's a turning point. It could either work for us… or against us."

Sofia stepped forward, eyes alight with intensity. "The seed technology can modify organic systems at a molecular level," she explained. "If we integrate it correctly, it could reshape the environment in our favor alter terrain, disable sensors, even create barriers. It could change everything."

Ghost leaned back against the wall, arms crossed, skepticism etched into his features. "And if it backfires? We could be unleashing something we can't control."

Maya flipped through a stack of notes, her tone analytical. "We need to understand its full potential first. If we can harness it safely, it could tip the balance give us an edge even against the military."

Marcus nodded solemnly. "Then we factor it into the heist. But before we deploy it, we test it. Small scale, controlled environment. No risks we can't manage."

The air thickened with a mix of excitement and dread. They all sensed the same truth this discovery could be their salvation, or their destruction.

Over the next few days, the team prepared tirelessly for the test. The lab became a symphony of mechanical hums and blinking lights, machines whirring in harmony with their heartbeat of urgency.

Gathered around the lab table, they watched as Sofia, hands steady but trembling slightly, lowered a seed into a vat of organic material.

Almost instantly, the seed reacted tendrils unfurling in a rapid, unnatural bloom that spread across the containment walls.

"Look at this!" Sofia exclaimed, her voice bright with awe. "It's adapting to the environment perfect for diversions or structural manipulation during the mission."

But the exhilaration turned to alarm as the growth became erratic. The vines began to twist violently, fracturing the containment glass with a sharp crack.

"Whoa, whoa, whoa!" Ghost shouted, stumbling back as the vines lunged outward.

"Shut it down!" Marcus barked. Sofia scrambled to cut power, the vines retracting with a hiss before collapsing into stillness.

"That was close," Sofia muttered, pale and shaken. "It works but it's volatile. If we're not careful, it could take everything down with it."

Marcus folded his arms, his jaw set. "Then we build a failsafe. If we're using this, it has to be controllable. No guesswork."

The next rounds of testing proved no less unnerving. Each experiment brought unpredictable results rapid overgrowth, chemical reactions, even brief surges of energy that distorted nearby instruments.

"We need to be cautious," Ghost warned, his brow furrowed. "This thing doesn't know friend from foe."

Maya took careful notes, her tone cool but intent. "We document everything growth rate, reaction times, external triggers. If we're going to use this, we have to know every outcome before we deploy it."

Days blurred together. By the end, the conclusion was clear the seed technology could be used, but only under precise, calculated conditions. It was power on a razor's edge.

And power, Marcus knew, always came with a cost.

With the discovery integrated into their plan, it was time to rehearse. The team gathered in a makeshift training area a dim storage room littered with crates and old machinery. Chalk lines marked the outline of the compound on the floor.

"We need to practice every detail," Marcus said firmly. "From infiltration to extraction every second matters."

Ghost grinned, holding up a smoke bomb prototype. "Let's see if this distraction works."

Before anyone could protest, he tossed it into the center of the room. A thick plume of gray smoke exploded outward, blanketing them in haze.

"Damn it, Ghost!" Sofia coughed, waving the air. "A little warning next time?"

"It's supposed to be chaotic," Ghost said with a shrug, a grin tugging at his lips.

"Too chaotic," Marcus snapped, his voice muffled through the smoke. "We can't communicate if we can't see each other. Fix it."

As the air began to clear, the team exchanged wary glances. Their laughter was strained, their smiles brief. Beneath the surface, tension simmered uneasy, volatile, ready to ignite at the smallest spark.

The plan was solid. The rehearsals were working.

But Marcus could feel it in his gut something wasn't right.

They were ready for the mission.

Yet somehow, they were walking straight into danger that had already begun to take root.

Maya grabbed a small fan from a nearby crate and began clearing the smoke. "We need better visibility. Can you adjust the formula so it's less dense?"

Ghost nodded, already recalculating. "Fine. I'll tone it down. But I'm keeping the noise component it's the best part."

"Just make sure it doesn't sabotage us," Marcus said, exhaling deeply as the haze thinned. "Let's keep running through the sequence."

Sofia busied herself with her array of tools, her expression focused. "I'm going to run a full systems check. We can't afford any surprises once we're inside."

Ghost was still tinkering, his voice cutting through the tension. "I've got a few tricks up my sleeve smoke bombs, noise traps, you name it. But we'd better rehearse every deployment. We don't get second chances out there."

Meanwhile, Maya took charge of the communications setup, ensuring their secure channel was flawless. "We need perfect timing," she said firmly. "If one of us gets into trouble, everyone else needs to know instantly."

The air grew heavy as they cycled through their roles, running scenario after scenario. The weight of the mission pressed down on them, the room charged with the hum of adrenaline and nerves.

"Timing is everything," Marcus reminded them. "Even one second off, and we lose the whole operation."

Hours slipped by in tense repetition. At one point, Maya stumbled over a loose cable during a simulated retreat.

"Damn it!" she swore, scrambling to her feet. "If that happens during the mission, I'll ruin everything."

"That's why we practice," Marcus said, helping her up. "We make mistakes now so we don't make them when it counts."

"Speaking of mistakes," Sofia said, holding up a dead communicator, "this one's fried. I'll have to rebuild it before our next test."

Marcus sighed, pinching the bridge of his nose. "Everyone double check your gear tonight. No surprises in the field."

Despite his calm tone, unease coiled deep in his chest. Beneath the structure of their meticulous planning, a darker question stirred *could he truly trust them all?* He pushed the thought aside. Doubt was poison, and they couldn't afford poison now.

The night before the heist, the team gathered for one last meeting. The room buzzed with nervous energy, the table littered with maps, notes, and gear. Every face was drawn tight, shadowed by the magnitude of what lay ahead.

"Alright," Marcus began, voice steady but edged with fatigue. "This is it. Final roles and emergency protocols."

He didn't get far before a loud *crash* shattered the tense silence. Everyone spun around. Ghost stood frozen beside an overturned crate, one of his smoke bombs rolling away and hissing faintly on the floor.

"Seriously, Ghost?" Sofia groaned, pressing her fingers to her temple. "Now is *not* the time."

Ghost hurried to scoop it up, muttering, "It's fine it didn't go off."

Marcus's glare could've cut glass. "Check everything. If that happens tomorrow, it could cost us everything."

The reminder hit hard. Silence followed, thick and uneasy, the scent of smoke still lingering in the air.

"Let's stay focused," Marcus said finally. "Mistakes happen here, not in the field. We tighten every screw, every plan."

Sofia straightened, determination burning through her fatigue. "We need to confirm our comms are secure. If something goes wrong, we have to reach each other instantly no interference."

"Agreed," Marcus said, locking eyes with her. "Maya, you'll monitor all channels. The moment anything sounds off, you trigger the alarm."

Maya nodded, her expression grave. "I'll run simulations tonight. Whatever happens, I'll be ready."

Ghost leaned forward on the table, his voice low. "And what if we're spotted by the military before we get in? Do we fight or retreat?"

Marcus's answer came without hesitation. "Retreat. We're here for intel, not a war. If we can slip away unseen, that's victory enough."

A heavy silence followed as each of them absorbed his words. They all knew the risks, but now the danger felt tangible real in a way it hadn't before.

"Remember," Marcus said, forcing a note of reassurance into his voice, "we're trained for this. We're prepared. And we have each other's backs."

From the corner of the room, Zara's quiet voice cut through the tension. "And if we don't come back?"

The question hung in the air like a lead weight.

Marcus met her gaze, his throat tight. "We will," he said at last, his voice quiet but firm. "We have to."

The meeting ended in subdued silence. One by one, they exchanged brief nods and quiet goodbyes some out of habit, others because they feared it might be the last time. The camaraderie that had once united them now felt fragile, stretched thin over the cracks of suspicion.

Marcus watched them go, the weight of their shared purpose pressing hard against his chest. They were walking into the unknown into danger, deception, and the possibility of betrayal.

As he stood alone in the flickering light of the lab, the hum of the city beyond their walls felt distant and strange. The countdown to the heist had begun, and with every tick of the clock, the invisible line between trust and treachery grew thinner.

Tomorrow would test not only their skill but their loyalty and Marcus knew, deep down, that one of them was already poised to break it.

## Chapter 15: Double Cross

The room was dark, shadows pooling in the corners as Leo sat across from Elder Valeria's agents. His fingers drummed lightly against the table, a rhythm he couldn't stop despite himself. The scent of something metallic lingered in the air or maybe it was just the taste of fear rising in his throat. His hands felt clammy, and he resisted the urge to wipe them on his pants. This was the moment he'd planned for, the moment he thought he wanted but now it felt like standing on the edge of a cliff, unsure whether to leap or step back.

The agents of Valeria sat across from him, their faces shrouded in shadow. One of them leaned forward; his voice was smooth, almost too relaxed. "You've done well, Leo. The information you've provided is... impressive."

Leo's throat tightened, but he forced himself to nod. His hands curled into fists beneath the table. "I…uh…just want to make sure... my team won't... they won't be in danger." His words came out uneven, each syllable feeling like a stone he had to push uphill.

He nodded, swallowing. "I understand; I just want to know my team will not be in jeopardy. We're all in on this together."

"Together?" The agent's laugh was soft but sharp, like a blade sliding across stone. "You misunderstand the nature of this arrangement, my friend. Your team... they were never part of the deal. They're collateral, nothing more."

Leo's breath hitched. His fingers twitched on the table, and he quickly clasped his hands together to still them. "That wasn't" He stopped himself mid sentence, his voice faltering.

"That wasn't what we agreed on," the agent said.

Leo's stomach twisted, his pulse pounding in his ears. He leaned forward slightly, his voice breaking. "What... what do you mean?" The words came out fragmented, weak, as if he were choking on them. He cleared his throat, but the desperation in his tone lingered, barely concealed.

The agent leaned forward, his voice dropping to a near whisper, though the weight of his words pressed down like a hammer. "Your little band of rebels? They're in the way. Consider this your final act of loyalty, Leo. Do this for us, and you'll have your guarantees. Safety, resources, a future. But only if you deliver them into our hands."

Leo's lips parted as if to protest, but no words came out. His nails dug into his palms beneath the table, the sting grounding him in the moment.

His heart hammered in his chest, his breathing shallow. The realization hit him like a fist to the gut he wasn't just a pawn, but the bait, the trap. "They trust me," he said, his voice barely above a whisper, a plea more than a statement. He shook his head, his words tumbling out before he could stop them. "You... you can't do this."

"Trust?" The agent's lips curled into a faint smile that didn't reach his eyes. "Trust is fleeting, Leo. And you abandoned it the moment you sat at this table. Regrets won't save you now. The trap is already sprung. There's no going back."

The agent's words hung heavy in the air, pressing down like a shroud. Leo shifted restlessly in his seat, legs twitching as if ready to flee, yet he willed himself to remain still. His eyes flickered toward the door, then back to the agents seeking reassurance but finding only the vertigo of a precipice. Trapped between forward and retreat, he ached to warn his team, but the agents' cold, unblinking gazes held him captive, silencing any thought of escape.

"Remember your role," the agent said, rising from his chair with deliberate slowness. His shadow stretched across the table, engulfing Leo. "Ensure the operation begins as planned. And, Leo?" He paused; his voice dropped to a lethal whisper. "If you fail us, you won't just lose your team. You'll lose everything."

Leo stepped out into the cold night air, the weight of the meeting pressing down on his shoulders like a physical burden. His hands trembled at his sides, and he shoved them into his pockets to steady them. The distant hum of the city sounded muffled, as if he were underwater. The clock was ticking, the heist drawing ever closer, and yet all he could feel was the ground shifting beneath his feet, threatening to swallow him whole.

Operation Beginning

Other times, at the rendezvous and upon, Marcus stood firm as his heart tucked and quickening of paces at the lengthening of the shadows. The night had arrived, and with it, the execution time of their plan. "Positions!" he shouted; though firm in his voice, a storm brewed within him.

Already at the technical station, Sofia's fingers danced over the keyboard with practiced precision, poised to deploy the critical backdoors into the military systems. Ghost held a vigilant watch from a high vantage point, his eyes piercing the perimeter for any sign of danger. Hidden in the shadows, Maya's gaze swept tirelessly for patrolling guards, every muscle taut with alertness. Beside Marcus, Zara stood firm an unyielding anchor amid the storm that roared beyond the compound's walls.

"Let's rehearse our parts one last time," Marcus whispered. "Sofia, you're on system breach. Ghost, diversions yours. Maya, you're calling targets, and Zara, you're with me on extraction. We move as one."

They got into starting positions, and immediately, signs of compromise began to show. First was Sofia's voice, crackling over comms: "I'm in the system, but it's got unexpected security measures they've locked it down since our last intel."

A cold knot was forming in Marcus's stomach. "What do you mean? New firewalls and added guards. I can get past them, but it is going to take longer than anticipated," she replied, urgency creeping into her voice.

"Stay focused," Marcus said, his heart racing. "We need to adapt fast. Ghost, can you create a diversion now?"

"Already on it," Ghost said, dripping assurance into his tone. "I'll set off a few smoke bombs near the east entrance. That should draw their attention."

Adrenaline stirred in Marcus's body as Ghost executed his plan they were mobile, but he felt something was entirely wrong. There, in thick air, was a silent specter, a growing feeling of betrayal waiting to come into view. "Something's wrong," Maya said, and her voice pulled tight. "We have to be on high alert."

Suddenly, an explosion resounded afar, accompanied by yelling from guards running in the direction of the noise. "Ghost, what have you done?" Marcus shouted, panic rising to his throat.

"Just a little detour!" Ghost said, shaking all over with excitement. "They are all going to the east. This is our opportunity!"

But as the team moved then it hit Marcus like a brick: his plan had been compromised all along; the fact that Leo had disappeared for such a long period left an enormous hole in the strategy. "Where is Leo?" His mind was racing he was supposed to be here. No sooner had the thought come than a cold voice filtered through the comms, making the hairs rise on the back of Marcus's neck. "You should have known better than to trust him." The voice was unmistakable: the agent for Elder Valeria.

"What is happening?" Marcus asked, fear stirring in his stomach.

"Your little operation is already over. You are surrounded," the agent darkly chuckled on. "You have walked right into our trap."

Panic ran wildly through him as he looked around madly. In the darkness, moving shadows flickered, and the clopping of shoes sounded in the distance. "Regroup!" he yelled, adrenaline spiking. "Marcus!" Zara's voice cut through the din, urgent. "We can't stay here! We have to adapt and move now!"

In that instant the team went into high gear. Though they had planned for emergencies, never had they faced anything at this scale. Marcus felt the weight of betrayal as they ran and weaved across the compound to gain cover and devise their way out of this tight corner.

"Stay close!" he yelped, his voice a rallying call above the chaos. "We can't let them cut us off!"

A heavy conviction settled deep in his chest as they moved an unshakable belief that it was Leo who had betrayed them. Now, they no longer fought for the mission but for survival. The night had transformed into a ruthless battlefield, where only swift adaptation could offer a fragile chance at life.

The burden pressed ever closer as Marcus took each step. They had come into this as warriors, playing a deadly game in which there was no longer room for trust. Time to raise the stakes: their freedom.

The air was electric with tension as Marcus and his team found themselves trapped inside the compound. What had begun as an adrenaline rush had flipped into overwhelming panic: heavy boots closed in along the corridors, signaling the arrival of security forces. They felt the walls closing in a vice clamping hard upon them in their fight against time and chaos.

"Everyone, stay alert!" Marcus shouted over the comms, his heart racing. "We have to regroup! We cannot let them split us up!"

As his gaze swept the dim corridors, one thing became clear they were scattered. Maya slipped off in a different direction, careful to avoid raising suspicion; Ghost melted into the shadows, preparing to create a diversion. At the technical console, Sofia worked feverishly, hacking toward a secure exit, while Zara remained steadfast at his side.

"Marcus, we have to go," Zara said, firm amid the chaos. "Any longer and we'll be trapped."

He nodded, the weight of their predicament pressing down. "We can't leave anyone behind. We have to find Maya and Ghost first."

Before he could move further, a resounding volley boomed down the hallway clear, sharp, jolting. "They're a lot closer than I thought!" he exclaimed, adrenaline washing over him. "We have to move, and we must do it right now!"

He fought deeper into the compound in a struggle to re establish contact with any remaining team members. "Maya! Ghost! Can you" Static swallowed the rest. Communications were dying beneath alarms and pounding boots on concrete.

A flash of fear crossed Zara's face, then steeled into resolve. "We have to trigger the emergency protocols; it's the only hope we have for communication with each other."

"Right," Marcus said quickly, mentally cycling back to their pre arranged code. "Alright, listen up, everybody! We initiate Protocol Alpha. If you can hear this, fall back to the secondary position the maintenance shed!"

The words hung in the air until it finally dawned on them all: they were no longer a team, only a group of people barely holding on. "We can't afford to wait and hear from everyone. We need to get to the shed before they lock it down," Marcus urged, tight and urgent.

"Come on!" Zara exclaimed, snatching his arm and pulling him toward a side door. "We'll find them on the way!"

Down dark corridors, the sounds of pursuit grew louder: shouting and staccato gunfire filled the air. Every corner threatened disaster.

Once in a clearer moment, Zara sat and narrowed her eyes, weighing their options. "Marcus, the course we're on is likely to take us right into a trap. We need to deflect them somehow."

"What do you suggest?" he asked, his heart thudding.

"We might activate one of the seed technology devices. Cause some chaos. It could give us enough time to get back to the others," she said steadily.

Marcus hesitated, weighing the risks. "But that could put Maya and Ghost in danger too. We don't know where they are."

"We have no time to second guess," Zara pressed, urgent. "Either we risk something now, or we're caught. It's time to do something fast."

Marcus let out a deep breath and nodded. "Alright. Let's do it."

Emergency protocols activated, they ran as fast as their legs could carry them toward the nearest lab, where they had stashed some of the seed technology. The air grew oppressive with the smell of chemicals and the hum of machinery. Zara grabbed a compact device from the cache, hands shaking slightly as she handed it to Marcus.

"Here," she said. "Set it to create a diversion."

He adjusted the settings with trembling hands, his heart pounding under the weight of what was to come. "On my mark, we blow it and then make for the shed. Ready?"

Zara nodded, alight with a fiery resolve that burned like flint. "Let's go!"

With a deep breath, Marcus hit the button, and the device roared to life, releasing a cloud of spores that expanded rapidly, filling the room with thick fog. "Now!" he shouted, darting out into the corridor as chaos swirled behind them. The spores spread fast, and soon the first shouts of confusion echoed from the guards.

"What is happening?" one of them yelled, startled by the sudden change in his surroundings.

"Secure the area!" another shouted.

"Perfect!" Zara exclaimed triumphantly, her tone urgent. "Let's use this chaos to our advantage!"

Down the hall they ran, through a maze of corridors, driven by a renewed sense of purpose.

The mayhem behind them swallowed their footsteps as they slipped through the shadows. "We need to find Maya and Ghost," Marcus said, already rounding a corner.

"Let's check the storage area first!" Zara replied, taking the lead. "They might have taken refuge there."

As they entered the storage area, the door swung open when she stepped out relief and urgency flooding her voice. "There you are! I thought I'd lost you both!"

"Maya!" Marcus exclaimed, pulling her into a quick hug. "We triggered a diversion. It should give us some time."

"Good thinking," Maya said, glancing over her shoulder. "But we have to go. Ghost's still creating a diversion, but he won't be able to keep it up much longer."

"Where is he?" Zara asked, scanning the area in all directions in case danger lurked nearby.

"He said he was going to meet us at the maintenance shed. He's trying to distract them from us," Maya explained, her wide eyes filled with urgency.

"Then we have to go. Now!" Marcus ordered, and the four of them took off at a trot toward the shed, their hearts pounding in unison.

They ran, the clamor of chaos echoing close behind. The path ahead was treacherous guards shouted, their footsteps thundering nearer.

"We must hurry!" Marcus urged, quickening his stride.

"Almost there!" Maya yelled as they closed in on the shed.

But just as they reached the door, a loud explosion rocked the compound, sending shockwaves through the ground beneath their feet.

"What was that?" Zara screamed, her heart pounding against her ribs.

"Ghost!" Marcus shouted, alarm rising in his voice. "He set off something big!"

They burst into the maintenance shed and found Ghost inside, panting heavily. Marcus felt a surge of hope shoot through him.

"Took you long enough!" Ghost grinned, his eyes full of urgency. "We need to move. They're regrouping, and they won't stay distracted for long."

"Alright, here's the plan," Marcus said, his voice firm amidst the mayhem outside. "We use the tools in here to create a makeshift barricade. If we can delay them, we can find another way out."

Maya nodded, scanning the shed quickly for supplies. "We can block the entrance with these crates and tools."

Zara grabbed a crowbar and began reinforcing the door. "I'll hold it while you two work on the barricade," she said, her tone brimming with determination.

As they worked together, the atmosphere shifted. The initial panic began to fade, replaced by a shared sense of purpose. They were a team and they were going to fight their way out.

"Once we secure the entrance, we'll need to find an exit," Marcus told Ghost, who stood beside him. "Do you know any exits in this place?"

"Yeah," Ghost said, brow furrowed in concentration. "There's a service tunnel leading to the back of the compound. It's a bit of a hike, but it's supposed to be the way out of here."

"Then that's our route," Marcus said, feeling the first surge of hope he'd had all night. "Let's finish this barricade and move out."

Footsteps and shouted commands grew nearer with every passing second, the tension inside the shed thickening like a suffocating fog. The walls seemed to close in around them, and with each creak of the floorboards, the weight of their situation pressed harder.

With the barricade in place, they sprinted toward the service tunnel, adrenaline flooding their veins.

"Stay low and quiet," Marcus instructed as he slipped through the narrow exit first.

The tunnel was dark and cramped. As they moved deeper, the chaos outside gradually faded.

"We're going to make it," Maya whispered. "We just have to keep going."

But with every step forward, the air seemed to grow thicker, charged with unease. Marcus couldn't shake the feeling they were still being watched.

"Keep watch," he whispered. "We can't drop our guard until we're out."

The twisted passageways of the tunnel curved and turned endlessly. Above them, faint footsteps and muffled voices echoed the guards were still searching.

"They're still looking for us," Zara whispered, darting her eyes across every shadowed nook.

"Just a little more," Ghost urged, urging them onward. "We're almost there where the exit's supposed to be."

Finally, they emerged into a narrow alley behind the compound, dimly lit and quiet. The cool night air brushed their skin  a chilling contrast to the suffocating tension of the compound they'd just escaped. They were out, but far from safe.

As they caught their breath, Marcus quickly assessed their surroundings. "We need to find a vehicle and put as much distance as possible between us and this place."

His voice carried calm authority, though the urgency beneath it was unmistakable.

"There's an old van parked a couple of blocks down," Ghost said, scanning their surroundings cautiously. "If we can get to it without being seen..."

"Let's move!" Marcus ordered, motioning for them to follow.

They slipped into the shadows, moving quickly but quietly as they made their way toward the street.

With every step, the tension ratcheted higher. Each sound rang sharper, every shadow seemed to shift with threat. As they reached the vehicle, Marcus hurriedly checked the doors. "It's unlocked," he said, relief flooding his voice more than he intended.

"Get in!" Zara exclaimed, jumping into the back as the others followed.

Marcus slid into the driver's seat and turned the ignition. His heart pounded as he glanced into the rearview mirror. "For the moment we've got it clear, but we really need to get out of here fast."

Time seemed to blur and vanish as they made their escape from the compound, chaos and danger striking at every turn. Yet through the fire, they moved as one battle worn but unbroken, a team forged in crisis. Still, in the quiet that followed, victory felt tainted. The ghost of betrayal lingered in Marcus's mind, casting a long, dark shadow over their hard won triumph.

They had managed to get away, but not without a price. The night was young, and their battle for survival had only just begun.

The air was thick with tension as Marcus and his crew huddled around a makeshift table, pale and drawn from the night's ordeal. They'd made it out of the compound, but no one needed to say the words aloud the shadow of betrayal loomed over them, dark and ominous as a storm cloud.

The dim light overhead flickered across the room as they sat in silence, each lost in the aftermath of what had just transpired. Still reeling from the emotional storm, Zara turned to her comrades. "I just can't believe Leo would turn on us," she said, her voice barely above a whisper. "I thought he was one of us."

A pang of guilt tugged at Marcus's chest. He had vouched for Leo once, had believed in his loyalty. "We trusted him," he said at last, the words heavy with regret. "Obviously, we weren't paying attention."

Maya crossed her arms, furrowing her brow in frustration. "We can't let his betrayal define us. We need to focus on what's next. We can't let them win."

Ghost nodded, the seriousness etched deep into his features. "We need to find a way to turn this to our advantage. If they really think we're out of the game, then it's time to strike."

Marcus straightened, his eyes lighting with determination. "You're right. We need to regroup and come up with a new plan. We can't let what Leo has done destroy everything we've worked for."

As they began to discuss their next move, a quiet surge of resolve rose within Zara. Thrust into a world of chaos and peril, she had not faltered. She had stood her ground unyielding amid the storm and now, something within her hardened into purpose.

"I want to join the team," she said steadily.

Marcus looked at her, surprised yet impressed. "You're sure? It's not an easy route, and after everything…"

"I haven't felt this alive in years," Zara cut in, her eyes blazing. "I want to fight back not just for me, but for all of us. We cannot let betrayal get the better of us."

Maya smiled, some of the tension easing from her shoulders. "Welcome aboard, then. We could use your skills you've already proven yourself."

With Zara officially joining, the mood shifted. A new sense of purpose filled the room an unspoken pact to move forward and defy the odds. They sat around the table, tossing ideas and strategies back and forth, each member contributing their thoughts and expertise.

"First things first," Marcus said, drawing a rough diagram of the military compound on a scrap of paper. "We need to analyze their security systems again. They'll be on high alert, but that might work in our favor."

Sofia leaned in, her brow furrowed in concentration. "If we can find weaknesses in the new protocols, we might be able to exploit them. It's possible they'll overcompensate since we 'got the better of them' last time and raised so much hell."

"Agreed," Ghost said. "We'll do diversions again but smarter this time. We can't afford to be caught."

As the planning continued, the despair that had once filled the room began to fade, replaced by resolve. No longer were they reacting they were preparing. This was no longer about mere survival; it was about reclaiming control.

Maya's fingers drummed lightly against the table. "What about the seed technology? It could still give us an edge. We can redeploy it, but this time with precision."

Marcus nodded. "We'll have to test it again make sure it works the way we need it to. If we can create chaos at the right moment, we might be able to slip in undetected."

For hours, they worked side by side, piecing together the plan each member offering their skills, insights, and instincts. They discussed escape routes, timing, contingencies every angle scrutinized, every possibility explored. The air crackled with energy, alive with determination and hope a stark contrast to the despair that had gripped them only hours before.

As the meeting drew to a close, Marcus felt a quiet pride swell in his chest, the burden of leadership lightened by the strength of the team around him. "We've come a long way, and we're stronger than ever," he said. "This isn't about revenge. This is about taking back our lives about standing up to those who tried to break us."

Zara met his gaze, determination shining in her eyes. "We're in this together now. Whatever happens, we face it together."

They began preparations for their final heist with high spirits and unshaken resolve. The night was long and dangerous, but they were ready to stand against it. Betrayal had sparked change and now, bound together, they would defy the storm.

## Chapter 16: Race Against Time

The first light of dawn was still a whisper on the horizon as Marcus gathered his team in the dimly lit safe house. The atmosphere buzzed with a mix of palpable tension and anticipation the weight of their impending mission heavy on their shoulders. This was it the moment they had prepared for, and failure was not an option.

"Listen up, everyone," Marcus began, his voice steady despite the adrenaline coursing through him. "This is our final briefing before we execute the plan. We've trained for this, and now it's time to put everything into action."

Zara stood beside him, her eyes scanning the faces of her teammates. Each one radiated determination, but she could sense the undercurrent of fear. They all knew what was at stake.

"Today, we split into three groups," Marcus continued, pointing to the makeshift map spread across the table. "Ghost and Maya will handle the distraction at the east entrance. Sofia, you're with me we'll infiltrate the central control room. We need to disable their security systems before they even realize we're there."

Sofia nodded, her brow furrowed in concentration. "I've gone over the blueprints a hundred times. I've got this. But we'll need to be quick. The moment we're detected, everything goes sideways."

"Exactly," Marcus replied. "And Zara, you'll be in charge of the extraction point. If we need to bail, you'll guide everyone back to safety."

"Understood," Zara said, her voice firm. "I'll be ready."

As the team broke into their assigned groups, the air crackled with tension like static electricity. Marcus led Sofia to their equipment station, where tools and devices were neatly arranged. "Let's double check everything," he said, running a hand across the table. "We can't afford any mistakes."

Sofia began inspecting her gear, her fingers deftly moving across the devices. "I've got the hacking module, signal scramblers, and the EMP device," she reported. "Everything looks good but we should also prepare for contingencies. If something goes wrong, we need to be ready to adapt."

Marcus nodded, feeling the weight of responsibility pressing down. "We will adapt. We've trained for this."

As they finished their checks, the reality of the moment settled in. "This is it," Sofia said softly. "We're really doing this."

"Yeah," Marcus replied, meeting her gaze. "But we're not alone. We have each other's backs."

The final moments before the mission were thick with emotion. The team gathered once more, the gravity of the task ahead heavy in the air. "No matter what happens, we stick together," Marcus reminded them, his voice firm. "We've come too far to turn back now."

Maya stepped forward, her eyes glistening with unshed tears. "I'm not ready to lose anyone today," she admitted, her voice trembling with emotion. "You all mean too much to me."

Ghost placed a reassuring hand on her shoulder. "We won't lose anyone. We're family now and family fights for each other."

Zara swallowed hard, her heart pounding. "If anything goes wrong, we'll adapt. We've trained for this. We know what we're doing."

Marcus felt a lump in his throat as he looked around at his team their faces a mixture of determination and fear. "Remember, we're not just fighting for ourselves. We're fighting for everyone who's counting on us. Let's make sure we're the ones who walk away from this."

With one final embrace, they exchanged quiet words of encouragement each of them fully aware of the risks, yet bound by a shared resolve to face them together. The air hung heavy with the unspoken weight of their farewells, echoing with emotion as they turned toward the unknown.

As the first rays of sunlight broke over the horizon, casting a golden hue across the landscape, the team gathered once more to synchronize their watches. "On my mark," Marcus said, checking his own. "We go in three... two... one... go!"

With that, they slipped into the darkness, adrenaline coursing hot through their veins. Marcus and Sofia moved in tandem toward the central control room, hearts hammering as they navigated the hostile terrain of the compound. The shadows seemed to close in around them, but with every step, their resolve sharpened purpose honed like a blade in the dark.

Upon reaching the entrance to the control room, Sofia pulled out her hacking module, her hands steady despite the tension. "This is it," she whispered, eyes fixed on the door panel. "I'll need a few moments to bypass the security lock."

"Just be quick," Marcus urged, scanning the corridor for any sign of movement. "We don't have much time."

Sofia nodded, her fingers flying over the device as she initiated the complex hacking sequence. The screen lit up with cascading lines of code, and she bit her lip in concentration. "Come on, come on," she muttered under her breath as the seconds ticked away.

Marcus watched her work, the tension thickening around them. "Any updates?" he asked, keeping his voice low.

"I'm in," Sofia replied, relief flickering across her face though her fingers hesitated briefly over the keyboard. "But it's worse than we thought. They've installed a counter intrusion system. If I don't disable it correctly, it'll trigger a full lockdown alarms, sealed exits, and an automatic alert to their patrols."

Marcus's stomach tightened. "How much time do we have before they detect you?"

"Not long," Sofia admitted, her voice steady but taut. "Every keystroke I make is being logged. If I make a mistake or take too long, they'll know someone's in the system."

"Just tell me what to do," Marcus said, ready to jump in.

"Keep an eye out for guards. And Marcus…" Sofia's voice dropped, the tension clear. "If the counter intrusion kicks in, I can't stop it. We'll have thirty seconds maybe less before they lock everything down."

Marcus's jaw tightened. "No pressure then," he muttered, positioning himself near the door, eyes scanning the corridor. The faint sound of footsteps in the distance sent a spike of adrenaline through him.

As Sofia worked on the hacking sequence, Marcus felt time slipping through their fingers. The tension was thick, every second stretching too long, and faint footsteps echoed ominously in the distance. "Hurry up, Sofia," he said, his eyes darting anxiously toward the door.

"I'm almost there," she replied, a faint tremor edging her voice. "But this system is fighting me every second I'm in, it's adapting. If I don't finish soon, it'll block me out and trigger a failsafe." Her fingers flew over the keyboard, and beads of sweat formed on her brow.

As she worked, the screens flickered, displaying real time surveillance feeds. "I can see their positions," she said, her eyes scanning the monitors. "If I can loop the feeds, it'll buy us a few minutes."

Marcus nodded, feeling a surge of hope. "Do it."

Sofia quickly initiated the process, her fingers flying across the keyboard as warning messages flashed on her screen: **"Intrusion detected. Countermeasures active."**

"Sofia?" Marcus asked, tension creasing his voice.

"I'm trying to loop the feeds, but the system's responding faster than I expected!" she hissed, eyes darting between lines of code. A moment later, the screens flickered, then froze, displaying images of empty corridors.

"Done!" she gasped, swiping a hand across her forehead. "The guards won't see us for now. But the system knows someone's tampered with it. We've got maybe five minutes before it starts rerouting to a backup."

"Nice work!" Marcus said, though his relief was short lived as Sofia's screen flashed another warning: **"Backup security protocols initializing."**

"Their system's rebooting," Sofia said, her voice tight. "If I don't shut it down now, it'll activate the failsafe and that means locked doors, armed guards, and no way out."

Marcus felt his pulse spike. "Then do it. We can't afford a single misstep."

Sofia's fingers danced over the controls, her heart hammering as she navigated the final layer of protocols. "I'm disabling the security systems now, but if I trip one more failsafe…" Her voice faltered for a split second before she continued, "They'll activate the automated turrets in the corridors. We won't make it out."

Marcus tensed, gripping the hilt of his weapon. "Then don't trip it. You've got this, Sofia."

But just as she began the process, the room shook with the sound of distant explosions, reverberating through the walls. "What was that?" Marcus shouted, adrenaline spiking as he exchanged a worried glance with Sofia.

"I don't know, but we need to move fast!" Sofia replied, her focus unwavering. "I'm almost there… just a few more seconds…"

As she continued to work, Marcus stood guard, his heart thudding against his ribs. The air crackled with tension, each passing second tightening the pressure around them.

Finally, Sofia's voice cut through the tension like a lifeline. "Got it! The security systems are down alarms disabled; surveillance offline!" She let out a shaky breath, hands trembling slightly as she leaned back.

Marcus exhaled deeply, relief washing over him. "Good work. Let's move before they realize what we've done."

"Let's go!" Marcus urged, feeling that surge of relief again. They had done it at least for now.

With one last look at the monitors, they understood the race against time was far from over. Stepping into the unknown, they carried with them a fierce resolve, ready to face whatever lay ahead. Fueled by the urgency to reclaim their lives and defy the forces threatening to unravel them, they moved forward unshaken and united.

## Chapter 17: The Heist Unfolds

The atmosphere crackled with tension as Ghost crouched behind a stack of crates, his eyes scanning the perimeter of the compound. The sun had fully risen, casting harsh light over the fortified walls, but he remained cloaked in shadows a ghost in the daylight. The final operation was underway, and every second counted.

With nimble fingers, Ghost set up explosive charges around the eastern entrance, carefully positioning them for maximum impact. He had spent weeks coordinating with mercenary contacts, gathering intel, and ensuring everything was in place for this moment. "Alright, let's make some noise," he muttered to himself, a slight grin creeping across his lips.

He clicked his comm device, connecting with Marcus and the others. "Charges are set. I'm ready to create the first diversion. Just give me the signal."

"Copy that, Ghost," Marcus replied, his voice steady. "We're in position. You have the green light."

Ghost took a deep breath, his heart racing with anticipation. He activated the detonator, and a series of explosions erupted in the distance, shaking the ground beneath him. Smoke billowed upward, cloaking the air in a dense haze that concealed his movements. Chaos erupted instantly alarms shrieked, and guards converged on the disturbance, abandoning their posts and leaving critical areas exposed.

"Now, let's see how well you handle a little distraction," Ghost whispered, watching through the swirling smoke as security forces scrambled to respond. He had created multiple distractions, each timed perfectly to draw attention away from the main objective.

With the guards diverted, he navigated the compound with practiced stealth, slipping through the turmoil toward his next objective. Ghost's military training took over, adrenaline coursing through his veins. Every step was deliberate, every breath controlled he was fully in his element.

As he moved through the labyrinthine paths of the compound, the sounds of confusion echoed behind him. "Ghost, how's it looking?" Marcus's voice crackled through the comms.

There was a brief pause a fraction of a second too long that made Marcus's stomach tighten.

"Just as planned," Ghost finally replied, his tone calm but missing its usual ease. "I've drawn away most of the security forces. They're too busy trying to figure out what just happened."

Marcus frowned slightly at the delay, glancing at Maya, who raised an eyebrow but said nothing.

"You should have a clear path to the primary vault," Ghost added, but Marcus couldn't shake the feeling that something was off about his tone.

"Understood. Keep us posted," Marcus said, his voice a steady anchor amid the chaos.

Ghost moved swiftly, planting charges at critical points to divert any lingering guards. Yet as he worked, his gaze drifted toward the central compound, where Marcus and Maya pressed forward. For a brief moment, his fingers hesitated over the detonator caught in a flicker of uncertainty.

"You're on schedule, right?" Marcus's voice cut through the comms.

Ghost's grip tightened on the detonator before he forced a casual tone. "Yeah, everything's going smoothly. They won't know what hit them."

Meanwhile, Marcus and Maya slipped through a narrow passage, their hearts pounding as they made their way toward the primary vault.

"How close are we?" Maya whispered, her eyes scanning for any sign of danger.

"Just a few more turns," Marcus replied, mentally tracing the blueprints he'd memorized. "With Ghost creating distractions, we should have enough time to reach the vault before they regroup."

As they navigated the dimly lit corridors, the weight of the mission pressed down on Marcus. "Remember, we can't trigger any alarms. We've trained for this, and we need to stay focused."

Maya hesitated for a moment, her lips pressed into a thin line. "You trust Ghost to keep the guards busy, right?" she asked quietly.

Marcus glanced at her, surprised. "Of course I trust him. Why?"

Maya shrugged, though her expression remained guarded. "Just feels like he's... holding something back. Probably nothing."

Marcus filed the comment away but said nothing as they pressed forward.

Maya nodded, her expression serious. She had studied the vault's design, using her archaeological knowledge to understand its ancient mechanisms. "If I recall correctly, there are puzzles we'll need to solve to access the vault's inner sanctum. It's not just a matter of brute force."

"Let's hope those puzzles are easier to crack than the security systems," Marcus said, forcing a grin. But Maya didn't laugh. Instead, her eyes darted briefly to the corridor behind them, as though expecting someone or something to appear.

"What is it?" Marcus asked, his tone shifting to concern.

"Nothing," Maya replied quickly, shaking her head. "Let's just focus. We can't afford distractions."

As they approached the vault door a massive structure adorned with intricate carvings Maya studied the symbols etched into its surface. "This is it," she breathed, her eyes wide with excitement. "If I'm correct, we'll need to align these symbols in a specific order to unlock it."

Marcus stepped closer, his heart racing. "Can you do it?"

"I've studied these types of puzzles before," Maya said, her fingers tracing the carvings. "But I'll need your help. We have to work quickly before they realize we're here."

They worked in tandem, Maya guiding Marcus as they traced the symbols. With every shift, the door resonated with a low hum, trembling beneath their touch. "Almost there... just a little more," Maya urged, her voice a blend of focus and urgency.

Marcus felt the pressure mounting as the sound of footsteps echoed down the hallway. "We don't have much time!" he said, his pulse quickening. "Hurry!"

Maya's fingers moved with precision, her mind racing to recall the patterns she had studied. "There! The last symbol should be aligned with the others just like that!"

With a final twist, the door creaked open, revealing the dimly lit vault beyond.

"We did it!" Maya exclaimed, relief and triumph flooding her voice.

"Let's move!" Marcus urged, stepping inside.

The vault was filled with artifacts glimmering in the low light, but they had no time to admire the treasures. Their objective lay deeper within.

They moved cautiously, avoiding the laser tripwires that crisscrossed the room. "Stay low," Marcus instructed, instincts kicking in. "We can't trigger any alarms now."

Maya nodded, her heart pounding as they navigated the maze of security measures. She had spent years studying ancient artifacts, and now that knowledge served her well. "Over there," she whispered, pointing toward a console at the back of the vault. "That's where we'll find the main objective."

As they approached, Marcus felt a surge of hope. "We're almost there," he said, his voice barely above a whisper.

But just as they reached the console, the sound of footsteps echoed ominously from the corridor.

"Marcus, we have to hurry!" Maya urged, her voice sharp with urgency.

As Marcus focused on retrieving the data, something caught his eye on the surveillance feed Sofia had looped earlier. In the distant corner of a hallway, just beyond the vault's perimeter, a figure shifted a shadowy silhouette, faint but unmistakably familiar.

"Is that…" Marcus began, narrowing his eyes.

Maya followed his gaze to the monitor, her expression darkening. "That's Ghost," she said, the words barely audible. "What is he doing there?"

Marcus's stomach twisted. Ghost was supposed to be far from this section of the compound, keeping the guards distracted. "Stay focused," he muttered, more to himself than to Maya. "We'll deal with it later."

"I'm on it," he said, his fingers flying over the console as he accessed the information they had come for. The clock was ticking, and they needed to act fast.

Just as Marcus retrieved the data they needed, the alarms blared to life, piercing through the tension like a knife. "They found us!" he shouted, scrambling to grab the artifact they had come for.

Maya winced, covering her ears as the sound reverberated through the vault. "How? Ghost said he'd neutralized the guards!"

Marcus's mind raced. Had Ghost's distraction failed or had it been intentional? The seed of doubt planted earlier now took root, but there was no time to dwell on it. "We have to move!"

Maya's heart pounded as they turned to flee. "We need to get back to Ghost now!"

With alarms blaring and footsteps echoing closer, they raced toward the exit, adrenaline surging through their veins. The heist had turned into a desperate race against time, and they could feel the walls closing in.

"Let's go!" Marcus shouted, leading the way down the corridor. His mind churned with questions he couldn't afford to ask: Had Ghost betrayed them? Was this part of Valeria's trap?

Maya kept pace beside him, her expression a mix of fear and fury. "If Ghost set us up…" she began, but Marcus cut her off.

"Not now," he snapped, his jaw tight. "We'll figure it out later. Right now, we focus on getting out alive."

Heavy with anticipation, the air hung motionless as Marcus and Maya confronted the ancient vault, their hearts pounding in rhythm with the distant wail of alarms. The faint glow of the emergency access panel cast ghostly shadows over the intricate carvings adorning the massive door. With a final, tense click, the great door groaned open, unveiling the darkness within.

"Ready?" Marcus asked, his voice little more than a whisper above the din of the alarms.

Maya nodded, her eyes aglow with determination. "Let's see what secrets lie within."

They stepped across the threshold and suddenly, an overwhelming silence swallowed the vault. Dim light illuminated the chamber, revealing rows of glittering artifacts and countless treasures from civilizations long forgotten. It was knowledge beyond belief and value but before them stood certain objects not of treasure, but of ancient security systems.

The walls of the vault were lined with intricate mechanisms and levers that gleamed with an otherworldly light. Some devices pulsed with energy; strange symbols seemed to shift and alter across their surfaces before their very eyes.

"What in the hell is this?" Marcus breathed, stepping closer to inspect one of the devices. "It's... uncanny like a total fusion of magic and advanced technology."

"Exactly," Maya said, eyes wide with awe. "These systems are protecting something truly valuable. We'll have to tread carefully. The wrong move, and we might trigger a defense protocol."

With every step deeper into the vault, an ancient power pressed heavily against their chests. Here, magic intertwined seamlessly with technology, its subtle hum resonating beneath their feet.

Maya reached out to touch one of the glowing symbols, and a sudden surge of energy coursed through her fingertips.

"Do you feel that?" she whispered.

"Yeah," Marcus replied, his brow furrowing. "It's almost like it's alive."

In the center of the vault stood a large pedestal, and resting upon it was a crystal orb that shimmered in every hue imaginable. It was breathtaking a beacon of light that drew them in.

"This must be it," Maya breathed, wonder filling her voice. "The true repository of this civilization's wealth. But what is it? What does it hold?"

Marcus stepped closer, his heart thudding in his chest. "Let's find out."

Energy snapped through the air as holographic images sprang to life around the orb flickering scenes of a vibrant world brimming with advanced technologies and awe inspiring vistas. They caught glimpses of people in motion, harnessing unseen energies and crafting marvels that defied imagination.

"This... this is incredible," Maya whispered, transfixed by the images. "It's a record of their history their achievements. Just look!"

But the deeper they gazed into the orb, the more the visions changed darkened. Scenes of destruction, conflict, and the misuse of power unfolded before their eyes. A cold shiver ran down Marcus's spine.

"Every civilization has its secrets," Marcus said, his voice heavy with realization. "And its consequences."

Lower down in the shifting images, the orb began to reveal its true nature an explanation unfolding before them of what it really was: the core of a civilization that, over time, had accumulated immense knowledge and power.

"You think that could help us?" Maya asked, raising an eyebrow skeptically.

"If we harness this knowledge, it might change everything."

"Or," Marcus countered, a grim note creeping into his tone, "it could blow us apart. Power like that... it corrupts."

In an instant, the atmosphere shifted the weight of a formidable presence settling over the chamber. The ground trembled faintly as a figure emerged from the shadows, cloaked in flowing robes, her features obscured.

"Foolish mortals," she intoned, her voice echoing through the space. "Do you truly dare to trespass knowingly into this sacred precinct?"

Marcus and Maya turned toward the newcomer, their hearts pounding. The figure stepped into the light revealing the Elder Va, ancient in power, her eyes glowing with the light of other worlds and heavy with authority.

"It is I who shall decide upon the fate of this knowledge," she declared, her voice carrying a resonance that seemed to shake the vaulted walls.

"Elder Va," Marcus said, forcing steadiness into his voice. "We came to understand the secrets of this civilization to learn from its past."

The Elder raised her hand, and the air around her shimmered, unveiling her true form: a majestic being, part human, part ethereal light, her essence swirling like a star strewn tapestry. The sight was both wondrous and terrifying, filling Marcus with awe and dread.

"You seek knowledge," she intoned, her voice reverberating through the chamber, "but knowledge without wisdom invites destruction."

"You don't understand what it means to carry that kind of burden," Maya said, stepping forward, her voice gaining strength. "We know the risks but we also know the potential for good. This knowledge could save lives and prevent further conflict!"

For a fleeting moment, Elder Va's expression softened but then it hardened again, etched with millennia of judgment. "You speak of noble intentions. History has seen that before. Yet this civilization fell not because of knowledge, but because of greed and lust for power. You think you are any different?"

A surge of defiance welled up in Marcus. "We're not like them. We want to learn from their mistakes, not repeat them."

"Do you?" Elder Va challenged, her gaze piercing. "How can you be so certain you are not racing down the same path to the same fate? Power is a seductive mistress it blinds those who seek it."

The tension mounted, the crystalline orb pulsing brighter and brighter between them.

"This portal," Elder Va said, gesturing toward the orb, "was devised to contain the power of this civilization. It serves as both a gateway and a prison for that knowledge allowing it to be accessed, yet safeguarding it from misuse."

Maya stepped closer, her eyes blazing with curiosity. "It's not merely a repository it's a key. A way to understand how to use that power responsibly."

Elder Va nodded slightly, approval flickering across her face. "Correct. Yet the path is perilous. To harness its power, your own intentions must be confronted first. Are you prepared to face the truth behind your desires?"

"What does that mean?" Marcus asked, his voice steady but uncertain.

"Power reveals the shallowness or depth of one's character," Elder Va said in her low, commanding tone. "Those who seek it often do so out of fear or desperation. It is a choice whether to wield it for the greater good or become enslaved by the desires it feeds."

Her words hung heavy in the air. Elder Va met Marcus's eyes, the weight of ages reflected in her own.

"We want to be better," Marcus said quietly. "To use this knowledge to help people to avoid the same mistakes that destroyed those before us."

Elder Va's stern features softened slightly, and for the first time, Marcus felt a glimmer of hope.

"Then prove it," she said. "Show me you are capable of rising above the temptation of power. Only then will you be worthy of the knowledge within this vault."

The words lingered like a sacred command as Marcus and Maya stood at the precipice of destiny. They faced not only the secrets of the past but the truths within themselves. Whatever awaited them next, they were resolved to forge a new history one defined by understanding, accountability, and the courage to change.

Suddenly, chaos erupted. The heavy doors behind them burst open as guards stormed into the vault. Maya turned sharply, the alarms screaming once more, drowning out thought. Fueled by adrenaline, she reached for her weapons the shield that concealed their hard won secret.

The first guard charged in, his eyes wide in awe at the treasures around him. In an instant, Maya moved dodging his lunge and countering with a swift kick to his chest that sent him sprawling backward.

"Focus!" she shouted at Marcus, who was still locked in a silent standoff with Elder Va.

"Just a minute!" he yelled back, eyes fixed on a new figure emerging from the darkness Aurelia, a towering presence that seemed to embody order itself, stepping into the light like the manifestation of divine judgment.

The sound of approaching guards lifted Maya's head heavy footsteps thundered and boomed, carrying ominous echoes through the vault. "We need to hold them off!" she shouted, urgency sharpening her tone.

Marcus slowly turned toward Aurelia, the silence between them almost a living thing. "You're not going to try to stop us, are you?" he said, determination etched in every line of his face.

Aurelia sneered, her eyes alight with a gleam of mirth and disdain. "You think you can simply walk out with the secrets of this civilization? You have no idea what awaits you."

With a sudden leap, Marcus dodged to the side, narrowly avoiding her strike. "We'll see about that," he replied, bursting forward with a flurry of blows.

They clashed in fierce combat a dance of strength and precision. Aurelia moved like liquid shadow, her agility allowing her to flow around Marcus's attacks with uncanny grace. Yet he matched her step for step, driven by urgency and defiance.

Meanwhile, the ancient security systems around them began to stutter and spark, lights flashing erratically.

"What's happening?!" Maya shouted, glancing at the heads up display as streaks of blue flame burst from the control systems. "It's overloading!"

"Ghost, what's going on?" Marcus yelled into the comms, parrying one of Aurelia's strikes with a grunt.

Static crackled over the line before Ghost's strained voice broke through. "I… I'm trying to stabilize the defenses, but something's interfering with the system. It's not responding like it should!"

Marcus's jaw tightened, instincts flaring. "What do you mean, 'interfering'? You're supposed to have control!"

"I know!" Ghost snapped back but there was a pause, a beat too long. "Just hold on. I'll get it under control."

Maya's eyes darted to Marcus, worry flashing across her face. "Do you think Ghost…" she started, but Marcus cut her off, shaking his head as if to banish the thought.

"Focus on the mission," he said, though doubt gnawed at the back of his mind.

"I don't know!" Ghost's voice came again, rising in panic. "The power levels are fluctuating and the defenses are turning on!"

A wave of dread swept over Maya. "We can't afford to lose control now! We have to finish our objectives before everything goes haywire!"

No sooner had she spoken than the walls came alive with radiant light. Ancient runes flickered to life, glowing with pulsating energy.

The air filled with electric static, and Maya felt a chill run down her spine. "What is it?" she breathed, watching the walls shift and reveal hidden mechanisms.

"Ancient defenses," Marcus grunted, blocking a heavy strike from Aurelia. "This place was built to protect its secrets!"

Before Maya could respond, the floor rumbled violently. Massive stone golems rose from the depths, their eyes glowing with otherworldly fire.

"We've got to work together!" Maya shouted, raising her weapon as the creatures lumbered toward them.

"Ghost, take them down!" Marcus barked, dodging another swing from Aurelia.

"I'm trying!" Ghost panted. "But I need more time they're drawing power directly from the vault!"

"Focus on the golems! We'll handle Aurelia!" Maya commanded, her tone sharp and unwavering. But as she glanced at the flickering lights along the vault's systems, her brow furrowed. "Wait... why would the defenses activate *now*? Ghost said he had everything under control."

Marcus didn't answer right away, his attention torn between Aurelia's relentless attacks and the chaos around them. "Maybe it's an automated response," he muttered, though unease crept into his voice.

"Or maybe someone didn't do his job," Maya shot back, her tone low but pointed. "He's been off comms longer than usual."

Marcus's grip tightened on his weapon. "We don't have time for this. Stay on task." Yet the thought lingered was Ghost stalling, or was something else interfering?

With a swift nod, Marcus lunged toward one of the golems, evading the crushing sweep of its stone arm.

"Maya, cover me!" he shouted.

Maya unleashed a volley of shots at the nearest golem; the bullets pinged off its rocky hide in a metallic chorus. "Aim for the joints!" she yelled, her heart hammering as the giant swung again.

As the fight raged, the group moved with desperate precision. Marcus and Maya fought in tandem, their rhythm fluid dodging, striking, and weaving through the chaos like a single force.

Amid the carnage, Marcus's focus cut through the haze. His eyes locked onto the main console flickering with streams of vital data. "Secure the primary objectives!" he shouted, his voice slicing through the din. "The technology and intel are right there!"

"On it!" Maya called back, sprinting toward the console. Her fingers flew across the controls as she initiated the data transfer. "This is our chance! We need to grab everything we can because after this, it might be too late!"

"Just a few more seconds!" Marcus yelled, struggling to fend off Aurelia as he monitored Maya's progress. Golems surged closer, forcing him into a frenzied defense.

"We can't let them overwhelm us!" he shouted.

While the console completed the download, Maya moved quickly, gathering fragments of ancient technology scattered across the vault. She scooped up several glowing devices, their surfaces humming faintly. "I've got the tech! Now let's get out of here!"

Marcus turned, panting, as guards closed in and the golems loomed nearer. "Go!" he roared, his voice raw.

With a powerful swing, he disarmed Aurelia, sending her blade clattering across the floor.

"You may have the upper hand now, but this is far from over!" Aurelia spat, her eyes flashing with fury.

Within minutes, Maya was scooping up samples of the treasures surrounding them artifacts, crystals, and relics that had lain undisturbed for centuries. "I got everything! Let's roll!" she shouted, her heart pounding as she prepared for departure.

From the console came an insistent beep: *complete.*

"Got it!" Maya exclaimed in relief, pulling out the chip.

"We have everything we came for!" Marcus yelled, his voice commanding as he led the charge toward the exit. But as the team moved, his comm crackled to life again.

"Marcus," Ghost's voice came through quieter this time, almost too calm. "There might be a problem at the extraction point."

Marcus skidded to a halt, his blood running cold. "What kind of problem?"

Ghost hesitated. "The reinforcements they're closer than I thought. I'm trying to redirect, but..." Another pause. "You might have to find another way out."

Maya's lips pressed into a thin line. "Another way out? Ghost, you said you'd secure the perimeter!"

"I'm doing what I can!" Ghost snapped, but there was something in his tone that made Marcus exchange a wary glance with Maya. "Just keep moving," Ghost added, his voice dissolving into static.

Marcus's jaw clenched. "We're on our own," he muttered, a flicker of doubt threading his voice for the first time.

"Wait! The seed technology!" Maya exclaimed, eyes wide with realization. "We can't leave without it!"

"Go!" Marcus shouted, covering her as she sprinted into the adjacent chamber. Inside, the seed technology pulsed with life colorful pods of energy glowing in rhythmic waves. She gathered as many as she could, realizing their potential as the key to everything that came next.

"Let's go, let's go!" Marcus urged, his voice taut with urgency as he fought off the remaining guards. With the seed technology secured and the data downloaded, they ran for the door, the weight of their mission pressing down on their shoulders. The vault shook violently, its ancient defenses still active, while the sounds of battle reverberated through the halls.

As they neared the exit, Maya's breath caught. "Wait," she whispered, eyes narrowing. "Why are there no guards here?"

Marcus slowed, instincts flaring. The corridor ahead lay eerily silent, broken only by the faint, distant wail of alarms.

"It's... too easy," he muttered, scanning the passage.

"Ghost said reinforcements were at the east wall," Maya said, her voice tightening. "But if they're not here... where are they?"

Marcus's comm buzzed again. Ghost's voice crackled through. "What's the holdup? Get to the portal!"

"Why are there no guards, Ghost?" Marcus demanded, his tone sharp and suspicious.

Ghost hesitated. "I don't know. Maybe they were redirected?" But the uncertainty in his voice was unmistakable. Maya met Marcus's gaze, her suspicion plain.

"We don't have time to question it," Marcus said quickly, though a cold knot of doubt coiled in his chest.

Suddenly, as they burst through the final door, the realization hit they weren't escaping to victory. What awaited beyond was the brutal aftermath of everything they had unleashed.

The chaos of the outside world crashed over Marcus and Maya as they emerged through the vault door, its weight slamming open with a thunderous clang. Alarms blared relentlessly, their echoes twisting through the narrow corridors. They clutched their prize critical data, ancient technology, and the luminous seed pods but their hard won success teetered on the edge of collapse.

"We have to go, now!" Marcus shouted, voice cutting through the din as he gripped his weapon and scanned their surroundings. Maya followed close behind, the burden of the recovered artifacts pressing against her back. Every step felt like a countdown behind them, the guards' shouts grew louder.

"Where to?" Maya asked, breath ragged as she cast one last glance at the vault, the shadows looming in its doorway.

"There's a service exit around the corner," Marcus said, forcing calm into his voice though his pulse hammered. "If we can reach it, we can rally with the others."

Their footsteps echoed down the narrow hall, mingling with the pounding of boots behind them. "They're right behind us!" Maya gasped, lungs burning.

"Go on!" Marcus barked, breaking into a full sprint. The guards' pursuit grew closer, their shouts and gunfire bouncing off the walls.

Bullets screamed through the air, ricocheting off stone with deadly precision. "This way!" Marcus shouted, veering sharply toward the service exit.

As he rounded the corner, he flicked his comm back on. "Sofia! Ghost! Do you copy? We're closing in on the service exit!"

"Copy that, Marcus!" Sofia's voice came through, strained and breathless. "We're holding the perimeter but hurry! Reinforcements are flooding in on the east wall!"

"We're moving!" Maya shouted, urgency thrumming through her voice as she ran. Every second felt like the difference between survival and disaster.

They reached the service exit Marcus heaved the door open to reveal a dark alley beyond. "Go! We have to regroup with the others!"

"Where's the portal?" Maya asked, scanning the shadows, nerves wound tight.

"Just ahead," Marcus said, pointing toward a small clearing where the faint shimmer of the portal glowed among the ruins. "We need to activate it before they catch up."

They surged forward, their breathing ragged as they reached the activation panel. Softly glowing inscriptions came to life under Marcus's fingers as he pressed his palm to the interface. A surge of energy rippled outward ancient, raw, and powerful awakening the long dormant gateway.

"Come on, come on," Marcus muttered, his fingers flying across the controls. The panel responded with a series of slow, agonizing beeps, barely audible over the rising noise of pursuit.

"Marcus, hurry up! They're right behind us!" Maya's voice quivered as she glanced back. The guards' shadows loomed larger, their shouts growing louder and more insistent.

"I'm trying!" Marcus yelled, heart pounding with every keystroke as he entered the final sequence. The portal flickered uncertainly, energy rippling across its frame as it fought to stabilize.

With a final surge one keystone command the gateway burst to life. A bright blue vortex spiraled open, pulses of raw energy flashing outward and flooding the alley with light.

"It's ready!" Marcus shouted, relief breaking through his voice.

But just as they prepared to leap through, the comm crackled to life once more.

"Marcus," Ghost's voice came through quieter this time, almost hesitant. "Are you sure you have everything? Did you check the side chamber?"

Marcus froze, his eyes narrowing. "What side chamber?"

"The one to the left of the vault," Ghost replied, his tone deceptively casual. "You might've missed something important."

Maya grabbed Marcus's arm, eyes blazing. "Don't listen to him he's stalling us!"

Marcus hesitated for a fraction of a second, his mind racing. Was Ghost trying to help or leading them into a trap? The guards' voices grew louder, their boots striking the stone like war drums.

"No time," Marcus said, his decision snapping into place. "We move now!"

Maya seized his arm and pulled him toward the portal. Heavy footsteps thundered behind them as they sprinted for the shimmering gateway, the heat of pursuit closing fast.

They leapt through just as the portal began to collapse, its light folding in on itself with a thunderous crack.

Behind them, the chaos of the vault vanished into silence.

For an instant, weightlessness consumed them then the world reshaped itself. Their eyes met mid flight, breath caught between fear and exhilaration. They had escaped with their prize, seizing a fragile freedom in the storm's wake.

But as the light faded and the new horizon stretched before them, both knew the truth that hung unspoken between them the real battle was only just beginning.

## Chapter 18: Seeds of Destruction

As Marcus and Maya emerged on the other side, they found themselves standing in a vast chamber thick with the scent of damp earth and aged wood ancient and breathing with forgotten life. Bright green vines clung to the walls, their phosphorescent leaves glowing faintly, casting shifting patterns of light that danced across the rough stone.

A deep rumble filled the air, reverberating beneath their feet.

"What was that?" Maya asked, heart pounding as her gaze darted across the chamber, searching for the source of the sound.

"I don't know," Marcus replied, his brow furrowed in concern. "But it doesn't sound good."

Before he could say more, a faint beeping rose from Maya's pocket a shrill, insistent alarm. She froze, pulling out the small device with trembling fingers. "It's the seed technology!" she gasped. "I must've activated it while we were escaping!"

The gadget pulsed erratically, its luminous interface flickering between vibrant green and an ominous, shadowed hue. Marcus felt the air shift around them a tangible pressure, as though the chamber itself was responding to the device's unstable energy.

Before Maya could react, a blinding flash of light exploded from the device, flooding the chamber in a harsh, unnatural glow. The green vines along the walls pulsed violently, their light surging in waves, as if something deep within the earth stirred in answer.

Marcus felt the hairs rise on his arms. "Maya, stop it! Shut it off!" he shouted, his voice muffled by the strange, resonant hum that filled the chamber.

The vines continued to pulse, their glow intensifying until the entire room throbbed with raw energy.

"Maya, what have you done?" Marcus cried, terror edging his voice.

"I didn't mean to! I just " she began, but her words were swallowed as the energy surged outward in a violent wave. The ground buckled beneath them, and the walls groaned with a deep, guttural sound that rattled the chamber.

The hum grew louder, a low, resonant drone that swelled into a roar. The air itself vibrated with power, each tremor stronger than the last. "We need to get out of here!" Marcus shouted, voice straining over the chaos. A sense of dread clawed at his chest an instinctive warning that something far worse was waking.

The ground suddenly split open before them, tearing into a widening fissure.

"Run!" Marcus yelled, seizing Maya's arm and pulling her back as the chasm expanded, swallowing chunks of the floor.

The rumbling deepened, and metal supports groaned under the strain. "The structure is failing!" Maya shouted, fear tightening her voice. "It's going to collapse!"

Energy coursed wildly through the vines, which writhed and snapped like living things serpentine and furious, lashing out as though caught in the throes of a storm. The chamber shuddered around them, and Marcus heard a low, ancient sound rising from beneath the earth something vast and old, stirring from its slumber.

"This isn't just a reaction," Maya whispered, her voice trembling. "It's *waking something up*."

"Maya, we have to get out of here!" Marcus pleaded, scanning the shifting walls for an escape. "If this place goes down, we're finished!"

"I saw a corridor on the other side!" she shouted, pointing toward a narrow passage half concealed by the vines. "This way!"

They ran, the floor trembling violently beneath them. The walls cracked and splintered, debris crashing down inches from their heads as they dove into the passage, shielding themselves from the falling stone.

Inside, the corridor was thick with dust each breath heavy, choking, as though the air itself had turned to ash. Shrill alarms wailed through the darkness, but beneath the clamor, Marcus heard something else: a faint, rhythmic vibration, almost like a pulse, echoing from deep within the earth.

"We're not out of danger yet!" Marcus shouted, his voice hoarse. "Keep moving!"

As they pressed forward, the walls seemed to constrict, the corridor narrowing with every step. Behind them, the roar of collapsing stone grew louder, chasing them like a living force.

"Maya, contact Ghost and Sofia!" Marcus called, fumbling for his comm. "We need to regroup find the portal before it's too late!"

"Ghost! Sofia! Do you copy?" Maya shouted into her device, desperation breaking through her voice.

"Copy!" Sofia's voice answered, crackling through the static, filled with urgency. "We're on the move! Heavy resistance, but we're closing in on your location!"

"Good! We'll meet at the portal!" Marcus replied, adrenaline coursing through his veins.

The corridor twisted and turned, drawing them deeper into the heart of the facility. The air grew warmer, the pulsing vibration intensifying. It wasn't just mechanical it *felt alive.*

Behind them, the sounds of pursuit grew louder: guards shouting, weapons clattering, the chaos of battle following close. Yet beneath it all, Marcus sensed something else moving a deeper, unseen presence, vast and awakening.

"Here they come!" Maya yelled, glancing back to see armed guards storming down the corridor.

"Make our stand!" Marcus shouted, stopping abruptly and raising his weapon.

They ducked behind a row of rusted machinery, breath ragged, hearts pounding in sync.

"Maya, cover me!" Marcus yelled, firing a burst toward the advancing guards.

"I've got your back!" Maya called, steadying her aim and letting off a precise volley. Bullets sparked and ricocheted across the narrow space, forcing the guards to scatter for cover.

Amid the chaos, Marcus's eyes caught a glint of silver a rifle resting atop a nearby crate, its sleek surface glowing faintly with alien light.

"Mine!" he shouted, lunging toward it without hesitation.

Behind him, Maya unleashed another wave of suppressive fire, keeping the enemy pinned and buying him precious seconds.

With the new weapon in his hands, Marcus felt a surge of renewed confidence. He powered up its targeting system; the rifle whirred to life, locking onto the nearest threat.

"This should give us an edge," he said, firing a precise burst toward the oncoming guards.

"Nice upgrade!" Maya shouted back, her voice brimming with adrenaline as they fought side by side.

Marcus could feel the tide turning the press of their attackers slowly weakening under their assault. Every second gained was hard won.

"We've got to get to the exit!" he yelled, glancing down the corridor. "Sofia and Ghost are waiting for us!"

"Let's move!" Maya replied, taking point as they pushed forward, weaving through the chaos. The sounds of gunfire and shouted orders echoed behind them, but neither dared to look back.

They had to reach the portal before time slipped away.

"Maya, left flank!" Marcus warned as another guard emerged from a side corridor.

Without missing a beat, Maya pivoted, raising her rifle. "Got him!" she called, dropping the soldier in one fluid motion.

Still sprinting, Marcus activated his comms. "Sofia! Ghost! We're nearly there. Can you meet us at the portal?"

"Just a few moments out!" Ghost's voice replied calm, steady, a strange calm amidst the storm. "We've created an opening, but it's getting crazy out here. Keep sharp!"

They pushed through the remaining resistance, moving like a single, synchronized force. Each knew the other's rhythm; every movement flowed seamlessly precision forged in fire.

But the deeper they went, the heavier the opposition became. Guards flooded the corridors, their faces hardened with grim resolve.

"They're everywhere!" Maya shouted, ducking behind a pillar as bullets tore through the air.

"We need to split up!" Marcus yelled, mind racing. "If we divide them, we can draw fire away and meet at the portal!"

"Are you crazy?" Maya cried, eyes wide with alarm. "We can't separate now!"

"It's the only way! Trust me!" Marcus shouted back, his voice burning with conviction. "I'll draw them off you get to the portal!"

Maya hesitated, then nodded reluctantly. "Be careful!"

Overwhelmed by the urgency of what had to be done, Marcus felt the full weight of his choice sink in as he turned away from Maya's side. Charging down a side hall, he fired over his shoulder to draw the guards' attention. "This way! Over here!" he shouted, his footsteps pounding through the echoing maze of corridors.

The ploy worked gunfire erupted behind him as the enemy shifted their pursuit toward his position.

Meanwhile, Maya sprinted toward the portal chamber, her heart racing as she tore down the twisting passageways. The sounds of battle rang behind her, but she refused to glance back. They had come too far to fail now.

Finally, she saw it far down the hall, a shimmer of light glinting like an otherworldly beacon. The portal.

But as she neared it, the ground beneath her began to quake, trembling in rhythm with the pulsing energy that coursed through the facility. A faint green glow traced across the walls like veins, carrying some malignant power deep within the structure.

"I'm almost there!" she shouted into her comm, her voice tight with urgency and unease.

But before she could reach the portal, the floor heaved again, the rumbling louder this time, the walls shuddering under the strain.

"Marcus, hurry!" she cried, as chaos erupted behind her.

A fierce determination took hold of her. It was a race against time, and nothing would stop her from reaching the portal. Summoning every last ounce of strength, she surged forward plunging through the gateway into the unknown.

Zara stood at the entrance to the portal chamber, her ears ringing from the relentless cacophony of the collapsing vault. The earth shook beneath her feet, a constant reminder that time was running out. Gunfire echoed down the corridors; shouts of guards filled the air. With every passing second, the weight of her choice grew heavier.

Her heart hammered in her chest as she took in the chaos. Marcus and Maya were already at the portal, their faces set with grim resolve. But a cold knot of instinct tightened in Zara's gut a primal warning that their fight was far from over. The guards would not relent.

"Zara, move!" Marcus shouted. His voice cut through the roar of combat, lined with urgency and fear. He fired in rapid bursts toward the advancing guards.

"I know!" she yelled back, but her legs felt rooted to the ground. This was the moment where a single decision could change everything.

The realization hit her like a wave: someone would have to stay behind, to hold off the pursuers long enough for the others to escape. They had fought too long and sacrificed too much for it to end here.

Zara took a deep breath, steeling herself, and turned toward Marcus. Their eyes met, a silent understanding passing between them.

"Marcus, I "

"Don't say it," he interrupted, his voice low but firm amid the chaos. "We can't afford to lose anyone else. We'll make it out together."

"Listen to me," she said, her voice trembling yet strong. "If I don't hold them off, none of you will make it. You have to get Maya through that portal. I can do this I *have* to."

"Zara…" Marcus's voice faltered. For a moment, the fire of battle faded from his eyes, replaced by something softer fear and admiration mingled in equal measure. He stepped closer, the weight of everything unsaid between them heavy in the air. "You're not just a teammate you're my friend. I can't let you go."

"I'm not asking," she said, her jaw set with quiet resolve. "I'm telling you what needs to happen. Promise me you'll get them to safety."

Marcus hesitated only a moment, then stepped back, his heart breaking with the truth of her words. "I promise," he said, a tear tracing down his dirt streaked face. "But you'd better come back to us."

Zara forced a small, bittersweet smile. "I will. Now go."

As Marcus turned to lead Maya toward the portal, Zara took a deep, steadying breath. Adrenaline surged through her veins as she gripped her weapon and faced the oncoming tide of guards.

The roar of gunfire filled the chamber again but this time, she stood her ground.

The realization of what she was about to do weighed heavily on Zara's shoulders, but she couldn't afford to falter. With a fierce battle cry, she stepped between the portal and the oncoming guards.

"This is where you stop!" she shouted, raising her weapon and firing on the advancing attackers.

A sharp hiss filled the air as bullets struck their marks. For a fleeting moment, satisfaction flared in her chest as the guards stumbled back but they didn't relent. More poured in, faces hardened with unshakable resolve. Zara fought with every ounce of strength she had left, weaving through the cramped chamber, dodging and striking, felling one opponent after another.

Amid the chaos, the weight of sacrifice rose inside her a tide she could no longer hold back. At last, she let herself feel it fully, the crushing truth of what she was giving up.

Every second she held them back bought Marcus and Maya precious time. Behind her, the portal's hum built toward ignition, glowing brighter as the ancient system came alive.

"Come on! We need to go!" Marcus shouted, his voice breaking through the chaos.

"Just a little longer!" she yelled, firing again as another wave of guards rushed in.

Gunfire, shouting, and the rising hum of the portal blended into a single, deafening symphony. Zara's muscles screamed, her lungs burned, and her arms trembled under the strain but still she fought. The guards pressed closer, their numbers overwhelming, yet she refused to yield.

"You will not take them!" she screamed in defiance, her breath ragged but her spirit unbroken.

The click of her empty weapon echoed like a death knell. Her last shot had been fired. Panic clawed at her chest, but she shoved it down. She had no choice she *would* hold the line.

"Go, now!" she shouted, her voice echoing across the chamber.

"To safety!"

"Zara!" Marcus called, desperation in his voice.

She shook her head, eyes blazing. "Just go!" she yelled again, louder this time. "You've got to make it back to Earth!"

With one last burst of defiant fire, she bought them the seconds they needed. The portal flared to full power as Marcus and Maya disappeared into its shimmering depths. Time slowed; her surroundings seemed to blur, colors bleeding together as the energy rippled through the air.

Zara turned sharply, steel in her gaze, bracing herself for the storm that was coming. Her heart hammered in her chest but she stood firm.

Meanwhile, Marcus and Maya crossed the threshold, the portal's energy crackling around them like a living storm. Electric pulses coiled through the air, casting the world in a kaleidoscope of shifting light and color.

"Turn it on!" Marcus shouted, his voice raw with urgency as he scrambled toward the controls.

Maya joined him, her fingers flying across the interface. "This is more complicated than I thought just give me a second!"

"Hurry!" Marcus yelled back toward the chamber, the echoes of battle still reverberating behind them. The last sound he wanted to hear was Zara's voice, still fighting, still defying.

The portal's mechanisms roared to life. A pulse of power surged outward, shaking the floor beneath them.

"It's working!" Maya cried, her tone fierce with focus. "But we need to move *now!*"

"You go first!" Marcus insisted, pushing her toward the portal. "I'll follow you!"

Maya hesitated, eyes glinting with fear. "What about Zara?"

"She's got this! We have to get to Earth!" Marcus shouted, his throat tightening around the words.

With a firm nod, Maya stepped into the portal, her body vanishing into the swirling vortex of light. Marcus watched as she disappeared, the colors flaring wildly in her wake.

Just as he turned to follow, a squad of guards burst into the chamber, weapons raised.

"Stop them!" one shouted.

Marcus spun and fired, cutting them down with ruthless precision. "Come on, come on!" he urged himself, squeezing off another volley as he backed toward the portal.

But the gateway flickered the energy around it destabilizing. Its edges shimmered, sputtering under the strain.

"Hurry, Marcus! The portal's unstable!" Maya's voice crackled through the comm, sharp with fear. "You need to get through *now!*"

"I'm coming!" he yelled, firing again, clearing his path. The light of the portal pulsed erratically, threatening to collapse at any moment.

"Go! Get through!" Maya cried.

With a final surge of strength, Marcus sprinted forward. Bullets sliced through the air as he dove headlong into the portal's shimmering light. Energy enveloped him searing, twisting, pulling him through a maelstrom of color and shadow.

Then, with a jarring thud, he landed hard on solid ground.

Gasping, Marcus pushed himself up. The world was dim, veiled in half light but through the haze, he saw Maya standing ahead, her face drawn tight with worry, eyes fixed on him.

"Where's Zara?" she asked, voice trembling.

"I " he began, but before he could finish, the portal behind him flared violently and imploded with a deafening roar.

A wave of energy crashed over them, hurling both to the ground. The shockwave tore through the air, scattering dust and debris like a storm.

Marcus staggered to his feet, his heart pounding in horror. "No! Zara!" he cried.

The dust settled slowly, drifting through the charged air like falling ash. The space where the portal had stood shimmered faintly, still humming with residual energy a ghostly echo of the power that had torn through it.

Silence descended, thick and heavy. Beneath their feet, the earth pulsed faintly, its rhythm uneven and strange as though the seed technology had rooted something deep within the planet.

Something ancient.

Something now awake.

They stood in stillness, eyes fixed on the space where the portal had once blazed a threshold now swallowed by shadow, a void where brilliance had been. Darkness pressed in, not only around them but within, as if what had passed through that gate had left more than memory in its wake.

"She didn't make it," Maya whispered.

A wave of sorrow crashed over Marcus, the truth sinking in like a blade. "She sacrificed herself for us," he said, his voice trembling with grief.

"We should have stopped her!" Maya cried, tears streaming down her face. "We should have done something!"

"There was nothing we could do," Marcus said quietly, his voice breaking as tears welled in his eyes. "Zara knew what she was doing. She was our shield."

They stood there in silence, consumed by the weight of loss. Their escape should have been victory, but there was no room for celebration only the hollow ache of absence. They had returned to safety, but at what cost?

"We need to regroup," Marcus said at last, his breath uneven. But even as the words left his mouth, he felt it again the faint vibration beneath the ground, subtle yet insistent. A reminder that their battle wasn't truly over.

"We have to make sure her sacrifice isn't in vain," Maya replied, her voice steadier now, though her eyes flicked nervously toward the faint green glow pulsing on the horizon.

"Agreed," she said again, wiping her tears away, her expression hardening with resolve. "We need to prepare for our return to Earth. We can't lose sight of the mission."

It wasn't until they began to take stock of their surroundings that they noticed it the land around them was unstable, the ground shifting in slow, deliberate movements beneath their feet.

"Something's wrong," Marcus murmured, his tone low and grim. The tremor wasn't random. It was rhythmic, almost alive. His eyes narrowed as he scanned the distance, where faint green tendrils twisted through the air like spectral storms.

"We're not safe here," he said.

Maya nodded, her face set with grim determination. "We need to find shelter and then figure out what comes next. Zara's sacrifice can't be for nothing."

As they pressed onward through the alien terrain, the fire within Marcus grew stronger. They would find a way back to Earth. They would complete their mission for her.

"We're going to return home," he said firmly, the words heavy with conviction. But even as he spoke, his gaze drifted toward the horizon. The faint green glow flickered like a heartbeat steady, unrelenting.

"For Zara," he whispered, eyes locked on the strange light. "We have to see this through to the end. Whatever we've unleashed... we'll face it."

And so, with sorrow as their burden and resolve as their guide, Marcus and Maya moved forward into the unknown. They would return to Earth but they would carry with them the weight of loss, and the unyielding memory of the one who had given everything so they could live.

## Chapter 19: Back to Earth

The world spun violently around Marcus and Maya as they emerged from the portal a kaleidoscope of color and sound unraveling into the muted greys of their new surroundings. The disorienting rush gave way to a jarring stillness. With unsteady steps, they stumbled forward and collapsed onto the cool earth.

Breathless, hands pressed to the ground, they sought anchorage in the silence something solid after the chaos they had torn through.

"Is anyone alright?" Marcus panted, propping himself up on his elbows as he looked around. The air was thick with tension, yet a strange sense of release began to wash over him.

"Yeah, I think so," Maya replied, her voice trembling as she scanned the area. The familiar landscape of their home base stood in stark contrast to the madness they had just escaped.

For a few long moments, they sat in silence, trying to steady their breaths. Then the realization began to dawn they had survived.

"We made it," Marcus whispered, a grin spreading across his face.

"We actually made it!" Maya exclaimed, her eyes shining with disbelief and relief.

Moments later, the sound of footsteps echoed around them. The others rushed forward faces that had been tight with fear now breaking into cries of joy.

"You're back!" Sofia cried, throwing her arms around Marcus in a fierce embrace. "We were so scared."

"We really thought you wouldn't make it," Ghost added, emotion thick in his voice.

Marcus turned toward Maya, who was laughing through her tears a fragile, trembling sound that pierced the quiet like sunlight through storm clouds. For a fleeting moment, the team fell into one another's arms, united by relief and sorrow alike.

"We made it," Marcus repeated softly, but the words wavered on his tongue, brittle with grief. His eyes drifted to the space where the portal had been now only stillness, and the echo of what had been lost. Zara's absence hung over them like smoke: heavy, unspoken, unbearable.

But the mission's weight pressed harder still.

"We need to focus," Marcus said, forcing his voice steady. "The seed technology's fallout could already be affecting the environment. We have to find out what we're dealing with."

As adrenaline ebbed, exhaustion and pain took hold. Marcus felt the ache in his muscles, the burn of bruises forming beneath his skin. He looked around, checking on the others. "Everyone okay? Any injuries?"

"Just a few scrapes," Maya said, tugging at her sleeve to reveal thin cuts and swelling bruises. "But are we really ready to face what just happened?"

"Agreed," Ghost said, rotating his shoulder with a wince. "But we need to take stock. We're not out of danger yet."

"Let's do an inventory," Marcus ordered, his tone sharp with purpose. The exhilaration of survival faded fast, replaced by grim pragmatism. Whatever they had brought back with them wasn't just a collection of relics it was something alive.

At the ramshackle table, they laid out their haul: seed pods, the data chip, and a shimmering crystal that pulsed faintly with energy.

"We need answers," Maya said, holding the crystal up to the light. "This isn't just a victory lap. Whatever we activated back there it's still alive, and it's not done with us yet."

Marcus nodded grimly. "We can't afford mistakes. Zara didn't give us this chance so we could waste it. Ghost, log everything. Maya, start analyzing the seed pods."

His mind raced. "We have to inspect every artifact carefully. Zara wouldn't have wanted us to take this lightly."

As they began sorting through the items, the atmosphere shifted. The earlier excitement dulled into a heavy quiet, reality pressing down around them. Each artifact felt like a reminder of what they had lost.

"Let's take a moment," Sofia said softly. "We owe that much to Zara. She gave us the chance to make it out alive."

For a heartbeat, silence ruled. The weight of Zara's sacrifice hung over them like a storm about to break. Then the faint pulse of one of the seeds shattered that stillness a dim amber glow casting flickering shadows across the walls.

"We don't have time to mourn," Marcus said quietly but firmly. "The longer we wait, the more dangerous this thing becomes."

It was then that Ghost noticed something strange. "Wait what's this?" he murmured, crouching beside one of the seed pods. He reached down and picked up a small object that had rolled free. "It looks like… a seed," he said, holding it up to the light. The tiny orb gleamed darkly, its surface glinting with faint, shifting patterns.

“Just a seed?” Maya asked, brow furrowing. “We’ve seen those before. They’re harmless.”

“Or so we thought,” Ghost muttered.

Marcus frowned. “Let’s not jump to conclusions. It could be connected to the activation sequence. We should study it before we do anything.”

The group exchanged uneasy glances. The air seemed to thicken, the temperature rising as the seed’s faint hum grew louder. Its amber glow deepened to a molten orange, light spilling across their faces.

A wave of heat pulsed outward. Marcus flinched as a shiver ran down his spine.

“It’s reacting to us,” he said, his voice tight. “Whatever this thing is it’s not dormant anymore.”

“Is anyone else feeling that?” Marcus asked uneasily, glancing around the room.

“What do you mean?” Maya replied, the defiance on her face slowly giving way to concern.

“It’s as if… something’s awakening,” he said, scanning the shadows warily. “We need to tread carefully.”

Before anyone could respond, the seed began to pulse its amber glow building with a rhythmic intensity. Within seconds, the entire room filled with light, each pulse syncing unnervingly with their heartbeats.

“What in the name of all that’s holy is going on?” Ghost shouted, stumbling backward.

“It’s going active!” Marcus yelled, trying to think and act at once. “We have to contain it!”

“Contain it? How?” Maya cried, panic rising in her voice.

They scrambled in the flickering light, hands darting over equipment and debris, desperate to subdue the surging power that seemed alive. Marcus grabbed a containment module, but the moment it touched the current, it sparked violently then went dead, useless against the swelling energy.

"It's too powerful!" he shouted, frustration boiling over.

Ghost hammered at his control pad, sweat streaking his temple. "I'm trying to stabilize it, but it's fighting back! It's like it has a mind of its own!"

"Everyone, focus!" Marcus bellowed, his voice cracking with strain. "We have to work together, or we lose everything!"

The air grew heavier by the second, each breath harder to draw. The hum of the seed deepened into a low, living resonance that seemed to crawl into their bones.

"This is my fault!" Maya cried, her voice breaking. "It's because of me because I pushed too far with this technology! It has to be stopped!"

"This isn't the time to point fingers!" Marcus snapped, the frustration breaking through his control. "We need solutions, not guilt!"

"You're right," Maya whispered, trying to steady herself. "But we have to face what we've done. This isn't a harmless artifact it's a threat."

Maya clenched her fists, tears spilling down her cheeks. "I didn't mean to "

"None of us did," Marcus said softly, cutting her off. "But we can't let guilt paralyze us. Zara wouldn't want that."

"Because of us, Zara's gone!" Maya shot back, her voice shaking with anger and grief.

"This isn't about blame anymore!" Marcus countered, his tone fierce. "We can't let her sacrifice mean nothing. This seed is waking up, and we're running out of time!"

"Enough!" Marcus shouted above the chaos. "Let's channel this energy into a plan. We must contain whatever this is before it's too late!"

Sofia nodded grimly. "We'll need a barrier around the seed. Ghost, can you rig something through the containment grid?"

"I'll try," he said, determination tightening his jaw. "But we have to move fast."

Tension clung to every motion as they worked side by side, the air thick with grief and unspoken anger. Marcus felt it in every glance, every silence the weight of loss pressing down like a physical force. This wasn't just the aftermath of a mission gone wrong; it was everything left unsaid, threatening to fracture what remained of their unity.

"What if it's too late?" Maya whispered. "What if we can't contain it?"

"We have to believe we can," Marcus said, locking eyes with her. "For Zara for all of us."

They continued their work, the atmosphere charged with guilt and determination. Every flicker of light from the seed cast distorted shadows across their faces, reflections of fear and hope intertwined.

Ghost glanced up from his device, his expression grim. "We can't lose anyone else. If this gets out of hand, it'll take all of us with it."

Marcus nodded, the weight of command pressing heavily on his shoulders. "Then we focus on containment. Emotions can't cloud our judgment now."

With tension simmering beneath the surface, the team rallied, working in frantic unison. The seed's pulse grew sharper, brighter, as if feeding off their desperation. Its glow painted their faces in molten gold, and Marcus felt its rhythm echo in his chest.

"Zara gave us this chance," he said, meeting Maya's gaze. "We can't waste it. Let's figure out what this thing is before it's too late."

But deep down, Marcus knew the true battle wasn't against whatever alien power they had awakened it was against the fear, guilt, and doubt threatening to consume them from within.

Zara's sacrifice lingered like a stormcloud unspoken, but ever present as they fought to regain control. Though they managed to stabilize the seed and contain the worst of its energy, the world beyond their base was already changing.

At first, the signs were subtle: a shimmer in the air, a tremor beneath the ground. But soon, the changes became impossible to ignore.

Days later, Marcus noticed the first clear sign. During a routine patrol, he saw the trees taller than before, their trunks warped and their leaves glowing with faint, iridescent hues. The air itself felt heavier, thrumming with an unseen current that made the hair on his arms stand on end.

"This isn't normal," he muttered, scanning the horizon. The once familiar landscape now seemed eerily alien.

"Maya, come see this," he called, his voice tinged with both awe and unease.

She joined him, her expression tightening as she took in the sight. "What in the world…?" she whispered, reaching out to touch one of the leaves.

It was warm beneath her fingers alive and it pulsed faintly, as if beating to the same rhythm as the seed.

"I don't think this is just some side effect of the seed," Marcus said quietly. "Something's changing here and it isn't just the plants."

The air itself felt different dense, electric as though the world were holding its breath. The sky was no longer the comforting blue they knew, but a strange, otherworldly hue that cast distorted shadows over the land.

As they walked back toward the base, Marcus and Maya watched the light dance across the sky in impossible colors. "Is it just me, or is the sunset different?" Maya asked in a hushed voice.

"It's not just you," Marcus said, a knot tightening in his gut. "We have to warn the others."

The changes hadn't stopped with the flora or the atmosphere. Reports began trickling in from nearby towns: strange lights streaking across the sky, low vibrations echoing through the night, and animals behaving erratically pets fleeing homes, livestock vanishing without a trace.

Ghost frowned as he scanned the latest data feeds. "This isn't just a local issue. Whatever's happening it's spreading."

"Something is definitely off," he added grimly. "People are starting to panic, and the last thing we need is for anyone to connect this back to the seed."

"What if they do?" Sofia cut in, her voice trembling.

"What if they think *we* caused it?"

A shiver ran down Maya's spine. "Then we need to get ahead of it before this spirals out of control."

As the strange phenomena intensified, so did public attention. Videos and images flooded social media vivid skies, glowing trees, flickering lights. Bewilderment and fear rippled across the globe.

Hashtags trended within hours: **#StrangeSky** and **#NatureGoneWrong.** Soon, news networks had seized on the story, replaying shaky footage of surreal landscapes and frightened citizens.

"We can't keep this under wraps anymore," Marcus said during a tense strategy meeting. "If the media runs with this, it's going to get ugly fast."

"Messy? *Catastrophic* is more like it," Maya replied, her eyes flicking to the wall of monitors, each showing a different news broadcast. Distorted environments, terrified faces the world was watching in confusion and dread.

"This could be the beginning of a new ecological crisis," one reporter announced gravely, her voice trembling as she stood before a warped, glowing forest.

"People are scared," Ghost said, running a hand through his hair. "They're going to demand answers."

"And they won't like what we have to tell them," Marcus replied grimly. "If we don't act fast, we'll lose control of the narrative and of the situation."

Thick tension filled the air as they met around the table. Just a week ago, the phenomenon had been a mystery confined to their lab. Now it was spiraling into a crisis that could engulf the entire world.

"We need to know the full extent of what we're dealing with," Marcus said, pacing the room. "If the seed is causing these transformations, we need to find out how far it's spread."

Maya nodded, her expression torn between resolve and fear. "We'll have to collect data, monitor every environmental change, and try to predict what happens next."

But before they could even begin, Sofia's voice broke through the growing tension. "We're getting warnings from the containment site," she said, pale. "The seed's energy signature is fluctuating it's stronger than we thought."

"Containment failure?!" Marcus barked, slamming his hand against the table. "We stabilized it!"

"Not enough, apparently," Ghost said darkly. "The readings show exponential growth. It's feeding off the environment."

A chill ran down Maya's spine. "If it keeps spreading, we'll lose control completely."

"It's already building momentum," Ghost warned. "We have to act now before it breaches containment."

"Then let's move!" Maya exclaimed, fire flashing in her eyes. "We can't sit here and watch it grow stronger. We contain it now, before it consumes everything!"

Even as they prepared to respond, a grim realization settled over them the seed they had brought back wasn't a tool or a discovery. It was a living force, volatile and uncontrollable. What they had seen as a triumph had become a catastrophe in motion.

The crisis deepened rapidly. Government agencies took notice, their presence felt before they were even seen. Black cars rolled up to the base, and men in sharp suits emerged faces expressionless, voices clipped and commanding.

"We're here to assess the situation," one said curtly.

Marcus exchanged a wary glance with Maya. A wave of unease hit him. "They'll want control," he murmured under his breath. "They won't care about fixing this they'll care about *containing* it. And if that means detaining us, they'll do it."

Maya's eyes widened. "We can't let that happen."

As government involvement deepened, tension skyrocketed. "We need to go public," one of the agents declared. "The people have a right to know what's happening."

"We don't want mass panic!" Marcus shot back, frustration boiling over. "We need quiet containment, not chaos!"

But the decision was already out of their hands. Press conferences were hastily organized, filled with evasive statements and half truths. Officials denied everything the team had warned about, framing the phenomenon as "natural atmospheric anomalies."

"They're painting us as the villains," Maya said, her voice shaking. "This isn't how it was supposed to go!"

A heavy sense of dread settled in her gut. "We can't let them silence us," she said fiercely. "We have to tell the truth before it's too late."

The team exchanged determined looks. The storm was already breaking online, in the media, and in the skies themselves. And as the world turned its eyes toward the inexplicable, Marcus felt the weight of inevitability pressing down.

Whatever they had unleashed was far beyond their control.

And it was only just beginning.

The world outside was changing fast and what had happened with the seed was only the tip of the iceberg. With the government moving in to take control and misinformation spreading like wildfire, Marcus and Maya knew they couldn't stand by. Something had to be done.

They needed to rally their team, confront the crisis as it grew, and make sure the truth saw the light of day no matter the cost.

"Whatever happens," Marcus said, meeting each of their eyes in turn, "we face it together. That's what we owe Zara and every person who's suffering because of this."

The words hung heavy in the air, yet they carried strength. One by one, the others nodded, resolve hardening behind tired eyes.

The stakes had never been higher. The world stood trembling on the edge poised between salvation and catastrophe.

And all that remained was their choice

to push it further into chaos,

or pull it back from the brink.

## Chapter 20: Global Impact

The world had changed rapidly since the seed came online its effects now reverberating far beyond Marcus and Maya's base. The news ran in a constant stream of reports, alarm following alarm, each more unsettling than the last.

### International News Coverage

Crouched behind a broken down truck on the outskirts of a nearby town, Marcus and Maya watched chaos unfold before their eyes. Crowds surged through the streets, faces twisted in fear and desperation. A woman sobbed, clutching her child both covered in grime while nearby, a man shouted incoherently about the sky turning purple.

Overhead, the sun burned with an unnatural hue, casting warped violet light across the turbulent scene.

"This isn't just panic," Maya said tightly as she watched people smash store windows and loot supplies. "It's chaos. People are turning on each other."

Marcus's jaw clenched. "And they're going to blame us for all of it."

From a nearby storefront, a newscaster's grave voice echoed from a flickering television, heavy with urgency:

"Authorities are investigating the origins of these strange events, which many fear may be linked to a recently discovered seed in the hands of a rogue research team."

Marcus stared at the screen, his heartbeat quickening as the reality sank in. "This is spiraling out of control," he muttered, turning to Maya, whose expression was a mix of disbelief, anger, and fear.

"It's not just panic it's chaos," she said again, shaking. "People are going to start blaming us for everything."

## First Public Panic Reactions

The panic was visceral inescapable. Marcus and the team stood at the edge of the town square, blending into the shadows as order unraveled around them. People screamed at the sky, their voices hoarse with desperation. A group of teenagers recorded the spectacle on their phones, capturing the eerie purple glow spreading across the horizon.

Nearby, a car alarm blared as a mob overturned the vehicle, their shouts blending into a cacophony of rage and fear. A man climbed onto the hood, shaking his fists at the heavens.

"The government's behind this!" he roared. "They've unleashed hell on us!"

Maya's hand tightened around Marcus's arm. "We can't just stand here and watch this happen."

"We don't have a choice," Marcus replied grimly. "If we step in now, we'll only draw attention to ourselves."

On Ghost's tablet, a feed showed footage of chaos erupting across the globe one man standing on a car, screaming conspiracies, the purple sun glowing behind him.

"See this?" Ghost said, motioning toward the screen. "There are protests in multiple cities. People want answers and they're looking for someone to blame."

"Blame us," Marcus growled. "They think we caused this nightmare."

## Government Agencies Mobilized

Military vehicles rumbled down the streets as Marcus and Maya slipped through an alleyway, moving cautiously. Soldiers barked orders, herding civilians toward makeshift checkpoints that had appeared overnight. Helicopters roared overhead, their searchlights slicing through the violet haze blanketing the city.

"The military's locking everything down," Ghost muttered through the comms, his voice grim. "If they find us, it's over."

Marcus peeked around a corner, watching a terrified family stopped by armed guards demanding identification. "They're not just locking it down," he said quietly. "They're preparing for war."

In a government conference room in Washington, D.C., officials crowded around a glowing map.

"We have to catch this team before they make any more changes," barked a stern faced general, his voice echoing through the room. "They're the only ones who can explain what's happening."

Across the world, similar meetings took place behind closed doors, all steeped in fear and uncertainty.

**Team Being Sought by Authorities**

Back at their temporary hideout, the team huddled in the basement of an abandoned building. The air was thick with dust, the silence punctuated by the distant wail of sirens and the rhythmic thud of soldiers' boots.

"They're looking for us," Maya said, peering through a crack in the boarded up window. Her eyes swept over the nearby checkpoints where guards interrogated anyone who passed. "We need to move before they figure out where we are."

"And go where?" Ghost demanded, tension sharp in his voice. "Every major city's under lockdown. If we stick our heads out, they'll have us in cuffs within minutes."

Marcus exhaled slowly, thinking aloud. "We can't just hide. We have to find a way to contain this before it gets even worse."

"Contain what, exactly?" Sofia asked. "Whatever's happening with the seed, it's spreading. I've seen reports of the same phenomena in Tokyo and London."

"Exactly," Marcus said. "If we don't understand what's happening, we'll be running forever."

**Initial Spread of Seed Effects**

The seed's influence had become undeniable. Across the world, entire ecosystems were mutating rampant growth overtaking cities, animals behaving with eerie intelligence, and once familiar landscapes turning alien.

As the team moved through a rural area, they came upon a farmstead in ruin barn doors hanging open, the air thick with the stench of decay. Inside, they froze. Pens stood empty, troughs overturned.

"What happened here?" Maya whispered.

Marcus knelt by the broken fencing, brushing his fingers across the dirt. "No tracks. Whatever took the livestock didn't leave any trace."

Ghost crouched nearby, holding up his scanner. "There's an energy signature here. Faint, but it matches the seed."

Maya's voice trembled. "It's spreading faster than we thought."

"Look at this," Ghost said, pointing toward the edge of the forest. He handed Marcus the scanner, its screen pulsing with sharp bursts of light. "It's not just showing on the map anymore. It's here."

The team halted. Ahead, the forest loomed trees twisted into spirals, their trunks bending at impossible angles. Leaves shimmered with shifting iridescence, and faint whispers drifted through the branches, low and haunting.

Maya stepped closer, her face pale. "It's alive."

"It's not just alive," Marcus said quietly, eyes narrowing. "It's hunting."

He turned to the others, determination hardening in his voice. "Then we have to contain it. Whatever it takes we stop this before it goes global."

**Government Response: Emergency UN Session**

As the situation deteriorated further, an emergency session of the United Nations was convened. Diplomats from around the world gathered in New York, their faces etched with exhaustion and fear. The atmosphere was tense, the air thick with the weight of an impending global catastrophe.

A representative from Brazil spoke with unwavering urgency.

"We must act immediately. The potential for ecological disaster is enormous. We cannot afford to lose time debating semantics."

"I agree," responded the German delegate gravely. "But we must find the right team. Somewhere out there, they hold the key pieces of the answers we desperately need."

Murmurs rippled through the chamber as translation headsets crackled. Words like *containment, biohazard*, and *mutation* echoed in a dozen languages, the weight of uncertainty pressing down on every conversation.

**Military Deployments Around the World**

In a desperate attempt to regain control, governments around the world mobilized their armed forces. Major cities erected checkpoints; armored convoys rolled down empty highways. Soldiers patrolled the streets beneath skies painted with unnatural violet hues.

At a hastily arranged press conference, a high ranking military official addressed the nation, his voice grim.

"We are working to contain the situation. Please remain calm. Stay indoors and report any unusual occurrences immediately."

Behind his composed tone lurked the fear of something far beyond military control.

Marcus watched the broadcast from their hideout, a pit forming in his stomach. "This is getting out of hand," he muttered. "The harder they try to control it, the faster it spirals."

## Scientific Community Mobilization

Meanwhile, the world's scientific community scrambled for answers. Laboratories across continents worked day and night, data streaming through encrypted channels as researchers raced against time. Papers were rushed into publication; emergency symposiums erupted across universities and research centers.

"Scientists are starting to connect the dots," Maya said, scanning the flood of new reports. "They're already theorizing about long term effects climate disruption, soil mutation, even shifts in atmospheric chemistry."

Marcus exhaled, tension lining his voice. "Which means they'll be looking for us even harder. If they think we're responsible, they'll come after us first."

The air in the room thickened, the weight of inevitability closing in on them. "We need to prepare for the worst," he said quietly.

## Public Containment Efforts

As the crisis deepened, governments launched public containment measures. Citizens were urged to report any "abnormal biological activity." Special task forces were deployed to investigate the flood of reports twisted trees, glowing animals, entire fields transforming overnight.

But instead of reassurance, the measures fueled paranoia.

"Every time someone reports something weird," Ghost said darkly, "it's another nail in our coffin. They're closing in on us."

Even amid chaos, fragments of cooperation began to form. Some nations realizing the magnitude of the threat set aside their rivalries to share data. A global task force was established to coordinate research, combining military precision with scientific urgency.

"We still have a chance," Maya said, her voice firm, rising above the hum of tension. "But only if we work together and that means sharing what little we know."

Marcus nodded slowly, though unease gnawed at him. "And what happens," he asked quietly, "when they decide that *we* are the enemy?"

## Team's Dilemma: Deciding to Separate Temporarily

Pressure mounted in the basement as a patrol vehicle rolled past, its spotlight cutting across the cracked windows. The team froze in silence, breaths held until the hum of the engine faded into the distance.

Marcus broke the silence, his voice a harsh whisper. "We can't stay together. They're closing in on us."

Maya turned sharply toward him, disbelief flashing in her eyes. "You mean we just split up? Leave each other to fend for ourselves?"

"If we stay, we're done," Marcus said firmly. "We'll cover more ground apart and regroup once we know more."

Ghost nodded reluctantly. "Then we need secure communication. If anything goes wrong, we check in immediately."

"So what, we just split up?" Maya snapped. "That's not a plan, Marcus we need each other."

"Perhaps we should disseminate the stolen technology," Ghost said evenly. "If we divide it among us, we can cover more ground and reduce the risk of losing everything at once."

The team exchanged uneasy glances but slowly began to agree.

"Fine," Marcus said, his tone heavy with resignation. "But we establish secure communication first. We can't afford to lose contact."

They distributed the stolen technology carefully each member receiving essential data and devices needed to keep the mission alive.

Maya's expression hardened with resolve. "We can't let this fall into the wrong hands."

"Agreed," Marcus said, nodding. "Secure channels only. Encrypted frequencies. No one outside this team hears a word."

Before parting ways, they reviewed every critical detail of the seed its signatures, its reactions, its potential behaviors.

"Stay alert," Marcus warned. "If you notice anything unusual, report it immediately. We need to stay ahead of whatever's coming."

Maya gripped his arm tightly. "We'll figure this out. We have to."

Ghost adjusted the controls on his wrist communicator. "We'll check in every few days," he said solemnly. "If anything feels off, we regroup no exceptions."

"Right," Marcus replied, the weight of leadership pressing on him. "Let's do this. For Zara."

With heavy hearts, they prepared to go their separate ways each carrying a piece of the mission and the burden of the world's unraveling.

"Remember," Maya said, her voice steady despite the tremor beneath it, "we're still together in this. However far we go, we find a way back."

They exchanged brief embraces and final words of encouragement before parting into the unknown. Marcus felt resolve solidify in his chest. The world was spiraling into chaos, but retreat was not an option.

They would fight to contain the disaster, to uncover the truth, and to reunite when destiny allowed. As Marcus stepped into the night, the echoes of their defiance rippled through the air. This was only the beginning of their long struggle, and he knew it.

The world outside was unrecognizable. As Marcus and Maya moved through a nearby town, they saw how the seed's influence had begun reshaping reality itself. Buildings were overgrown with vines that pulsed faintly, glowing from within as if alive. People argued in the streets some hoarding supplies, others demanding answers no one could give.

A low hum filled the air, deepening as they approached a tree whose leaves shimmered like gold. A crowd gathered around it, mesmerized.

"Don't," Marcus warned, grabbing a man who reached out to touch it. "You don't know what it'll do."

The man yanked his arm free, eyes blazing. "This is a gift! You can't stop us from taking it!"

Maya tugged Marcus's sleeve urgently. "We need to move. This is going to turn ugly fast."

It wasn't just the twisted vegetation or erratic wildlife that terrified the world. A new anomaly had appeared *Money Trees.*

First sprouting in parks and public squares, these strange trees bore clusters of leaves that resembled shimmering banknotes. To onlookers, it seemed miraculous a divine answer to poverty and need.

But wonder turned swiftly to chaos.

"Look at this," Maya gasped, watching a live broadcast on a nearby screen. Citizens swarmed a city park, tearing at the golden leaves and stuffing handfuls of cash into their arms. "They think it's a blessing but this will destroy everything."

Marcus stared grimly at the footage. The promise of effortless wealth had turned into madness. Humanity driven by greed and desperation rushed to harvest the Money Trees as if salvation could be plucked from their branches.

"It's not possible," he murmured under his breath, despair flickering in his eyes. "Money doesn't grow on trees."

News coverage exploded. Reporters spoke over chaotic scenes of riots and economic collapse.

"The very fabric of global finance is unraveling," one analyst said live on air. "Inflation will soar currencies will collapse. The consequences are catastrophic."

Within days, stock markets crashed worldwide. Banks fell into chaos as investors demanded withdrawals, and economies ground to a halt.

Marcus watched the red ticker lights flashing across the screen, his expression hollow. "This is a complete disaster," he whispered. "People are going to lose everything."

Ghost dropped into a chair beside him, scrolling through a dozen reports on his tablet. His voice was tight. "They're blaming us," he said slowly. "They're saying this all happened because of our experiments that *we're* the enemy."

The words hung heavy in the air, echoing against the crumbling certainty of the world outside.

And as the Money Trees multiplied, currency values crumbled. The once stable U.S. dollar faltered, black markets for physical cash erupted, and desperation spread faster than the vines that now covered the earth.

"People are treating the Money Trees as a panacea," Sofia said grimly, eyes locked on her tablet as streams of social media updates flooded in. "But what they're ignoring are the long term aftereffects hyperinflation, collapse of trade, entire economies imploding under their own weight."

Her words hung heavy in the air. Outside, society was unraveling.

Protests ignited across major cities not just against governments, but between desperate citizens themselves. Fights broke out over access to parks where the trees had taken root. The thin fabric of order that once held civilization together now stretched to its breaking point.

Marcus's jaw tightened as he stared at the wall of monitors, each one showing another fragment of chaos. "We're losing control," he said through gritted teeth. "If this keeps up, it'll be a free for all. Anarchy."

The team gathered around him in the dim glow of the underground base. The noise of sirens and shouting filtered faintly through the vents above a constant reminder of the world they had helped unmake.

"We have to do something," Maya urged, her voice cracking with desperation. "We can't just sit here and watch everything fall apart."

"Like what?" Ghost shot back, frustration boiling to the surface. "What can we possibly do when the *entire world* is coming apart at the seams?"

Marcus's fists clenched at his sides. "We show them the truth," he said sharply. "Expose the illusion before it destroys us all. The Money Trees aren't salvation they're poison. People need to understand that."

A silence followed, thick with the weight of guilt and realization.

"If we hadn't taken that seed back…" Marcus began, but his voice faltered before he could finish. The unfinished thought lingered like smoke.

Maya looked down, her voice barely above a whisper. "We thought we were helping. That this could change things for the better."

"Good intentions mean nothing," Ghost muttered darkly. "Not when the world's on fire because of us. We didn't just unleash chaos we engineered it."

The words hit like a hammer. No one spoke for a long moment. Each of them felt the crushing truth: they weren't just witnesses to destruction they were its architects.

Then, suddenly, the secure channel beeped. Sofia's head snapped up. "Incoming transmission," she said, eyes widening. "It's from the other survivors."

Marcus leaned forward, pulse quickening. "Other survivors? From the portals?"

Sofia nodded, fingers flying across the console. "They want to talk."

The screen flickered to life, revealing a familiar face Alex, one of the original operatives lost during the portal collapses. His voice crackled through static, edged with urgency.

"Marcus. Maya. We've been tracking what's happening. The seed isn't just affecting your world it's spreading into others. Whatever this thing is, it's cross dimensional."

The team exchanged stunned looks.

Alex continued, voice steady despite the chaos behind him. "We've started organizing a resistance. Survivors from other sectors are joining forces. We can't let this spiral any further. We need to act now."

A spark of hope flickered in Marcus's chest for the first time in days. "If we coordinate," he said slowly, "we might have a chance. We share intel, resources work together."

Alex nodded. "Exactly. We'll send what we know about the energy signatures and containment breaches. Together, we can find a way to shut this thing down for good."

As the connection stabilized, a map bloomed across the monitor nodes of survivors scattered across the globe, each beacon pulsing faintly. The scope of their mission loomed before them: vast, daunting, yet finally within reach.

Marcus exhaled, resolve hardening in his chest. "Then we move fast. This isn't about us anymore it's about humanity. We need to turn the tide before there's nothing left to save."

Around him, the team straightened grim faces illuminated by the glow of their screens, the spark of determination reigniting in their eyes.

They would join the resistance.

They would unite the scattered survivors.

And they would fight not just for redemption, but for the future of the world itself.

The hour to act had come.

Retreat was no longer an option.

Together, they faced the gathering storm, ready to stand against whatever fury awaited beyond the horizon.

## Chapter 21: The Hunt

In a dingy motel room under weak, flickering light, erratic shadows danced across the peeling wallpaper. The television blared with a harsh blue glow, its screen flashing with breaking news.

Marcus sat motionless, the remote forgotten in his hand, his pulse hammering as one familiar face appeared under the headline:

### WANTED: INTERNATIONAL TERRORISTS RESPONSIBLE FOR GLOBAL ECONOMIC COLLAPSE

Grainy footage of the museum heist looped relentlessly each frame edited to perfection, every shadow twisted into guilt. Their images, once heroic, now branded them as the architects of ruin.

"They've turned us into monsters," Marcus murmured, his voice hollow, as hotline numbers scrolled across the screen.

He was no longer a scientist, no longer a soldier of progress. He was a scapegoat for a world collapsing under its own fear. The weight of that realization pressed on his chest until he could hardly breathe.

Outside, searchlights swept through alleyways as special forces raided suspected hideouts. Every second counted. The world's most powerful nations were hunting them, and the net was closing fast.

### Scattered Team: Underground

Elsewhere, the team clung to survival in fragments.

Sofia crouched in the narrow confines of a freight car, her mobile rig spread out before her in a tangle of cables and screens. Her fingers danced furiously across the keyboard, every keystroke erasing another digital footprint. "You won't trace me," she muttered through gritted teeth, sweat trickling down her temple as the clatter of wheels echoed beneath her. "Not yet."

Ghost fared worse. The man who had once built networks of secrecy now lived among the unseen sleeping under bridges, trading what little he had for food and silence. Every flicker of movement brought a rush of paranoia. "They're after me," he whispered into the night. "But they won't find me."

Maya's life had narrowed to a stall near the border, selling trinkets to passing tourists. Her hair was dyed, her accent changed, her eyes always darting toward the nearest checkpoint. "Just one more day," she whispered to herself, pressing a false smile as she handed out bracelets. "Just one more day."

Interpol red notices plastered their faces across every continent.
Marcus, hidden deep in an abandoned subway tunnel, stared at the cracked concrete walls that surrounded him. The air was damp and heavy, his thoughts darker still. "I can't live like this forever," he muttered, watching the faint glimmer of daylight through a fissure in the ceiling.

Nobody on the team slept more than two hours at a stretch. The unspoken enemy wasn't just pursuit it was fatigue. The shadows in their lives were constant companions, and every heartbeat felt like a countdown.

Though miles apart, the team remained connected through a fragile web of coded signals a lifeline spun from ingenuity and trust.

Each dawn, Marcus scanned the classified ads in local papers. A phrase like *"Vintage camera collection, mint condition"* whispered that Ghost had secured new documents; *"North Star visible tonight"* signaled a newly established safe house. Mundane words that masked messages of survival.

Across the cities, Maya turned her art into language. Her murals weren't just camouflage they were messages. Three blue stripes meant *safe passage.* A red circle meant *watched location.* Her colors painted warnings across crumbling walls.

Ghost's method was more ephemeral: chalk marks scratched on corners of doorways and lampposts vertical for "clear," horizontal for "danger."

Sofia managed their digital world from her shifting sanctuaries, weaving layers of encryption through forgotten networks. "Remember the museum's third floor?" she'd say in coded transmissions shared memories now transformed into secret keys. Each reference from their past became a phrase of survival only they could understand.

Their daily check ins became sacred ritual. At precisely 7:13 every evening, each sent their signal: Marcus placed a chipped coffee cup in a windowsill; Maya posted an innocuous review of a street vendor; Ghost nudged a dumpster a few inches left; Sofia triggered a one second flicker in the city's power grid.

Each act whispered the same phrase across miles and borders:
**"I'm alive. I'm still fighting."**

"We're still a team," Sofia would remind herself each night, her hands trembling as she entered the code. "Distance can't break what we built."

But close calls were constant. One night, while rerouting signals from a moving train, Sofia detected a breach someone was tracing her connection. "Not today," she hissed, yanking the plug and fleeing down the narrow stairwell just as agents boarded the carriage. Her lungs burned, but she didn't stop running.

Ghost sprinted across the rooftops, the night wind slicing against his face as boots thundered close behind. "I can't get caught," he panted, the words tearing from his throat as adrenaline surged through his veins. The city blurred around him a sprawl of steel and shadow as he vaulted a gap between buildings, the dull thud of impact rattling through his bones. Behind him, a voice shouted through a comm: "Target in sight move in!"

His pulse roared in his ears. *Not today.*

Marcus crouched in the darkness of an alley, pressed against cold brick as law enforcement swept the nearby street. Flashlights carved through the gloom, slicing across rain slick pavement.

"We've got to find them," one officer barked. "They can't have gone far."

Marcus held his breath. The pounding of his heart was so loud he swore they could hear it.

At the border, Maya faced her own reckoning. A guard's question cut through her trembling calm: "Do you have any weapons or restricted items?"

"Just a few trinkets," she replied, forcing a smile as she held out her satchel. "Cultural artifacts. Tourist stuff nothing valuable."

The guard examined her carefully, suspicion flickering across his face before waving her through. Maya exhaled, her pulse finally slowing.

But she knew that was too close. Far too close.

Days bled into each other. The team's network once intricate and reliable was unraveling. Burner phones were compromised; dead drops under surveillance. Every meeting point felt poisoned.

"We're losing contact," Sofia said, panic rising in her voice as static filled the line. "I can't reach Marcus. If we're cut off"

"Meet me at the old warehouse," Marcus replied, though even saying it felt reckless. "We'll regroup there."

Every conversation was now a risk. Every signal could be a trap.

Zara's face haunted Marcus's dreams, her memory flickering like static. "What have I done?" he whispered into the darkness, night after night.

Sofia's paranoia gnawed at her. "What if one of us is compromised?" she murmured, eyes darting over her encrypted screens aboard the freight train. "We can't trust anyone anymore."

Ghost fought his own breaking point. Years of military discipline were all that stood between him and panic. "Focus," he told himself again and again, but the fear clawed at him, whispering of mistakes and ghosts long buried.

Maya, too, felt the weight. "I never signed up for this," she murmured. "I just wanted to save history not destroy it."

The walls were closing in.

Each narrow escape chipped away at their resolve. The once unbreakable team had fractured into survivors, bound by fear more than faith.

They weren't heroes anymore.

They weren't even fugitives.

They were ghosts haunted phantoms clawing through a world they'd accidentally broken.

Yet even in the depths of despair, fragments of hope flickered. The world above spiraled into chaos sirens, riots, fear but Marcus refused to surrender. They had to adapt, or vanish completely.

Their salvation came from the most unlikely source the invisible networks of the forgotten.

Marcus moved through alleyways and beneath overpasses, the smell of smoke and decay heavy in the air. "We need eyes on the streets," he said quietly to a man huddled beside a dumpster. He handed over a wad of crumpled bills. "If you see anything police, military vehicles, surveillance drones you tell me first."

The man studied him with wary eyes before pocketing the money. "I can listen," he said. "But information doesn't come cheap."

Marcus nodded. "Then we'll pay."

Fragile alliances were forged in whispers and cigarette smoke. The homeless, the forgotten, the unseen they became the team's watchers, their informants in a world too chaotic for official order.

Sofia worked her magic in the digital realm, spinning a web of misinformation to keep the authorities chasing phantoms. "They'll be too busy chasing shadows to find us," she said, her eyes flickering with equal parts excitement and dread.

With every false lead planted, with every fake signal broadcast, they bought themselves time. "If we can keep them busy, we might actually regroup," Marcus said, though guilt weighed heavy on his words.

Deep cover identities became their last defense.

Marcus drifted through the city under a new name, a man erased from history. Maya resurfaced as a muralist, her art a coded language on forgotten walls. Ghost took refuge among repair crews, a faceless laborer in the background of rebuilding zones. Sofia became a freelance tech consultant, her digital presence scattered and untraceable.

"Keep it loose," Ghost said during one of their rare encrypted calls. "We can't afford a single mistake. Slip once, and it's over."

Each day was a balancing act living between lives, breathing between identities. Fear was constant, but so was the fragile thread that still tied them together.

Their faces were on every screen. Their names were curses whispered in government halls.

Yet beneath the fear, something unbroken remained.

A spark.

A promise.

A vow that when the time came, they would rise from the shadows and finish what they started.

Desperation had stripped them of choices. The team once protectors of history now bartered it away, piece by piece, to survive.

Through dim corridors and smoke stained dens, they traded ancient relics for passage, for silence, for the smallest edge against the tightening noose. Each exchange was a cut into their conscience.

"This isn't what we envisioned," Maya whispered, trembling as she handed over a rare artifact a relic that once symbolized her life's work. "We're bartering away our morals."

"Survival is the priority," Marcus replied, voice hard but hollow. He avoided her eyes as the dealer's greedy hands snatched the piece. Every deal felt like sinking deeper into a moral abyss from which there would be no return.

They sought alliances in the underworld arms dealers, smugglers, data brokers. Men and women who thrived in chaos. "Just remember," Sofia warned during one meeting with a particularly dangerous contact, "we're not like them. We can't forget who we are."

Ghost's jaw tightened. "If we do, we won't make it out alive."

The air in that room had been thick with distrust, lit by a single bare bulb swinging from the ceiling. They were no longer scientists or soldiers. They were survivors trapped in a world where every shadow hid a potential betrayal.

Then came the broadcast.

"Ten million dollars," the anchor announced coldly, "for information leading to the capture of the fugitives responsible for the global economic collapse."

Marcus stared at the screen, unable to breathe. The bounty was enough to fracture every alliance, to turn friends into predators.

"They've just weaponized the world against us," Sofia whispered.

From that moment, the hunt entered a new phase. Private military contractors joined the pursuit, their armored vehicles rumbling through the streets like war machines. Tactical teams flooded cities; drones scoured the skies. Marcus felt it the weight of inevitability pressing down like gravity.

"They're getting serious," he muttered, the words tasting of dread.

Soon, facial recognition systems came online across the continent. Cameras peered into crowds, scanning every face, every movement. "We're running out of places to hide," Marcus said, pacing their cramped hideout. The walls seemed to breathe with them, alive with fear.

Borders closed. Cities locked down. Escape was no longer possible.

The consequences rippled outward, tearing through their personal lives.

Marcus watched his family's home from afar, hidden in the shadows. Agents patrolled the perimeter, their presence constant, their rifles gleaming under porch lights. "I can't let them get hurt because of me," he thought, his heart breaking under the weight of guilt.

Sofia's voice trembled through a cracked phone line. "They raided my mother's house," she whispered, tears streaking her face. "They're looking for me for us. What if they find something?"

Ghost's old contacts brothers in arms from his military past betrayed him for money. "I can't trust anyone anymore," he spat, the anger trembling beneath his breath.

And Maya... she had learned her former research partner had been captured, questioned for days. "This is all my fault," she whispered, the guilt anchoring her like a chain. "I never should have brought the artifacts out."

Every tie to their past was unraveling. The lives they once lived were being erased methodically, ruthlessly until nothing remained but the hunted.

Then, one night, it all came crashing down.

Coordinated raids erupted across cities. Helicopters tore through the skies, floodlights carving into the darkness. The airwaves crackled with reports of "suspected terrorist hideouts neutralized."

Their final secure server lit up with red alerts. "They've breached our systems!" Sofia shouted.

Marcus's blood turned cold. "Activate emergency protocols now!"

Panic erupted. They scrambled to purge data, destroy equipment, and flee. Sirens wailed in the distance closer each second.

Maya clutched her bag of remaining artifacts. "We can't split up!" she cried. "We need to stick together!"

Ghost's voice cut through the chaos. "We won't survive if we stay clustered they'll corner us!"

A flash of blue lights sliced through the window. Marcus made his decision. "Follow me!"

They tore through side streets, chased by the echo of boots and gunfire. Shouts ricocheted off concrete walls. "This way!" Ghost barked, pulling them into a narrow alley just seconds before a tactical team swept past.

They stumbled into an old passage Marcus had mapped weeks ago an entry to the forgotten tunnels beneath the city. The air was thick with dust and history, every surface slick with moisture. Their footsteps echoed like heartbeats.

"Keep moving!" Marcus urged. "Don't stop!"

At the tunnel's end, among the debris of another age, Marcus's flashlight caught the edge of an ancient map wedged into the wall. It was one of Zara's something she had hidden long ago.

His hands shook as he unfolded it. Faded ink lined the paper, and within it, an encrypted code her handwriting unmistakable.

"She knew," Marcus breathed. "Zara… she knew all of this."

The message revealed more than coordinates. It hinted at a deeper truth a conspiracy woven long before the team's mission began. The seed, the vault, the heist none of it had been coincidence.

"They used us," Sofia said, realization dawning like a curse. "We were part of something bigger something they wanted to activate."

Marcus clenched the paper, fire igniting in his chest. "Then we stop running."

He looked at each of them tired, bruised, but still standing. "We fight back. For Zara. For everything they've taken from us."

The decision was made in that underground tomb of concrete and ghosts.

They would no longer flee.

They would expose the truth, even if it meant their lives.

Outside, the sirens still screamed. Helicopters scoured the night. But in that moment, something shifted the hunted became the hunters.

"The game's changed," Ghost said, loading his weapon with renewed resolve.

Marcus nodded, the map clutched tight in his fist. "Then it's time we changed the rules."

The war for the truth had begun.

## Chapter 22: Legacy

The sun was low, casting long shadows across the museum's grand façade the place where it had all begun. Once a sanctuary of knowledge, a temple to human curiosity, it now stood as both monument and memorial. To the world, it was merely a building. To Marcus and his team, it was the sum of everything they had fought for, everything they had lost, and everything they had finally come to understand.

Marcus drew a slow breath, his chest tight with memory and meaning. "We need to understand what we've done here," he said softly. The words hung heavy in the air, echoing through the quiet courtyard.

The others stood beside him, silent, each bearing their own reflections.

Maya stepped forward first, her gaze tracing the weathered columns. "It feels unreal to be back," she murmured. "Like the walls remember us their shadows, our choices." Then, with quiet resolve, she added, "But we can't live in the past. What matters now is what we build from it."

"Agreed," Ghost said, his voice low but steady. "We've seen the best and worst of what we're capable of. This time, we act with purpose."

They crossed the marble threshold together. The museum's echoing halls felt haunted not by ghosts, but by echoes of discovery, conflict, and sacrifice. The memory of Zara lingered strongest here, her courage stitched into every stone.

Sofia ran her fingers along the cold glass of a shattered display case. "The seed didn't just open a portal," she said quietly. "It opened our eyes. It showed us how fragile the balance is between creation and destruction."

Marcus nodded. "Then we make sure we never forget that balance again. Knowledge isn't power it's responsibility."

They gathered in a small corner room, its walls lined with artifacts from civilizations long gone. A sense of renewal began to take root among them.

"Why not start something?" Maya said suddenly, her eyes bright with conviction. "A foundation one dedicated to preserving culture and promoting ethical technology. That could be our legacy."

Sofia's face softened. "Or work with governments. Help write the laws that prevent another crisis like this. We can use what we've learned to guide others."

Ghost crossed his arms, thoughtful. "It won't be easy. Power always finds a way to twist knowledge. But together, we can keep the balance."

Their words carried no idealism now only experience, resolve, and the quiet strength born of loss. They were no longer fugitives. They were something greater: custodians of the lessons carved from their mistakes.

As the sun dipped below the horizon, golden light filtered through the tall windows, draping them in warmth. One by one, they spoke not to each other, but to the memory of who they once were.

Marcus broke the silence. "I've learned that leadership isn't about making decisions it's about carrying their weight. I'll live with that, and I'll live honorably."

Maya smiled faintly. "I've learned my worth isn't tied to my research or recognition. It's in what I give back. It's in the good I choose to create."

Sofia looked up from the holographic tablet flickering in her hands. "I used to think every problem could be solved with technology," she said. "Now I know the real solutions come from people from empathy, connection, and conscience."

Ghost's gaze was steady, his voice rough with feeling. "Strength isn't about walls. It's about what you let through them. The vulnerable aren't weak they're the ones who stay human when everything tries to strip that away."

Their eyes met in quiet understanding. What had once been a fractured group bound by fear had become a family bound by trust and shared purpose.

"Together, we're stronger," Marcus said, the words carrying a weight that felt eternal.

"We've been through hell," Maya added, her voice firm, "but we came out as a family. Let's make sure our story means something that it inspires others to choose wisdom over power."

"Every action causes a ripple," Sofia said softly, as the final rays of sunlight stained the museum's portico gold. "We have to be aware of the waves we create."

Outside, the world was healing. The chaos the seed had unleashed was giving way to balance. Governments, humbled by catastrophe, began enacting new safeguards for technology laws that valued ethics over ambition.

Communities rebuilt together, finding strength in cooperation rather than competition. Knowledge became shared, not hoarded. Economies shifted toward sustainability, and people finally began to understand that progress meant nothing without compassion.

The world was far from perfect, but it was learning.

And as Marcus stood at the museum steps, watching the horizon glow with the promise of morning, he felt for the first time in years something like peace.

Zara's sacrifice hadn't been in vain.

"Let's begin again," he said quietly.

And as the first light of dawn touched the world reborn, they walked forward not as fugitives, not as survivors, but as builders of a new future.

Humanity was seeding an era of evolution one forced upon it by the weight of its own mistakes. At last, people began to understand that every stride toward progress came with a cost, each innovation a lesson sown deep into the soil of civilization.

Standing outside the museum their beginning and their rebirth Marcus and his team looked out over a city slowly healing from the scars of its chaos. The wind carried the scent of renewal through streets once choked by fear.

Marcus's eyes glimmered with quiet hope. "We've only scratched the surface of what's possible," he said, a faint smile tugging at the corner of his lips.

"We can inspire change," Maya replied, her voice steady, confident. "We can help humanity evolve into something more."

With resolve forged in the crucible of adversity, they turned toward the horizon ready to transform their trials into a legacy that would shape generations to come. They no longer ran from their past. They walked into the dawn, determined to leave their mark not as fugitives, but as visionaries.

As the first stars shimmered above them, they knew one truth would endure: whatever lay ahead, they would face it together. Their story had become more than survival it had become a gift to all humankind, a testament to resilience, unity, and the boundless power of connection.

Weeks later, the museum's research wing buzzed with renewed energy. Once a sanctuary of relics and forgotten histories, it now thrummed with the pulse of discovery. Marcus and his team stood gathered around an ancient tablet, its carvings faintly glowing under the soft hum of the lab's lights.

"Look at this," Sofia said, her voice trembling with awe. "These symbols they describe a *network* of portals. Not just one… an entire system linking to other worlds."

The others leaned in, eyes wide with wonder. Etched spirals and constellations traced pathways through unknown dimensions, mapping connections between civilizations long lost to myth.

"If we could activate them," Maya whispered, almost reverently, "we could reach those worlds. Imagine what we could learn what we could share."

Ghost's brow furrowed. "Or what we could unleash. We don't know what's on the other side. It could be another war waiting to happen."

Marcus studied the carvings, the light flickering across his face. "Maybe. But if other civilizations exist, we could find allies cultures that value preservation and knowledge as we do."

Maya nodded, her mind already racing ahead. "A coalition of worlds. Shared wisdom across dimensions."

Ghost shook his head, practical as ever. "Not every civilization will welcome us. Some might see us as invaders."

Sofia's eyes never left the tablet. "Then we prepare. We learn their languages, their science, their art. We build bridges before others build weapons."

Marcus smiled faintly. "We can be more than just survivors. We can become guardians of knowledge a network of civilizations united to protect culture, technology, and life itself."

But even as the words left his mouth, the ground trembled violently.

The museum's lights flickered, alarms shrieking to life. Sofia's console flared with crimson warnings. "We've got a problem," she said, her fingers flying across the controls. "Someone else is trying to access the portal network."

"What?" Maya gasped. "How is that possible?"

"The energy signatures…" Sofia's eyes widened. "They're identical to the seed's. It's *them.*"

Marcus felt his stomach twist. "The Organization."

The shadowy syndicate that had manipulated global markets and technological systems after the collapse they had been watching, waiting for this moment.

Ghost's display lit up with tactical overlays. "Three strike teams inbound," he said grimly. "Heavily armed, using energy dampening tech. They're surrounding the building."

"If they gain control of the portal network first," Maya said, her hands trembling as she began securing the artifacts, "they could weaponize it. They could drain resources from other worlds or destroy them entirely."

Marcus's mind raced. "Then we stop them here."

He snapped into command mode, the old rhythm returning like muscle memory. "Sofia create a digital labyrinth. Feed them false portal signals through the sublevels. Ghost, reinforce the entryways. Rig traps along the main corridors.

Maya, start the activation sequence we can't let them seize control of the real portal."

The team moved with precision born of countless trials. Sofia's fingers blurred over her keyboard, spinning a web of false data through the museum's network. Ghost repurposed the old security systems into a deadly grid of energy barriers and traps. Maya knelt before the portal interface, deciphering its ancient code through trembling determination.

"Energy surge at sixty percent," she called out. "Three minutes to full activation."

An explosion rocked the lower levels. Ghost's traps had engaged. "They're breaching the east wing!" he shouted.

Sofia intercepted communications her face turned pale. "They're not just after control," she said. "They want to siphon entire worlds. To harvest them."

"Not if we get there first," Marcus said, steel in his tone. "We're going to warn them every civilization we can reach. We'll build an alliance before the Organization can corrupt it."

The portal pulsed brighter, symbols glowing with life as if awakening after eons of silence. The air shimmered with energy, bending light and sound around them.

"This isn't just exploration anymore," Maya said, steadying her breath. "It's preservation."

"Then we finish what we started," Marcus said.

The floor quaked again, dust raining down from the vaulted ceiling. The hum of the portal crescendoed into a resonant roar, light blooming outward in fractal patterns across the room.

Sofia's voice rose above the chaos. "Activation complete!"

Marcus turned toward the swirling vortex of energy green, gold, and violet light spiraling into infinity. He looked to his team: Maya, Ghost, Sofia all scarred, all unbreakable.

"This is it," he said. "Our next beginning."

They stood together on the threshold of the unknown united not just by survival, but by purpose. Behind them lay the story of a world rebuilt from ashes. Ahead stretched a destiny unbounded by space or time.

The portal flared, its light enveloping them, and for one fleeting instant, Marcus thought he heard Zara's voice echo through the radiance:

"Every ending is just a door to another beginning."

And then, together, they stepped through.

A whole universe stretched out before them, waiting to be unveiled through the portal network a vast, uncharted canvas where treasures and dangers alike awaited discovery. Each world promised lessons that could deepen their understanding of themselves and of the fragile balance they now swore to protect.

"What if we meet those who know of technologies far beyond our learning?" Maya wondered, a fire kindling in her                                                        eyes.
"We could learn from them," she added softly, "or at least share what we've learned."

"Or we could blunder into a war between civilizations," Ghost countered, his tone measured. "We'll have to be strategists, not just explorers. What we do here could shape the course of cosmic history."

The weight of that truth settled over them, heavy but exhilarating. From the seeds of catastrophe had grown a new sense of purpose. Each carried the scars of their past but also its wisdom.

In the weeks that followed, they prepared with relentless focus. Marcus would guide diplomacy; Maya would safeguard culture; Sofia would master the technology; Ghost would stand watch against unseen threats. Together they gathered equipment, provisions, and relics tools for a mission that blurred the line between discovery and destiny.

"Our first destination should be a world of history," Marcus said, conviction bright in his voice. "A place untouched by time. We need to make a good first impression." "And prepare for everything," Ghost replied, eyes narrowing. "Never underestimate what waits beyond the horizon."

As departure day neared, the air inside the lab thrummed with tension and anticipation. They had come full circle, from fugitives to ambassadors of a newborn era.

"This isn't an adventure it's a responsibility," Marcus reminded them. "What we do now can shape not just our world, but others yet unseen."

Maya stepped forward. "We've become family through this journey. Whatever happens, we face it together. I'm in." Sofia nodded, resolve glinting in her eyes. "We've seen the cost of our mistakes. I want to make sure we never repeat them."
Ghost's expression hardened into determination. "Then no half measures. We look after one another and anyone else who needs us."

Their shared vow forged them anew. They were no longer the hunted; they were pioneers.

"We'll be ambassadors for our world," Marcus said, his voice carrying through the chamber. "Protectors of knowledge, guardians of what connects us all. Our heritage will be the lessons we've learned."

Each of them met his gaze and answered with silence the kind that meant absolute commitment.

Sofia turned back to the console, fingers steady as she initiated the sequence. "This is it," she breathed. "The moment we step into the unknown."

"Then let's be ready for anything," Ghost said, checking his gear one final time.

The portal ignited, a storm of color and light unfurling like the dawn of creation itself. Its radiance spilled across their faces an invitation, a challenge, a promise.

"Ready?" Marcus asked, his heart hammering.

"In this together," Maya replied.

"Always."

They took one last look at the world behind them, then stepped forward. The gateway enveloped them, its swirling brilliance sealing shut as they vanished into its heart.

They emerged as pioneers of infinity explorers of the unseen, bearers of hope. Their legacy was no longer one of mere survival but of connection, compassion, and courage. Through every choice they made, through every world they touched, their story would ripple outward reshaping not only their destinies, but the very fabric of reality.

And somewhere beyond the stars, the universe waited to answer.

## Epilogue

### The Money Tree   Vault of Verdancy

Months later, the world above the ruins moved on. The headlines had faded, the tremors stilled, and the sands reclaimed the broken gates of Money Tree City.

Yet beneath that silence, something remembered.

In a chamber no instrument could detect, the last seed pulsed faintly, each rhythm slower, deeper, more deliberate. Threads of light drifted through stone like veins of molten gold, mapping patterns too complex to belong to any age of men. Still, it pulsed.

Far away, in a forgotten observatory, a single monitor flickered to life. Lines of code bled down its screen not language, not numbers, but equations that bent logic into faith. For an instant they formed a single word before dissolving again: **Ledger.**

A whisper crossed the dark, neither sound nor code, carrying the promise of another awakening.

And somewhere, far from the sand and the silence, a man still dreamed of gold that wasn't meant to shine but to remember.

The City had only begun to breathe.

## About Author

**Randeep Pahwa** is an author and technologist who writes at the intersection of myth, science, and the human search for meaning. After spending more than fifteen years leading global digital transformation programs, he turned his focus to exploring how technology shapes belief and consciousness through story.

His debut series, The Money Tree, is a cinematic trilogy that examines the cost of creation, the greed of discovery, and the fragile truths that bind civilizations.

He lives in Canada, where he divides his time between innovation projects and the imagined worlds that continue to grow from his desk.

www.ingramcontent.com/pod-product-compliance
Lightning Source LLC
Chambersburg PA
CBHW070618300726
48975CB00006B/1851